PERFECT

A Breathless Novel

SAVANNAH KADE

Published by Griffyn Ink

www.griffynink.com

For ordering information or special discounts for bulk purchases, please contact Griffyn Ink at Mail@GriffynInk.com.

There should always be fine liquor on hand, you never know when a gentleman might want some. You never know when you might need some yourself.

"BAILEY ANN MAYFAIR, WHEN ARE YOU GOING TO MARRY ME?"

Bailey spun around on the street, looking for the voice that was a pure blast from her past. The sound was both sweet and spun with regret. She peered into a wind that felt far more bitter than it should have, but that was likely just her mood.

He'd asked that same question of her more than once before. He'd asked it in jest and in full sincerity. And now he was asking on the street of Breathless, Georgia, where anyone could hear. But Bailey Ann hadn't seen him in at least five years.

Her eyes searched the street until she landed on him. She didn't recognize him by sight, but she knew just by feel that the broad-shouldered form standing down the street was Finn Malloy. Her face lit up; she could feel it. "Finn! I didn't know you were in town."

She fought the urge to run and throw herself into his arms, to sink there and let him lift away all the world. But she was out in public, so she couldn't do it. She'd also answered that same question in the negative before—a good indicator that he wasn't going to take kindly to her using him as a crying shoulder if she tried it.

He walked closer, the straight nose and bright eyes so familiar. The broad mouth almost smiling, but not quite. Typical black Irish coloring marked him. His hair was so dark as to be inky, his eyes blue enough to be startling. She'd once told herself she couldn't marry a man with prettier eyes than her own.

Even in his twenties, he'd been slim but cut. Something had happened, and he now filled out that suit he was wearing. She blinked. "You're wearing a suit."

"Yeah," his mouth got closer to smiling, but still didn't quite achieve it. "I do that. I wear a suit."

She only nodded, because what else could she say? That she didn't think he'd been the type? That she'd never seen him in one before? Weren't jeans more his style? It all sounded vaguely insulting and she'd been carefully taught to never insult someone unless she meant it. Tears pushed at the back of her eyes, and Bailey fought them back. "Are you doing something specific here?"

Breathless wasn't the kind of place a person visited without a purpose. It was full of families and homes and schools. The shops were cute, the diner was full-scale Southern with a capital S, and the main street was named "Main" and lined with the basic stores with pretty lettering, but it wasn't a tourist town.

"I'm taking care of my parents' house," he finally answered her, the words not quite sinking in.

"Oh, did they move out? Somewhere flatter?" She was thinking of old knees and all the stairs in the house. It was a kind way of asking if they'd been moved to a nursing home, or more, when she noticed he was looking at her oddly.

"No. The house is all that's left. They died in a car accident about a year ago."

"What?" She stopped cold. "They . . ." She couldn't bring herself to say it. She'd had no idea. How had she had no idea?

Finn nodded solemnly. "Single car. They went into the big tree over on Kellar, but neither of them made it."

"Oh, my God, Finn, I'm so sorry." Truly, she was. But she was just as sorry that she hadn't known. That she hadn't come back and attended their funerals. Mrs. Malloy had no more approved of Bailey being her son's girlfriend than Bailey's own mother had approved of "that immigrant boy." Still, it didn't seem right to not attend. It was worse to not have known.

He just nodded. "After your mother passed, I figured you probably weren't getting the news." He shoved his hands in his pockets, the conversation awfully awkward for two people who'd had some of the most amazing sex she'd known existed. For someone who'd asked her to marry him on multiple occasions.

This time, he was the better person and bridged the silence for them. "When is the service for your father?"

Just being asked, just having to think about it again pushed the tears forward. "Saturday morning at the church." She took a beat before she realized she wasn't being clear. "Our church, First Methodist on South Main. We'll have a reception at the house afterward."

He nodded again. Though she hadn't gotten the news about an accident with both his parents, and though she had family and friends in town at the time, somehow Finn—with no family left around town—had heard about her father passing within just a few days.

She stepped in. "Are you planning to attend?"

It was all so formal and stilted, she thought. This was Finn. Finn Malloy who'd sat behind her in seventh grade English class. Mayfair. Malloy. They'd been placed next to each other that whole year and the next, too. Finn Malloy, the boy she'd accepted a shy request for a date from. Finn who she'd lost her virginity to before heading off to college. Bailey Ann pushed her hands down into her pockets.

"Am I invited?"

It was a silly question and he probably knew that. Of course, he was invited. The whole town was. Breathless wasn't that big. People who'd known Con Mayfair would simply show up at the church and many, if not most, would follow Bailey Ann and her sisters back to the house. "Of course, you're invited, Finn."

"He didn't like me all that much."

"He didn't like anyone I dated," she retorted quickly to put Finn at ease, but realized quickly that her offhand remark bore a disturbing resemblance to the truth. She covered it with a smile and a straighter spine.

Finn graciously changed the topic. "Are your sisters coming in?"

"I don't know if you heard, but Harper Rose lost her husband about six months back." She didn't add that it was a big fat mess and her little sister had slowly been learning that her husband had no money, they didn't own the house, and he appeared to have no real job. "She's got three little girls to bring with her."

Harper Rose followed in the family footsteps but had her kids much closer together than their parents had. Bailey Ann had yet to find the man to make her a wife. So here she was at thirty-four, talking to Finn Malloy who was gracious enough not to ask if she was still single. She was so boringly single that she'd quit her job and dropped everything to come home when her Daddy called her. She didn't want to dwell on that. "Emma Kate should be in soon, too, but she's working on getting her classes squared away."

At least, Bailey Ann hoped she was. Somehow, she was now the de facto head of this little family of sisters.

"Well, I'm here if you need me." He had his hands still in his pockets but gestured with the flaps of his coat. "It was good to see you, Bailey Ann. It always is."

With that, he turned and walked down the street away from her as she watched. From behind, the wool coat covered the suit that had been a surprise. She saw now that he had on polished shoes and his haircut had been far more expensive than the ones he'd had in school. When she'd known him, he'd been a jeans and t-shirt kind of guy.

When they'd dated, he'd been creative—picnics, hikes, drives out of town. Only rarely did he take her to the movies and even less often to dinner. In the beginning, she'd thought it was just Finn. When he wore the same pair of slacks the second time they'd gone out somewhere nice, she'd started to get a clue. Later, when she'd been in his house, she'd understood.

The Malloys didn't have the extra money for those things. They weren't poor per se, but it seemed they'd spent all their money on the house on Sparrow Road. Their son was in a good neighborhood of a small town, and he was getting a good education at the public school, but they weren't eating steak every week. They weren't getting the threadbare carpets replaced or the front door painted. And Finn wasn't giving her the impression that one day he'd wear wingtips with his perfectly cut suit and fine wool coat.

Then again, he'd always been a surprise.

Bailey found her first smile that day and headed further down the street away from Finn. Toward the corner pizza shop to get a slice and a coke. She needed it. The bad-for-you lunch would provide three of the four food groups—salt, sugar, and grease. She could get the fourth—alcohol—when she got home. She'd decided she was going to open the decanter to Daddy's whiskey and take her first drink of it.

Not that she hadn't had whiskey before, but Daddy had never let her drink in front of him, and he'd never let her have even a sip of the stash he kept at the house. Today, she might need the whole bottle. She had a funeral to plan and a man to get off her mind.

Bailey Ann drove to the airport for the second time in three days. It was morbid, but she thought of her Daddy lying in the morgue, waiting on them to have his funeral. She'd gone into Atlanta both times, since both her sisters weren't willing to pony up the extra cash to fly to a smaller airport closer to Breathless.

Harper Rose was coming in with all three girls—not about to leave any of her children behind after they'd lost first their grandmother, then their father, and now their grandfather. Bailey understood. On the other hand, Emma Kate was just in her twenties and still in school. She was burning through her school money and her student loans. Flights were expensive last minute, and though they'd all known Daddy was going downhill, they hadn't expected it now.

As she took one of the many turns into the Atlanta airport, she maneuvered the lanes like a pro. Her brain was in other places. Wondering how Emma Kate was doing out at UCLA. If her sister was finally staying on track now. Bailey Ann couldn't imagine how her youngest sister was taking this. Emma Kate didn't take much of anything well. While they'd all been Daddy's girls to an extent, Emma was the youngest. She also hadn't been home much this last year, hadn't seen how Daddy had just emotionally disintegrated without Mama. Bailey's arrival had made the household run smoother, but it hadn't changed anything for how he felt.

He'd gotten the flu, which hadn't really worried anyone. Then it had become pneumonia, which had. Then he was gone. That was it. Bailey Ann turned her thoughts with the car's wheel and started looking for her sister at the pick-up curb.

She tried to stop thinking about Finn Malloy and whether he'd show up or not. She tried not to think about the last time she'd run into him and whether or not they could call it a one-night stand since they'd gone together for over a year in high school.

The hand waving emphatically caught her eye and she looked up. It could have been anyone, but it was Emma Kate. She knew her own sister. Bailey inched the car forward trying to get into a closer pickup space. Her little sis walked the last few feet, a bright smile on her face and a small rolling suitcase behind her.

It hadn't hit her yet. Bailey Ann could tell.

Putting the car in park, Bailey climbed out and wrapped her sister in a big hug. She'd just entertained the thought of taking Emma Kate home to let Mama tell her the news, since her sister clearly hadn't absorbed the shock yet. But Bailey was in for her own shock. There was no Mama waiting at home to soothe a hurt heart. There was no Daddy either—not so good at soothing but always ready with a gruff command that surprisingly helped. No. It was just Bailey Ann now. Sudden matriarch of the Mayfair Clan.

"Emma Kate, it's so good to see you."

"Em," her sister reminded her, never having liked the full two-name moniker Della Mayfair had bestowed upon all her girls. Emma was also an "Emerson," another point against the name. Bailey Ann thought it was a shame to chop such a pretty name down to what sounded like a single letter.

She'd been ten when her baby sister had been born, and she'd loved the infant with everything she had. Enough not to be too jealous that her little sister had a prettier name than she did. Nor did she get jealous when Emma Kate turned into a beauty. Willowy and sporting long, blond hair, Em could have been a model with a few more inches on her. She had mossy green eyes and freckles on pale skin, and she didn't seem to take note of any of it.

What Bailey Ann thought was the best part was that Em's best friend was their cousin, Lennon. Though she was half African-American, she looked far more black than white, and Em had constantly longed for Lennon's ebony coloring, tight curls, and volume in her hair. Lennon was a beauty of her own and the pair turned heads when they were out.

Even now, people were looking. Not at her, she knew. Bailey Ann had brown hair—mahogany if she was being generous. She had brown eyes, a squarish face, and was passably attractive on her good days. Em here wasn't wearing any makeup, had paler eyelashes than Bailey Ann and was still getting looks. Bailey had come to accept that a long time ago. "Let's get in the car before they start honking at us."

She lifted the little suitcase wishing it were bigger but knowing that it couldn't be. Em had to get back to her classes. She was in her senior year, though Bailey had heard no word about how that was going. Yet another thing that Mama and Daddy had kept tabs on that was now going to fall to her. She hadn't decided how much of her sister's keeper she was going to need to be. Maybe this weekend would tell.

They climbed in and shut the doors in perfect unison, just like sisters.

"Is Harper at the house?" Em used only the first of her sister's two names.

Bailey nodded. "With the girls."

"I can't wait to see them. It's been too long." She rested her elbow on the car window and settled her chin in her hand.

Bailey didn't bother pointing out that she actually lived closer to Harper Rose and the girls than she herself did. It wasn't that far from Los Angeles to San Fransisco, but Em never made it out. Maybe she was studying too much. Maybe Bailey would buy that pile of crap later, but not today. She decided silence was the better part of valor and kept her mouth shut. Besides, no one needed a fight at Daddy's funeral. Wouldn't that keep the gossip mill turning for a while?

They stopped at a drive through for a snack, since Emma Kate said they hadn't fed her on the plane, and Bailey managed to put ranch dressing on the front of her shirt. "Good lord."

She tried to watch the road, clean up, and not think about the damage to a nice blouse she probably shouldn't have been wearing to drive to the airport.

"Good one, Bailey."

"I guess I'm not wearing this under my gray sweater for the service," she sighed.

"Why do you even own a gray sweater?"

Bailey Ann deflected that question. "Tell me you brought something appropriate."

"No, ma'am, I just thought I'd borrow your gray sweater. I didn't know you were planning on wearing it." Emma Kate looked back out the window. "No worries, I'm sure you have more than one."

"I do not!" She always rose to the bait. Her little sister was plenty smart and knew exactly where her buttons were. Brown hair, brown eyes, gray sweater, old maid. She did not own two gray sweaters. It was a cardigan, too. She sighed to herself. The blouse had to go to Mr. Waddell at the dry cleaners.

"So how is school going?" She tried to start a conversation.

"Do you really want to know?"

Well, crap. Maybe she didn't. "Do I?"

"I don't think I can finish this year," there was not so much disappointment in her voice as there was resignation.

"That's a shame." Bailey decided not to chide the way Daddy

had. Daddy believed in "getting things done." Bailey had at least been the best at that. Mama would have guilted. Daddy would have reminded Emma Kate exactly how much money was left in her college fund. Bailey wasn't either of them, she hadn't achieved that status. Hell, she hadn't even found a decent enough boyfriend to marry yet.

"Yeah, my thesis is not coming together. I should have had my preliminary work done and I can't even find enough background information to support the idea yet." She was still looking out the window though Bailey Ann detected something more in the set of her sister's shoulders. She couldn't quite place her finger on it.

"Can you finish over summer?" Bailey took the exit that led into Breathless. Once the town had been called Mayfair, after some great-great ancestor of theirs, but that had changed when most of the buildings and homes were destroyed in the war. There was a plaque in the middle of town about it, and everyone knew, but that was about it. It had been called Breathless since it had been rebuilt.

"I don't think so. My committee probably won't be around then."

That, Bailey Ann understood. Her own senior year had been a whirlwind. She'd been doing her capstone project, prepping for her new job, and she'd been a bridesmaid three times over. Emma Kate wasn't even in a sorority, a fact Mama had lamented repeatedly. *Where had she gone wrong with the baby?*

Well, Bailey Ann didn't know the answer to that, or that it required one. She pulled into the driveway and under the carport in the back of the house, bracing herself for the cold from the car to mudroom door. Like a good sister, she held the door for Emma Kate and her little suitcase. Then she watched as her baby sister walked into the light and into the waiting arms of three little girls yelling "Auntie Em! Auntie Em!"

They didn't get the irony.

Harper Rose came up and hugged her next, only she didn't

ask about school or anything, she only said, "You look good, baby sister."

Bailey Ann could learn a thing or two.

Emma Kate smiled back. "How's San Fran treating you?"

"They have no manners."

Bailey Ann laughed.

*Every funeral had best have a reception afterward in the relatives'
home. If there isn't fried chicken and Co-Cola cake, the deceased
hasn't been sent off properly.*

BAILEY ANN LOOKED AROUND THE LIVING ROOM, THEN
turned to her sister. "Harper Rose, do we have everything?"

"Please, Bailey, this is the one time it doesn't matter."

Correct as usual, she thought. No matter how hard Bailey tried
to do everything right, she couldn't live up to her middle sister.
Harper Rose was a natural. She showed up flawless and ready to
every event, and she knew when to show her flaws, too, without
seeking attention and only looking human rather than actually
flawed. It all just worked out for her. She'd graduated summa
cum laude, married her boyfriend, and had three beautiful
daughters. Everything right on time. *Except the early widowhood.*
Bailey shut her uncharitable thoughts down and stepped back.
"You're right. Are you ready?"

"That doesn't matter either. There's a car out front and we
are on whether we are ready or not." Harper Rose smiled and
shook her head. Her dark coppery hair curled to perfection,

resembling a modern version of a fifties star. Her dress was dusty teal, complementing her coloring. She'd shown up to a funeral in green, and she'd looked far more appropriate than Bailey Ann had. She regretted the gray sweater. Harper Rose was a classic no matter what she did.

Sucking in a breath, Bailey Ann opened the front door.

It was a good thing too. Her mother's old friend, Mara Lamont, didn't have a hand to knock with. She was holding a huge platter of fried chicken. "Hi, baby, just tell me where to put this."

"We've got the kitchen table cleared off for food," Bailey gestured toward the formal dining room and Emma Kate came and took the platter out of the woman's hands.

Em had donned a dark brown skirt that swirled around her legs, a white button-down blouse she'd borrowed from Bailey, and some bamboo, three-quarter sleeve, slouchy sweater in almost the same shade of brown. It had a hood, and she was wearing snakeskin heels to her Daddy's funeral. She was herself, that was for certain. Harper Rose told Em she looked good again. Bailey held her tongue.

By the time she turned back to the door, three more people were on her front step. The Markmans and Mrs. Winchell down the street. Bailey Ann started ferrying the food back and forth, saying her hellos in between as she could. She hugged her visitors when warranted and leaned a head on shoulders when her hands were full. She said her thank-yous, and even accepted one crushing hug while she was holding a tray with a ring of Jello-salad. Lord knew how she didn't manage to smash it into her chest. Her mother would have called it a Christmas Miracle, despite the fact that it was neither. It would have been a miracle if she could have gotten a legitimate excuse to change out of her dull black and gray outfit and not have to eat a bite of that damn Jello salad then lie about how she'd enjoyed it.

Bailey didn't like lying, not really in any form, but she disliked disappointing her elders more. Mama and Daddy had drilled it into all three of them. It hadn't really taken with Emma Kate much at all. All the lessons seemed to have bounced right off the baby of the family. Harper Rose absorbed them, then picked and chose and let some of them go. Only Bailey had taken all the lessons to heart, unable to make them her own. Even though both her parents were officially gone as of today, the need to please them clung like vines around her heart.

She was smiling at Mrs. Naman and admiring her beautiful East Indian funeral garb—brought out special for Con Mayfair's passing—when Bailey Ann felt the shift in the air. She'd thought it was a remnant of high school. She'd thought she was over such foolish things as crushes and sighs, but she turned.

In her doorway stood Finn Malloy, holding a platter with a creamy colored cake. His eyes caught hers for a second and she felt a flash of heat, followed by a surge of sympathy. He'd been in this same place himself, only he'd lost both parents at the same time and unexpectedly. She also had not come to comfort him. But why would she? They were an old story, finished and done.

She was walking toward him when he was intercepted by Harper Rose. As she watched, Harper said something, thanked him, and headed over toward the table. With a small smile, Bailey met up with her sister and began re-arranging the already too-full table to accommodate yet another dish. There was no making it happen.

Harper Rose sighed, then did that mother thing where she looked around the room until she spotted each child. She must have been checking a list and each child passed, because she looked back at her older sister and said, "We have to move some of it."

Bailey Ann was already on it. There were china dishes on the sideboard, knicknacks that her mother had hoarded and displayed. Scooping them up, Bailey wondered if they'd ever get put back. It took three trips to clear all the ceramics, small plates, and passed down teacups that had adorned the top of the sideboard and mostly created some very complicated dusting problems. By the time she returned, Harper Rose had moved the salads to the sideboard, creating only a small extra amount of space.

She stood back, hands on her hips in that fashionably thrown back teal dress. "If more than just a few more people show up, we'll have to do this again."

"I'll get the card table," Bailey was on the move already, heading up the stairs to their old bedrooms. She passed the door that held the bunk beds in the small room Emma Kate and Harper had shared. Now it held Harper's three girls, one on an inflatable mattress. Bailey Ann had left her own door open, the queen bed perfectly made, a handful of guests having taken her up on tossing their jackets or purses onto the bed. She'd given Harper the master bedroom, unable to take it over herself for any number of reasons.

She was staring into the hall closet when she felt him behind her.

"How can I help?" Finn's voice rolled over her, warm and comforting.

She sighed though, not letting him know how good he made her feel. It didn't matter anyway, there was nothing to be done about it. "There's supposed to be a card table in the back of this closet."

She couldn't see it, and watched as Finn tilted his head, bent down to peer into the bottom section and basically did everything she'd just done. "I don't see it."

"Thanks," she commented wryly.

"Sorry." He at least had the decency to step back and look sheepish. "Where else could it be?"

She crossed her arms. She'd lived here for three months now, and still had no idea about some things. She'd moved out for college fifteen years earlier and not really looked back. She'd known Harper Rose had taken over her bedroom then, leaving Emma Kate in the bunks by herself. But the rest of it? Unless it was out and open, like Mama's teacups, she didn't know where it would be. "The shed out back? In the basement? My closet, Daddy's? It could be anywhere."

"So, how important is this card table?" He was looking at her as though this was a legit question.

"I don't know. It's a funeral reception. We just need a place to put more food if it shows up."

"Gotcha. No worries, then. Go back down and talk to people. I'll be back in a bit."

He didn't give her time to ask, and she only got a second to admire the breadth of his shoulders as she frowned at his back. He disappeared down the hall and out the back door before she could say anything.

She wasn't quite ready to face everyone again. Besides, Harper Rose and Emma Kate were holding down the fort just fine. Actually, they were doing a better job than she had been. So she stood in the hallway and leaned her head back against the wall. She felt tears on her face a moment later and ducked into the bathroom to wash them away. Without Daddy here, she looked at the space as no-longer-his-and-Mama's. Until today, she'd been living in their house again. The pastel blue of this bathroom hadn't bothered her when it was theirs. But now, it was hers and her sisters' and it was so out of date.

Mama hadn't changed with the times. She hadn't updated the decor. But could Bailey blame her? It had turned out later that Mama had been sick a lot longer than she'd let on to any of them. Only Daddy had known. Probably her bathroom color scheme wasn't at the top of her list. But seriously, it had been fading out of date before Bailey left for college. Maybe it was just her, just the funeral, just the final loss of her last parent. She turned away and went into her bedroom.

She'd updated this room since she'd come back. Took down the posters Harper Rose had hung in her last years of high school. Bailey Ann had even painted the room and brought her own bedding. But now she didn't look at any of it, just headed over to the window to catch the movement out there.

There was Finn, walking along the top of the low, stone retaining wall that separated the yards in their neighborhood. His house was two over on the street behind theirs. But here he was, a grown man, still coming over to her house balancing on top of that silly wall. This time, he had some kind of folding table under his arm. She felt her heart twist with thanks, and even so, watching him navigate the uneven stone took her back.

✣ 4 ✣

Finn was back in the dining room, talking with Emma Kate, by the time he saw Bailey Ann coming back downstairs. He and Em were catching up while they pulled the legs out on the skinny plastic table he'd brought over from his own home. Or was it really just his parents' home? He didn't know and figured Bailey Ann was grappling with the same problem.

"Here," she held out the tablecloth she'd brought from the upstairs closet. Her tone was rough but he decided to attribute it to the fact that she was still at her father's funeral and the wound was fresh.

Bailey shoved the cloth at her younger sister, frowning and looking back and forth between him and Em. The look was disapproving, but maybe that was just what filtered out from under the sadness. She couldn't think he was flirting with Emma Kate. He was way too old for that. He was a year ahead of Bailey in school, and there was over a decade gap between Bailey and her little sis. Not okay.

He smiled at Bailey as if to reassure her he was just being nice. Still, her feelings were running across her face in waves. He'd always been able to read them, but now they looked jumbled, and there was nothing he could do. Nothing he should do.

Lifting the table, he helped Em fold the tablecloth in half then drape it over the small surface, tucking it against the wall to make space. He'd found a long, skinny table, and even Bailey Ann would have to admit it was perfect for the job. It fit in the back of the room without causing the need to move the big table, which would have been a pain.

Despite all that, she was still frowning. Then her full lips opened and her sad words tumbled out.

"I just expected to see Mama's card table out here. I know it would have been awkward and all wrong for the space. But . . ."

He nodded. His table was perfect, but she resented it. He could tell.

"Thank you." She squeezed the words out and then turned away as he and Emma Kate looked at her oddly. He fought the urge to follow her out of the room. Instead, he watched as she turned and spoke to the people who'd come to pay respects to her father.

Lennon and Jackson Mayfair—the sisters' cousins—came through the door just then. Finn recognized the family and the family's famous Co-Cola cake that Lennon carried. What people wouldn't suspect was that Jackson was the one who'd made it.

"Cousin Jax! Lennon!" Harper Rose jumped up to greet them, so Finn hung back and watched as the brother and sister came in through the door trailed by their father, Dex Mayfair. Her uncle. Daddy's brother. Uncle Dex—Finn had picked up the moniker from Bailey Ann back in high school—was holding the hands of two little dark-haired, dark-eyed girls—Jackson's kids. He'd married young and his wife had died young, while giving birth to the twins, leaving Jax on his own to raise them. The girls looked a lot like Jackson, mixed race.

Uncle Dex had always liked Finn and been better to him than Con and Della Mayfair had been. But then again, Bailey Ann wasn't his daughter. Also, he'd been the first Mayfair to marry outside his race, but he hadn't stepped outside the boundaries of marrying a belle. Aunt GiGi was a magnolia to her toes. Her mama had been Mayor of Breathless for a while, too. Spines of steel on that side of the family. Dex Mayfair had always been more open minded than his brother. Finn had more than once wished Bailey Ann was his daughter rather than the child of the man they were burying today.

Con's youngest sibling, his sister Westerley Mayfair Weaver trailed in the door behind her brother Dex. Her husband Dawson, and two of their children, Carlisle and Charlie, followed her. Five minutes later, their oldest, Christian, showed up with his new fiancé, Riley, on his arm. Bailey Ann couldn't help but smile at them as they entered. Christian was definitely of the more introverted and maybe even reclusive type, but even Finn could see Riley brought out the best in him. Finn looked from Riley to Bailey and from Christian to himself and tamped down the envy that tried to hit.

Hail, Hail, he thought, *The Mayfairs have all arrived*. It was uncharitable thinking, he knew, but he'd always been a little jealous of the family, too. He had only his parents and his sister. Bailey Ann had that plus four cousins she loved and had grown up with, two sets of aunts and uncles, and even still had Nana Rue. She may have lost both her parents, but she still had a huge support system.

Finn was here for the funeral, but he didn't have a lot of love lost. Con and Della were part of the reason he and Bailey Ann weren't together now, and—gone or not—he struggled to forgive them for the wedges they'd driven in.

"Lenn!"

"Em!"

Everyone turned as they watched the two youngest Mayfair cousins shoot across the room, meeting in the middle, embracing in a wash of colors and contrasts. Their tone did not match the fact that they were at a funeral, but even Bailey Ann didn't protest. As far as he could tell, the two hadn't seen each other in a while.

A minute later, Aunt GiGi came through the door with Bailey's Nana Rue, Con and Dex and Westerley's mother. Everyone in Breathless knew all the Mayfairs. They were small town royalty. So Finn could easily name Bailey Ann's grandmother, her aunts and uncles, cousins and so on. Nana Rue had been good to him, too. He'd appealed to her at one point while Bailey Ann was still in high school, but she'd pointed out that there was nothing anyone could do when Della Mayfair made up her mind. Now, he understood she'd lost her son this week. None of it seemed right.

Bailey Ann smiled but he could see her heart was in a twist. Nothing was okay for her. No one else really seemed to see it. And there wasn't anything he could do. Not here. Not now.

They were celebrating a life well lived, but not lived nearly long enough. Though Harper Rose and Emma Kate seemed to accept the situation, the way Bailey Ann's smiles didn't reach her eyes told him she wasn't taking it well at all.

She was making her way around the room, not paying overt attention to him at all. But he wanted to believe she knew where he was as she made her way closer. When she sent Jackson to help Nana Rue with a plate, she was close enough to smell her perfume. Finn had noticed before that it was the same one she'd worn in high school. Luckily, she'd been a classic even then, and it still fit her perfectly. He tried not to think about the memories it brought back.

"How are you holding up?" He asked, watching as her spine straightened at his words.

Totally the wrong time and place for his feelings, but that had always been the case for them.

"I'm doing okay." She shrugged her reply but didn't turn around to look at him.

"You're a terrible liar." He leaned in close to her ear to

whisper it and watched as she tried to ignore the arc between them.

"I am not."

"So, you're a good liar?"

She just stood there, not turning around and not answering. Not until he prodded her. "What's really wrong, Bailey Ann?"

He always used her full name. She'd always liked it and he'd keep doing it until she told him not to.

Turning to face him, she crossed her arms and he watched her eyes start to fill. "What? My Daddy died and I'm at his funeral and I'm in need of another reason?"

He felt like crap for pushing, but she stared at him as though she were sad, not angry. He leaned back against the front closet door, the only place left not crowded by Con Mayfair's friends and family come to pay their respects. "No, you don't *need* another reason, but you *have* one. Tell me."

He hadn't even laid eyes on her in over five years. Why did she tear him up like this?

"It's too early," she protested the whole problem. "Daddy died too young. Mama did, too, you know?"

He nodded but let her go on and she did, keeping her voice low.

"Mama was at least sick. There was an explanation. But Daddy?" She shook her head like she was shaking off a bad feeling, and Finn started to get one, too ". . . He just let go!" That was the other thing bothering her. He could see it. "Why does everyone think that's okay? It's not."

She uncrossed her arms and crossed them again. Now her discomfort looked almost painful.

Finn shifted on his feet, his eyes scanning the crowd for anyone paying attention to them. Only Harper Rose seemed to have noticed her sister's tiff, and she offered him a nod and moved on to handle the crowd.

Keeping his voice low, he tried to be soothing, but heard the hint of Ireland coming through. It always happened when he felt something strongly. No matter how much he'd tried to remove the accent, it came back when he least needed it. He must feel something now, because he could hear the brogue brushing the edges of his words. "Maybe he loved your mother so much, he couldn't go on without her. You know, some people never get to have that kind of connection."

There was a small pause from Bailey Ann as her eyes blinked and he could only wonder if she was thinking what he was. But he talked over his own thoughts. Now was not the time or the place for his own feelings about the woman in front of him. They were too complex for one conversation anyway. "I think you're right that his life was too short, but I think people are beginning to accept his death because his life was well lived. He took care of your mother, he raised three girls into adulthood. Worked his job, was a central figure in the community. He always lent a helping hand." Finn shrugged, "I'm not sure there's more he could have accomplished."

Bailey Ann's chin trembled. "He didn't stick around to see his grandkids."

"Aren't the H's his granddaughters?" Finn sounded confused.

"The Hs?" He watched as she deflected with a smile and waited while he struggled to remember all Harper Rose's girls' names.

"Hannah, Hayden and . . . Not Hoyden—"

"No, not Hoyden!" She almost said it too loud. He'd almost made her laugh at her Daddy's funeral.

"Holland." They said it at the same time. But Finn continued. "They're his grandkids."

"He won't see Emma Kate's kids or mine. I guess it wasn't worth hanging around for." Despite the laugh a moment ago, her lips quivered again, and he wanted to kiss her and take that pain away. He wanted to yell and say it was her own fault she hadn't had kids before her Daddy died.

"So you don't have kids?" Finn raised one eyebrow.

"Of course not."

"Well, Em's a bit young for that, isn't she?"

"Yes. And he should have stuck around. We should have been enough."

"Bailey Ann, maybe it was enough that he saw how strong and capable you are. Maybe it was enough to know that you were in a good place and he'd set you up well. Sometimes people are in pain we don't know about."

That got her attention and for the first time, she turned to look at him. "You sound like you know what you're talking about."

He was nodding his head when she heard the voice.

"Bailey Ann, you get over here." Aunt GiGi didn't bellow anything, but her voice commanded respect. "I haven't gotten to give you the hug you so desperately need. More than your sisters even."

With that, she was pulled away from him and enveloped in the kind of embrace that she clearly needed and he couldn't give. She wouldn't take it from him even if he could have offered it. With that thought, Finn turned away.

B ailey Ann held the crystal tumbler out toward her youngest
sister.

"Daddy's whiskey?" Emma Kate exclaimed, but she didn't
hand back the tumbler. "I've never touched these." She sounded
almost in awe.

"Touched what?" Harper Rose asked, coming down the steps
in stockinged feet. The teal dress still looked good, but the
woman looked a little worn down, having taken off her smile
with her shoes.

"Bailey Ann is giving us Daddy's whiskey in Daddy's glasses!"

Bailey was pretty certain that—like her—neither sister had
ever touched this stuff except to dust the decanter if he'd been
traveling.

"We aren't allowed," Harper Rose protested.

Bailey only raised one eyebrow. By God, if she could get
through her father's funeral in her dull black and gray outfit and
choke down a little of that Jello salad with every canned fruit
known to man inside, then she could drink her Daddy's whiskey.
"Look at it this way, if he protests from the heavens, at least we'll
get to hear his voice again."

With that proclamation, Harper Rose accepted the third cut

glass and raised it. "To Daddy. Wherever he is, he's mad that we're drinking his whiskey."

"To Daddy," Em added, "May he rest in peace, probably at one of his time shares."

Bailey almost laughed, but she sombered as she added her own bit. "To Daddy. He went too young."

"He's with Mama now." Harper Rose held the glass out and stared at it.

"What?" Bailey asked, taking a sip and letting the very expensive amber liquid soak into her tongue before it even made it down her throat.

"That's some good shit." Her sister's voice was a little hoarse from taking too big a first sip and Bailey did finally laugh. Harper Rose continued. "No wonder he didn't let us have it. We'd have become alcoholics." She tipped up the glass, finished off what little she had left and poured herself another. Then she looked up at her sisters. "Oh, don't mind me. I've lost my mother to a massive battle with cancer. Then my husband to a freak accident. And now my Daddy, all within one year. I have three small children and no relief. I'm drinking this."

She raised the glass with a smile and at least this time, she didn't pound it back. She did reach up and pull out whatever clip she'd been using to hold her hair up and proceeded to massage her head while she drank herself to a good buzz with her eyes closed.

Bailey Ann, always the oldest, but now the leader of this little family, decided it was time for a serious discussion. "We have the will to deal with Monday morning."

"I can't," Emma Kate was the first to get out of anything. Had she gotten away with it all along because she was the baby? Bailey Ann couldn't really remember. If that was the case, then surely she was partly responsible. She'd been part and parcel to spoiling the cute youngest sister.

Now, she looked at that baby, all grown up, and wondered if

they'd gone wrong. For God's sakes, this was the reading of her Daddy's will. "Why can't you?"

"I have class. My flight back is tomorrow evening."

"You can't take one day off?"

"I couldn't afford a Monday flight!" Em protested. "I'm a poor college student, remember?"

That, Bailey understood. She did remember. She turned to Harper Rose.

"Don't look at me." She was shaking her head as she stepped up to the cart and poured herself yet another two fingers. Bailey Ann was still on her first. Harper Rose frowned. "Don't judge me. Thiss iss my lasst one."

The creeping lisp made one side of Bailey's mouth quirk. She wasn't sure she'd seen Harper Rose even a little drunk since high school. Then her middle sister sighed. Not a sweet release of tension, this was big. Weary. Burdened.

Bailey understood. Harper Rose had lost everyone but her sisters and her own clutch of little girls. But Bailey wasn't prepared when Harper Rose glided over to the table and sat down. "Y'all should come sit to hear this."

Bailey topped off her own drink, but Emma Kate refused, clutching her glass to her chest and clearly starting to worry. Bailey would have reassured her, but she had no idea what was coming.

When they were all three seated at the table—a clean cloth set out by Aunt GiGi after she put away all the food—Bailey set her arms on the table. Elbows off. She simply could not bring herself to rest her elbows on the table lest the ghost of her late Mama reach out from the beyond and smack her.

Harper Rose didn't beat around the bush. "I can't come to the will either. The girls and I fly out tomorrow, too."

"*You're leaving me to do this all alone?*" Bailey did not have control of either her mouth or her emotions. She blamed the whiskey.

"I can't stay." Harper looked up at the ceiling. "I have to get the girls back into school and find a job and . . ." Another sigh. "So when Thad died, I was a mess for a week or so."

"I remember." Bailey Ann had flown out and stayed with her sister for two weeks. It was part of the reason she'd quit her job and come back to Breathless to live with Daddy. She'd taken a leave of absence for Mama too, and she didn't have any days left. She remembered sitting at Harper Rose's side. Em had come out, too, able to drive to San Francisco from Los Angeles. Those thoughts pierced Bailey's heart each time she had them.

"Well, I lied to you all." Harper dropped a mini bomb that would detonate when she told them what she lied about. "I didn't mean to lie, but I did. When I called the life insurance place, I found out he'd let it expire. He hadn't paid it for two years."

"What!" Both Bailey and Emma reacted like shattering glass, but Harper Rose stayed calm. Apparently, she'd weathered this storm already.

"Oh yes, but it gets worse. Our savings is gone. The house is owned by a shell corporation, not by my husband and not by me. I had no idea!" She gestured wildly, gracefully almost sloshing out some of her whiskey.

"Are you okay?" Bailey was leaning forward now, very concerned. She'd always thought Harper Rose had it all. Her middle sis had done everything right. She'd married her college boyfriend right after graduation. She'd had Hannah right away, never having gotten a job with her childhood education and music degree. They'd lived in the big, pretty house in the beautiful neighborhood in the expensive city, and the only thing Bailey had ever seen wrong was that they'd had to move so far away.

"I'm okay. I'm fighting to keep the house. At least to be able to sell it and keep a portion of the profit. But I don't know. I don't want to move the girls if I don't have to. And I have to get a job, right away."

"Ouch," Bailey Ann commented, though she'd been working

at her job in finance ever since she'd graduated and turned down Todd Hooker's proposal. He'd done the right thing—proposing at graduation—but she'd thought there was something better out there. And she was pretty convinced she could not go through life as Bailey Ann Hooker. A later relationship had drug on until that man proposed to her, but Ray Haley had not been the man of her dreams either, and she'd broken it off. That time she'd even told him she would never be Bailey Haley. But Harper Rose had struck gold with her first shot. Or so they had all believed.

"I let him handle the money, you know, the way Mama and Daddy split it up. I took care of the kids, the house, and us, and he was supposed to pay the bills. Except he hadn't been paying them. He'd gotten into a lot of debt. Apparently, we couldn't really afford that house in the first place. I didn't know that, but he'd gotten it financed. Then he bought us a car we couldn't afford—certainly not on top of the house payment. But he wouldn't have me work for money and he wanted to have the best of everything. Well, he got it. I put him in the ground in a super expensive casket because I didn't know I needed to save my money."

That hurt. Harper Rose had loved Thad, but now she sounded bitter about the man. Though Bailey had to admit she understood that. Thad seemed to have taken everything and left her sister holding the bag.

"Do you need help?" She thought about the savings she had and that it was dwindling. But Harper Rose and her daughters probably needed it more.

"No, but like Emma Kate here, I can't afford Monday tickets. Not for four of us."

Bailey Ann cringed. It hadn't occurred to her that Harper would be strapped for cash.

"The one thing you can do is take care of this, that would be a big help." Harper Rose gestured to the house they were sitting in and Bailey Ann looked around. First, she looked at her sisters

—both had plans they had to get back to. She had none. Then she looked at the walls. Burgundy striped wallpaper climbed above the once-stark-white chair rail. Below the middle piece of molding, the wainscoting ran around the room. Wood grain showed beneath the burgundy paint and Bailey Ann had second thoughts.

"Do you want me to sell the place? They had those time shares. And I'm assuming it's all going to be divided evenly between us in the will. It might get y'all some cash."

Harper Rose looked around the room and drained her glass. "Have you been to the beach time sshare lately? It hasn't held up well. And this place? It's not gonna net us enough cassh to save the day. Do whatever you think is best."

Emma Kate nodded, and Bailey Ann found herself in charge of her parents estate alone.

🐾 6 🐾

If you've got a to-do list that's bad, pick the worst thing first. It's called "eating your frog." If there's a frog on your list, eat it first.

PULLING HER BLUE JACKET OFF THE HOOK IN THE MUDROOM, Bailey Ann headed out the back door. She was happy to leave the house behind for a while.

The day before, Harper Rose and the girls had decided to go to the airport early with Emma Kate. Honestly, Bailey Ann wouldn't have had time to get down to the Atlanta airport twice in that time frame. The only solution was for them to go with Auntie Em and hang around for several hours. She didn't envy her sister being stuck in the airport for that long with three small kids to entertain. At least Em would help while she could.

But the house had felt so empty last night she almost couldn't stand it. She'd had another drink of Daddy's whiskey, noticing how low the amber liquid had gotten in the crystal decanter. That would have to be her last for at least a while. It wasn't because she was worried about becoming a lush or anything. It was because, if she drank any more, she would have to refill it. She'd never drunk any of it until this last week, and she'd never filled the decanter either. It was Daddy's. She wasn't ready.

Last night had been a hell of a pity party with only one glass of whiskey. The house was empty. She had no job. No husband. No kids and no parents to take care of anymore. Just an uncertain future looming in the same small town she'd grown up in. She liked it here. Liked that she remembered Daddy's lawyer from church. Delia at the Sun Up and Shine knew her breakfast order and gave her pulp free orange juice without her having to ask. Bailey Ann liked the street she'd grown up on. There was a school across the street—an elementary that often had kids out at play. She liked that she could walk a lot of places and everything was close. But she was utterly alone.

Even Daddy, poor company that he'd often been, had been *something*. So she'd spent the evening staring at the TV in the cabinet, most of the things in there out of date. Daddy insisted on watching his football live, and Thad had convinced him to come around to HD TV, but they'd never managed to talk the man into a recorder. *Mama would have liked one*, Bailey Ann thought, but what Daddy didn't care about, Mama didn't care about.

She sighed and climbed into the cold car, wishing she'd thought to run out and start the engine earlier. She'd parked herself in the spot closest to the back door, having moved Daddy's old Cadillac into the far spot several days after he died. It was another thing she hadn't wanted to do, but she'd done it, knowing it was better to rip the band aid off.

Shivering as she put her small sporty car into reverse, Bailey Ann backed out onto the street. Her father had taught her to drive here, now she had a Caddy to sell. Her sisters hadn't wanted it. It wasn't antique or anything, just another thing on a growing to-do list.

She was at the lawyer's before she'd even thought about it, and she parked and ran in, shaking off the cold. She greeted Mrs.

Treackle where she sat behind the desk. In Nashville, she would have given her name. Here, Mrs. Treackle already knew it.

"Honey, he's waiting. Just go on in."

The blessing and the curse of the small town. Nowhere to hide. No time to catch your breath. Bailey Ann smiled her thank you and headed down the hall. She took a moment to pretend she was looking at the pictures, when really she was gathering her thoughts and thinking about the cheap wood paneling they'd never upgraded in here. The carpet was old and starting to show the wear. Even Mrs. Treackle was getting up in years. Still, the service was solid, the old ties strong. She pushed through the doorway.

"Good morning, Mr. Ball."

The lawyer smiled up at her then hid the frown that flashed across his features. "Are you the only one we are expecting?"

"Sadly, yes," she sighed. She explained about the girls and school in San Francisco, about Emma Kate and exams in Los Angeles. Bailey Ann had come when Mama was sick. She'd come back when Daddy was sick. So why shouldn't she be the one to do this, too? "They decided I should handle it." She paused. "Actually, I think Daddy named me the executor of his will. Is that right?"

He and Mama both had done so when Mama got sick. Not because they didn't trust each other, but because Mama had foresight and knew Daddy wouldn't do the work to get it changed after she was gone. It also had soothed Bailey Ann, thinking they were both doing it because it needed to be done, not because Mama was dying or anything. Instead, it had been exactly because Mama was dying. Bailey moved to the job at hand. She could hear Mama's voice telling her to eat her frog. "Shall we get started?"

"And finished." Mr. Ball smiled.

"I'm sorry?" She'd barely gotten her coat off and she frowned up at him.

"Con wasn't a man of many words, you know that. He was

much the same, legally." Bailey was getting it now, but she let Mr. Ball keep talking. "I have papers that he was of sound mind, that kind of thing. But mostly, his will states that all possessions be shared equally between you three girls."

Bailey Ann raised one eyebrow. "Well, I guess I should have expected that. Now I get to spend the next five years finding out what all these things are."

"There, I can help. I did get him to give me a list."

Bailey nodded, *good*. Daddy had just nodded off one night in his recliner and not woken up the next day. Bailey Ann was playing this blind.

Mr. Ball pushed the papers across the desk. "I can do an actual reading of the will, but it seems silly with just the two of us." He explained the will itself. It wasn't as short as Bailey had thought from what he'd said before, the legalese added to Daddy's words. Still, she could hear his terse comments in there. He'd probably just walked in, taken off his hat and demanded Mr. Ball "just give it all to my girls." He might have even walked right out after that, thinking he'd said it, so it was done.

Mr. Ball was still talking, so Bailey pulled herself out of her little daydream.

"This is the additional documentation. Here's his list of assets."

Bailey barely looked at it. She'd check it later when she could get out a pen and search the house for whatever items her Daddy had considered assets. She looked up again at Mr. Ball who was now asking her if she had a death certificate and explaining what paperwork she would need to be able to get into the accounts.

"The bank accounts and the assets are all jointly held in both his name and your mother's. So you'll need both sets of paperwork to get control of them."

"He never took Mama off the account?" she asked it before she even thought. Of course, Daddy hadn't. Why would he? She sighed. In about five more minutes she'd been handed all the copies that were hers in a nice manila envelope and she'd left.

She tossed the envelope on the seat of the car beside her, thinking it looked sad to have Daddy's life wrapped up in such a tiny package. Then she decided that it didn't matter, and she needed pizza for lunch. She headed over to Bobby's.

There was usually a wait, but she was alone and it was early. She got lucky and got a table right near the front window and ordered a small pie with extra cheese, mushrooms, and pepperoni. Her stomach grumbled despite the fact that she'd eaten a decent breakfast. It must be the smell. It must be the cheesy, greasy calories hanging in the air. She'd been here far too often since she arrived. Bobby's was incredibly local—a chain with this place and the little take out down the street from her house and restaurants in each of the nearby towns. But all in all, Bobby only owned seven stores. He was local famous and so was the pie. It was probably solely responsible for the five pounds she'd gained since she returned home. She'd been exercising better and stressing out and she should have lost weight, but Bobby's was sending her the other way. She didn't care today.

She'd been looking at her phone and not paying attention when she sensed him.

Finn Malloy slid into the seat across from her and grinned. "What are you doing in here eating pizza all alone?"

"Well," she snarked back, "I was eating pizza all alone."

7

Finn sat and watched as Bailey Ann bit into the best pizza in town. He'd sat himself down and was waiting for his own order to arrive.

Though he waited like a gentleman, not even asking for a slice from her order, she eyed him cautiously. Then again, he hadn't asked if he could join her, so his gentleman status was shaky at best.

By the time his order showed up, he was past ready from smelling the pizza at the table. She watched him as he ungracefully bit into the melted cheese too soon. Everyone in town had burned the roof of their mouth on a slice of Bobby's.

Her eyebrow popped up. "Have you not learned?"

"Never." He grinned through the pain. "It's worth it."

Bailey Ann clearly disagreed but didn't say so. She just changed the subject. "So how long are you in town for?"

Opting for more decorum for the rest of the meal, Finn waited until he finished chewing his bite, then wiped his mouth with a napkin and leaned back. "I really have no idea."

"Do you have plans?" She took another bite. This was her real talent: small talk with a side of southern manipulation when she wanted it. What Finn really wanted to know—and what he likely wasn't going to get out in public—was the knowledge of whether she was really interested in what was going on with him, or if she was just using her patented skills.

He wanted to believe she really wanted to know about him. So he answered as though she did. Or he tried. "My mom and dad left me the house—"

"They didn't split it between you and Sioban?" Bailey Ann shocked him by interrupting. Maybe she really did want to know.

He almost smiled. "Well, yes, but . . ." He took a moment to frame it. There was a lot of family history that he couldn't quite wedge into a discussion over pizza. "She'll get part of the sale. They seemed to understand that neither of us would be living there. That it wasn't going to be our family home for generations to come like back in the country."

Bailey had been around him long enough to know "back in the country" meant *Ireland*. Normally he would have explained, but not to her. She'd been around his parents enough to learn to understand their relatively thick accents. Finn—who remembered some of his early childhood "back in the country"—had worked hard to shed much of his accent when they'd been in school. "So, they asked if I wanted it after they were gone. They suggested I renovate and sell it." He took another bite of pizza. "It took a long time to figure out if that's what I wanted to do, but then I hit a wall and the decision was made."

"Hit a wall?" Was she running her small talk again? Or did she want to know?

He told himself he didn't want to spill his guts. He wanted to play this closer to the vest with her. So he only said, "With work."

The confused look passed quickly on her face, replaced by what looked like fear. It took him a moment to gather the pieces of his heart back together. She didn't know what he did. Had no one ever commented to her about him? Because everyone loved to keep him up to date on what Bailey Ann Mayfair was doing these days. He knew when she'd graduated, what city she lived in, which bank she'd worked with. But she didn't know about him . . .

"Don't panic. I'll tell you." He pushed a smile forward and leaned in. "I'm an architect."

"What?"

She not only hadn't known, it hurt a bit that it surprised her. Finn talked through it. "I went back, got my masters in it even." How had it happened that Bailey Ann Mayfair, Homecoming Queen of Breathless, was not up to date on her gossip? Maybe he wasn't gossip-worthy. "My parents were proud. It's what we came here for. There weren't enough jobs back in the country. Not enough work so my parents could pay for college, not enough for Sioban and me to get the kind of jobs we wanted. So this is good."

"So what wall did you hit?"

He looked up over her shoulder, felt his eyes glazing for a second, and thought about all the tiny things that had built up. "I do a lot of historic restorations. I do new homes, too, in older styles. It's trendy in wealthier neighborhoods." It took a moment to sort out what to tell, what to keep, what she might want to hear. Then he looked back at her. "I was doing a new house in an old neighborhood. The original had burned, the new one needed to fit in."

Taking another dainty bite of her pizza—his had disappeared —she nodded at him to go on.

"There's a lot of paperwork associated with that kind of work. But we got held up because of a church down the street. They were sheltering homeless people and the neighborhood had taken up a cause to get rid of them. Lots of NIMBY stuff."

"NIMBY?" She asked, wiping her fingers on the small, thin napkins delivered with the pizza.

"Not In My Back Yard." He shook his head. "Laws that keep the poor people out. The undesirables. The house got held up three different times, because the neighbors were passing ordinances trying to *stop* the church from doing good work. There was a bridge nearby—the neighborhood was on the river, and the bridge seemed to attract homeless people. The pastor was occasionally walking people from the bridge to the church building. The neighbors didn't want these people walking by their pretty homes. Then the neighborhood decided the church should move. To a place where they could be helpful, but away from the *nice* people. They built a fence between the bridge and the neighborhood . . ."

His voice trailed off as the resentments poured back in. He'd thought he'd shaken it off. But clearly, he hadn't. "They were kicking the homeless people out of the shelter?"

"Not really, but . . ."

"Effectively, they were. Who does that?"

He shrugged, but she wasn't wrong. "I run into NIMBY laws often enough. Rich people have the money to get it done. They want the homeless people helped, but not where they have to see it. God forbid their view have something bothering it. I saw one place that got a bridge re-done because they looked at the side of it and it was ugly. Not because they were worried about the people driving over it or anything. And I saw one community vote down a windmill farm. I was going to incorporate it into some of the design, but they got it voted down."

"Why would anyone vote down windmills? Like the turbines?"

He nodded.

"They make clean energy," she countered. "We have so many mountains stripped from coal mining, who could complain about windmills?"

He frowned at her as she clearly still didn't get it. "They disturb the view."

"What about the strip mining? Doesn't that disturb the view?" She was incredulous. She'd never heard of this before.

"They don't have to see it. It's on the *poor* mountains."

"Jesus," Bailey muttered then tossed her napkin onto the

little paper plate that had come with her pizza. "That's definitely a wall to hit."

"Too many times. So, I decided it was time to come do something that I could make all the decisions on. Not run into NIMBY laws. Design it myself without someone telling me they want a formal living room they never use." He leaned onto his elbows and grinned at her. "What about you? Are you heading back to Nashville?"

She shrugged. "Eventually?"

Finn heard the question mark at the end of the word and wasn't quite sure how he felt about it. If he'd been asked the same question, he would have answered the same way. He was "between jobs" in the purest sense of the term. He could end up staying or take a position across the country. Hell, he could go back to Ireland. But the woman across the table made him want to rethink that. She always had.

Tipping his head at her, he asked, "How long can you take leave?"

"Forever," she quipped. "I quit. I was out of vacation and personal days after Mama and then Harper Rose losing Thad like that. So, when Daddy got sick, I just quit. I haven't even really been spending much of my savings." Bailey Ann likely had a good healthy savings. She was in finance, after all, and she'd always done the right thing even if it didn't suit her.

"Are you staying in town for a while?"

"I think so. Us three girls inherited the house—I just came from reading the will—by myself."

Finn heard the bitter tinge in her words, but she was talking before he could ask.

"I'm the only one here to sell it. And I don't think it will sell too well now without some upgrades."

"Upgrades?" he frowned. "I thought your parents took good care of the place."

"Oh, they did," she informed him. Then she leaned in like she was sharing a secret. "They just had old taste."

He'd seen the place. It was sturdy, the kind he'd refer to as "good bones," and the choices weren't bad. Maybe . . . *classic?* But he wanted to know what Bailey Ann thought. "Old?"

"They don't understand new colors. I'll have to stage it with all new furniture, which means moving all the current, out-of-date stuff, and sell it or give it away. I may have to paint."

Finn frowned at her. "I remember the colors in your house being . . . fine."

"Yeah, fifteen years ago it was! It's . . . It's . . ." She struggled for words.

Finn just grinned. "Show me what you mean."

❧ 8 ❧

"It's not . . . that bad."

Bailey Ann cringed at his tone. He must not have paid any attention when he was here at the funeral. Now Finn looked around the room with his hands shoved in his pockets, and he had to be lying.

"Everything is out of date." She sighed and looked at the room with fresh eyes. Then she admitted what bothered her. "What hurts is that you were right—it's all well-tended. I can't just claim it's old and bad and throw it away. I mean these chairs are in great shape."

"Can you get them reupholstered?"

Her thoughts jerked, and she slowly nodded. "I hadn't thought of that. They are really good chairs. They're just—" she cut herself off and didn't say it.

"What?"

"Mama at least didn't follow trends," she murmured to the chair. "Mama called the color something close to 'pickle,' though why anyone would want their furniture pickle-colored is beyond me." She took a breath in then threw her sister under the bus. At least it was a small bus. "Harper Rose always called it 'booger.'"

"Oh." He nodded and rocked back on his heels. "I can see

that in this shade of green. Yup." Then he started laughing. After a moment, when he got himself together a little more, he looked around and added, "It just needs some work."

Bailey Ann sighed. "That's true, but 'some work' is actually 'a lot of work.' Everything has to go." She looked at the couch and matching chairs. She could re-upholster them, but did she like them better than the ones she'd put in storage in Nashville? She didn't think so. The dining room was burgundy and while the sideboard was beautiful, she wasn't sure who would want it. Maybe Aunt Gigi? Lennon? But Lennon was just finishing her graduate work—hardly the time to be obtaining a family heirloom sideboard. And who used a sideboard these days anyway? Even Mama had mostly covered the tops with her figurines.

They were yet another matter. Bailey Ann huffed out her breath at the thought of all the work before her. She'd been volunteering at Riley's elementary grades class, so had her cousin Christian. But with the work on the house getting more involved every time she turned around, Bailey was thinking she couldn't make the commitment anymore. All of this sucked.

Finn grinned at her. "Want to feel better?"

She blinked. "What are you proposing, Finn Malloy?"

"Put on some jeans and sneakers, come over and see my parents place with me and you'll see."

For a moment she looked at him and wondered if he was up to something. Then she decided she wouldn't know until she went over and found out. Besides, what was she going to do now? Read all the tedious paperwork from her father's estate? It was barely past lunch time. She could use that to keep her going tonight when she was sitting in front of a TV that offered up no good fare.

With only a slight nod, she disappeared upstairs and changed out of her skirt, hose, and heels. What had she been doing, dressing up to go to the lawyer's office? Then again, it had been about her father's will and she'd been the only one there. She at least had represented well. Still, she slid into her jeans and sneakers pretty easily and thought about changing her sweater out, too, but in the end she left it. As she grabbed a nice jacket, she realized she was still probably overdressed for the situation.

Back downstairs, Finn told her to get her keys and follow him. Surprisingly, he led her out her back door and it took only a second to realize what he was doing.

"Finn, we can't."

"Why not?" He kept up his long stride across her back yard.

"We aren't fifteen anymore," she protested even has he put his hands on the top of the low stone wall and hopped up.

He leaned down and held his hand out to her. "It's still the best route between our places. Are you going to walk all the way around the block?"

She considered it. She was an adult now, though clearly he wasn't, despite being a full year older than she was. But then she decided *what the hell?* It was the best route between their houses. She reached up and grabbed his hand, letting him pull her up.

In that moment, she paused at the feeling of having her hand in Finn's again for the first time in years. And she almost missed the step up onto the wall.

"You good?" He frowned at her.

"Fine," she responded, finding her feet on the uneven surface. How many years had it been since she'd stood up here? It had to have been the last time she headed over to Finn's from home.

She let go of his hand, shaking off his hold and the feeling that she was doing something wrong. Her mother hadn't liked this, hadn't liked her walking along the wall even though the neighbors always said hello and smiled if they were out. Mama hadn't liked her dating Finn. Told her to marry a man. A man she met in college—though Bailey Ann hadn't found any men there. Just frat boys.

Finn didn't seem to take offense as she motioned for him to turn and go. He looked over his shoulder once. "Watch your step."

"I've walked up here just as much as you."

"Not that." Again, it rolled off him like a duck and she wished she could do the same. It seemed everything stuck to her these days. "It's that the Millers sold the house and the new people haven't kept up the wall."

"What about the Johnsons?" She asked, making her steps more tentative now that there was a genuine reason.

"They're too old."

"What?" She said it before she calculated the years. "Oh." Despite having been back in town with Daddy for a while, she hadn't seen the Johnsons. There was a lot she hadn't done.

Daddy's cholesterol and his blood pressure had gone wild and she'd simply packed up her own life and come home. Only it wasn't home. She stepped on a loose rock and felt her ankle turn, but she didn't fall.

"Thank you." She looked up at Finn where he'd reached out and grabbed her upper arm.

"Might leave a mark," he cringed.

"Better than a twisted ankle." She meant it and hoped her face showed that. She should have been better to him. There just wasn't much in the handbook about how to treat an ex that didn't feel quite enough like an ex.

"Hold my hand? We'll balance each other."

This time she obliged, and they made it safely to the corner of his back yard, where he hopped down and reached up to grab her around the waist. Her hands gravitated to his shoulders, just as they had when they'd been dating in high school. Only then it had been a rebellion against her mother as much as a desire to be with Finn. Now there was no envelope to push, no boy to catch her, just a man who didn't seem to be offering more than friendship.

Her feet hit the grass and she could see the yellow patches the Malloys had let form in the yard. Finn wasn't blind to it. "They got old, you know?"

She sure did. Her parents had, too, and they were a good ten to fifteen years younger than Finn's parents had been. Apparently, things had been tough in Ireland and they'd held off starting their family until they were almost too old. But they'd had Finn, then Sioban.

He didn't let go of her hand as he led her across the back yard and up the old deck steps. Were there ruts he was worried about? Or was he simply holding her hand? She couldn't tell.

Then he started talking. "So, I obviously have to re-do the deck."

"Can you replace pieces of it?"

He shook his head. "The pillars are okay, but the rest is just too far gone. The number of boards I could keep would look odd. It'll be easier to do the whole thing." He turned the knob on the back door, pushing it open without unlocking it.

Typical small town, Bailey thought, but she followed him inside.

When he flipped on the light she saw the house as she'd seen it so many times before. "What are you going to do with it?"

She couldn't imagine. It was what it was; she couldn't see anything different in this space. But Finn was looking around, and he could see something she couldn't.

He gestured excitedly with his left hand, as his right hand was still holding hers. "I'm going to take out this wall—it's not load bearing—and open up this space." He looked up. "I'm adding skylights in the living room. Not the bedrooms, though. That's just mean."

He pulled her along into the main room where one wall had already been stripped down to the studs. "I'm going to replace the front windows. They date the house and I'm going to open them up. I'm going to remove a lot of the markers from the seventies and eighties."

She saw it then. The thin, tall windows indicative of the era. The split level design. The way the eaves hung out over the windows just a bit farther than was currently fashionable.

"It doesn't have a lot of floor space, so I'm going to make it a roomy two-bedroom rather than a cramped three bedroom." He headed up the stairs, his voice working through an excitement she didn't have about getting her own parents' house on the market. He went on about the bathroom remodel and let her get in a few questions.

Then he turned to her and took both her hands in his. "So, will you help me? I could use a backup set of eyes for colors and such, and someone to handle budget." He smiled. "In exchange, I'll help out at your place. Including taking out that wall between your kitchen and dining room."

"I don't need a wall taken out."

"Yes, you do," his smile spoke for itself. "Say yes."

Bailey Ann shrugged, wondering what she'd gotten herself into. But she never really had been able to say no to him. "Yes."

His smile made it worthwhile, whatever she'd gotten herself into. Then, he leaned in and kissed her.

❦ 9 ❦

The touch of his mouth to hers brought Bailey Ann to a standstill.

It yanked her back to the past in a way she'd not thought was possible. She could have been under the bleachers, with the roar of a high school football game beyond the feet overhead. She could almost smell popcorn and cotton candy, feel the polyester of her cheerleading uniform against her shoulders and Finn's hands touching the bare skin at her waist.

Now, his hands held hers, tugged hers forward, pulling her into him. She didn't lean in purposefully, but she didn't resist either. She couldn't fall into the feeling. It wasn't who she was anymore, but she couldn't push him away either.

Only their hands and mouths touched, his lips tracing hers, pulling her soul to the surface. Each soft, searching movement dragged her deeper under. Her muscles fought the sense memory of reaching up and twining her arms around his neck. The sensation of kissing Finn flooded her.

Bailey Ann gasped, suddenly not sure she'd felt like herself any time in the past three months. Not since she'd come home to take care of her father. She'd disappeared into the role, and now the role had disappeared.

Finn seemed to be the first person who looked and saw Bailey Ann Mayfair, not the dutiful daughter. He didn't see the successful financial analyst from Nashville. He didn't calculate the years she'd been the unmarried woman who, by all accounts, had done everything right and should be driving a minivan with two kids in it.

Finn kissed the woman she was. And that woman kissed him back.

At least, she did until she realized what she was doing.

Stepping back, Bailey Ann broke the contact, dropping his hands. She was opening her mouth to say, "We can't do this."

Finn stopped her cold, again, with a question. "Do you remember us?"

He looked at her then, his eyes and soul open, waiting for her answer.

There were so many things she could say. "We aren't those kids anymore." "We broke up for a reason." "We already know we don't fit." But the look on his face stopped her from saying anything like that. Instead, the word escaped without her permission.

"Yes."

His mouth smiled, just a little. Not a big grin saying he thought they were an item now. Not a smirk that said he had any hold over her. Just a smile that he was happy with her answer and he was willing to leave it at that.

So Bailey left it at that, too. But she took another step back. Then another. She was looking for an out, and he gave it to her.

"I'll see you tomorrow to get started on that wall." He grinned at her, seeming to know he was letting her go with that line. Setting her free, but only until tomorrow.

"Okay."

She turned then, letting herself out the back door. She crossed the deck, this time analyzing the quality of the wood and finding it lacking like Finn did. She traipsed down the steps and headed to the corner of the yard.

She'd said "okay." Finn Malloy robbed her of her ability to speak clearly and with purpose. He stole her ability to use multi-syllabic words. He took away her depth of thought. She hadn't thought at all, she'd just agreed because Finn Malloy wanted her to.

In the corner, she hopped up onto the wall without his help, and yet she wondered if he was watching her leave. Or if he'd managed to kiss her then let her go without further thought.

Could he do that? Could he shake her up like he always did with no cost to himself?

Bailey Ann looked down at the wall, thinking about the loose stones and the time that had passed without her here. Without Finn. She walked the whole distance that marked the line between the Johnsons' and the Millers' properties without thought and she was at the back corner of her own yard.

It was her own yard now—not Mama and Daddy's anymore. Bailey still hadn't come to terms with it not being Mama's house anymore. It was easier to understand that her father had vacated the premises.

She pushed open the back door, realizing that, like Finn, she hadn't locked up. Not in Breathless. Even though it was stupid not to, she hadn't done it.

As she moved into the room, she started to see the space as Finn did. And she understood the exact opposite, too.

The reason it was hard to believe her mother had vacated the premises was because the woman hadn't. Mama had painted the living room herself. It was Mama who'd chosen that shade of green that Harper Rose dubbed "booger color." No one else had loved it as she did. No one else thought a room should be done in shades of "pickle green." But it was Mama who'd added pale and mid-bold pinks with just a few shots of burgundy that made it work.

The colors had never been popular, yet Mama still managed to have picked dated colors. Though her house didn't have the same tall, narrow windows that Finn's did, it was definitely out of style.

Bailey didn't have to go outside to know her home was cream-colored with a roof so dark a brown it was almost black. Each window was bracketed by non-functional shutters too wide to be current. The windows were double hung, the back patio a perfectly square slab of concrete. The dining room and kitchen both closed in enough to feel small.

Shit. Finn was right.

Bailey Ann remembered when her family had moved into this house. Harper Rose had been a toddler. Emma Kate hadn't even been conceived, but Bailey Ann was five, just old enough to know the neighborhood had still been new. And the problem with living in the new neighborhood was that it wouldn't be new forever. The very things that made it new and fresh at the time were what made it feel old and outdated now.

She'd wandered the ground floor, examining it with new eyes and a removed perspective. As she looked out the window now, she could see the early sunset of the late winter months. It was Georgia, it wasn't going to snow, but the wind could still get a good bite. The humidity that sweltered in the summer lent a sharpness to the winter that made it harsher than it should be.

Time to make dinner.

She was working to keep a schedule. Day one on her own and she was already fighting to maintain anything resembling regularity. In the kitchen, she looked in the fridge. This was hers. Not her mother's.

Mama cooked casseroles, opening canned vegetables and premade soups. She made meats and added boxed sides. Easy was good.

Bailey Ann had broken with that. Her best friend in high school had been the daughter of a caterer. Mira's mother taught Bailey about fresh fillets of fishes, about using wine when she sautéed. Hell, Mrs. Withers had taught her about sautéing in the first place. Mama only boiled.

This fridge bore no signs of her Mama. Daddy was here, his six pack of beer, five left, lingering in the corner. Bailey Ann grabbed one and then reached for the brown paper wrapped sausages she'd bought from the grocery deli. She opened the drawer and pulled out a pack of thick cut bacon and fresh green beans.

She wasn't hungry, but she laid it out on the tile counter—which would also have to go—and started chopping. She wondered why she was cooking when she wasn't hungry. Why did she have to keep the schedule?

Used to living alone, the schedule had always grounded her. Or had it hemmed her in? Dates on Friday or Saturday nights; she wouldn't be late to work. She had dinner with a friend usually one night a week. She ate at the table, often with a book or a boyfriend, depending on her dating life at the time.

But she'd always had a job. Single, not a mother, she had to have a job. Here, her job had been taking care of Daddy. She'd run his errands and taken him to doctors' appointments and filled the remaining space like a daycare worker, putting in activities to stretch the time.

Now, she didn't even have that.

She was adrift again, and she hated it.

She'd drifted that last summer before college. She'd broken up with Finn, citing college as the reason. It was a crap excuse and he'd known it. They'd stayed together through his first year at university, so why not through hers? She'd never explained. He'd never asked.

She'd drifted again after college. She'd graduated with honors but without an engagement ring. Both goals had been equally important to her Mama. Bailey Ann could have gotten both, but she hadn't been able to say yes to any of them. None had held up to the standards she'd set. So here she was alone. Maybe Mama hadn't been right about standards.

Making two servings, Bailey Ann set each out on its own plate, leaving the second on the counter to cool before she would put it into the fridge later. Taking her plate to the table and sitting amid the burgundies her mother had used in the dining room, she opened the envelope from the lawyer that morning and started sorting through the last of Daddy and Mama's things.

The bank account had a code and she logged in on her phone while eating marinated sausage. There wasn't much in the checking account, which didn't surprise her. Clicking over to the savings did.

There was a stock account as well and that shocked her more. Then she found the property deeds. Her parents had bought a third timeshare somewhere along the way. They'd gone into two of them with friends, not even buying a whole share. But the third they'd bought full out for retirement.

As Bailey Ann looked at the estimated values, her eyes widened.

❦ 10 ❦

T *he Belle secret to playing the stock market is: buy low, sell high.*

BAILEY ANN WOKE UP THE NEXT MORNING IN THE QUEEN BED she'd spent her high school days in. She stared at the ceiling and found that to be lacking, too.

Torn amongst a trio of conflicting thoughts, she lay there in the bed unmoving. First, that the ceiling had a popcorn coating; it had to go. Second, her Daddy had died basically a millionaire; the property added up . . . to a lot. And lastly, she'd lost her virginity in this bed, to Finn Malloy on a night her family had been out.

The memory, which she'd successfully avoided for months, now came at her with a vengeance. They'd come in here, tearing at each other's clothing, wanting each other in a way she could only associate with teenage love and with Finn. She remembered that evening. They'd had to get dressed in a hurry as they'd heard her parents pull into the driveway long before they were expected.

They'd laughed their way through their fumbles, then

tumbled out the front door in perfect timing to her family coming in the back.

Finn had lost his virginity that night, too. He was only eight months older than her. She remembered that still. Remembered his birthday. Remembered every time they'd been together.

She tried to remember the men she'd been with in between. Todd Hooker had been good in bed. But she remembered it like a phrase, *he was good in bed.* She couldn't remember him touching her. Couldn't remember what it had made her feel like.

She remembered dinners with Ray. Remembered parties in cocktail dresses and trying to coordinate their lives. She remembered that they had slept together, but for the life of her, she couldn't remember actually doing it.

But, God, she remembered Finn.

Bailey Ann forced her gaze back up to the ceiling. Popcorn coating. She had to think about the house rather than the man. She had to scrape the ceilings. Maybe Finn would know a good contractor for that.

Throwing the covers back, Bailey forced herself out of bed. She was in an adorable set of flannel pajamas. Cute. Not sexy.

Telling herself she didn't need sexy, she headed to the shower. At the last minute she swerved. First order of business was the removal of wallpapers and borders. That was the grunt work, she could take breaks to go pick new colors, talk to Finn about *not* taking out a wall, and calling contractors to discuss the outside of the house—which she could absolutely not do herself. She should shower after.

She dressed to head out, pulling her hair up into a ponytail and throwing on an old pair of jeans. Even now she couldn't leave the house without being at least some level of put together. Even in death, her mama disavowed it. Mama disavowed cereal, too, but that was in the house now that Bailey Ann was running it. She ate her bowl of puffs standing at the counter, another no-no that Bailey suddenly didn't let get in her way.

Then she was shrugging into her thick jacket and heading

out into the day. The cold always found its way under the carport, but the sun never did. Bailey Ann had always thought that was a bad system. She jumped into the driver's seat, trying to minimize her exposure and started the car, once again regretting not warming it up.

Breathless was a nice town, mostly middle-class based, but not big. She was at the hardware store before she knew it. The only reason it took time to get her supplies was two employees expressing their concern for her and their condolences over her Daddy.

"Con was a good man," one of the green-aproned employees said.

"Thank you." She was trying to be kind though she didn't want to talk about her Daddy. She'd done that plenty on Sunday and the topic was worn out. But a lady didn't say so, and Bailey Ann kept her sad smile in place and tried to slide in a question about how to remove wallpaper.

It should have been a ten-minute task, but it was a good hour before she was back home. In that time, she'd comforted four different people—two employees at the hardware store, one other shopper, and the barista who got her coffee at Bean Around the Block—about the loss of *her* father. She'd answered one person's questions about Emma Kate's school and another about her cousin Christian's sudden engagement. She'd needed the coffee, but she should have been given the tip.

It was still warm by the time she got home.

She hauled the equipment inside though it would have been easier to leave it, but she wasn't willing to have to come back out in the cold again. If there was anything Bailey Ann Mayfair was good at, it was eating frogs.

She almost spilled the coffee, but she got everything inside. She changed into her oldest clothes, pulled her ponytail into a bun that wouldn't catch on anything, and then grabbed Harper Rose's old high school sneakers out of the closet. If her sister had left it in the room she'd taken over when Bailey Ann moved out, then Bailey Ann wouldn't feel guilty for using it now.

Finally, ready for the job, she headed downstairs and hooked up the spray bottle. It took three tries and a run to fetch an old towel to get it right. Then she ran the little piercing device over the wallpaper her mother had so loved. She stabbed it in little lines, making patterns as she rolled the piercer over it. The burgundy wallpaper had strings of white cabbage roses essentially making stripes running vertically on the wall. Green leaves and vines threaded the roses together.

That was when she saw it.

It had been almost twenty-five years since her mother had hung this wallpaper herself. She'd had two young girls and not enough budget to hire anyone after they'd made the down payment on the house. Bailey Ann hadn't understood that at the time. Now she understood the necessity of down payments to the economy.

All that and she'd never seen it. The vines and leaves were a certain shade of green. Maybe pickle. Maybe booger. But Mama had so loved this wallpaper she'd used it in here and then carried the colors into the living room. This was the burgundy that only showed up in small accents out in the main room.

The pale pink on the living room walls was the same shade as the shadows nestled in the petals of the white cabbage roses.

Stopping dead, Bailey Ann pulled the roller back. She almost couldn't do it. The only thing that kept her going was that she'd already started it. Too late now. So many years it had clung to the wall and she'd never seen it. Of course, she figured it out now, when Mama was gone, when she'd already ruined it beyond salvage. She grabbed a chair and climbed up to reach the top, destroying the ugly burgundy and roses wallpaper her mother had so loved.

She'd finished the whole wall before she realized her next problem. The sideboard was always there, how could she have missed it? Maybe the same way she'd lived here so long and not seen where her mother had pulled that hideous shade of booger green from.

That sideboard would have to be moved and it was a hippopotamus of a piece of furniture. She wasn't going to be able to move it by herself, but she was going to try.

Hopping down from the chair, she reached out to the end, where her hands could prop shoulder width apart and see if she could push it. But she still had the piercing roller in her hand. *Shit.*

Not a frog she could eat. She turned back to the short wall where she'd started and decided she could do a second layer of spray. That was something she could accomplish.

Turning back to the sideboard, Bailey Ann attacked the problem as she did everything else: A good plan and some possibly misplaced confidence. She could solve this.

It took a moment, but she realized she needed to pull out the drawers. They surprised her with just how heavy Great-Grandma Brown's silver was. The drawers themselves were a good part of the weight.

When it was stripped, she thought about the next step and went to get Daddy's chamois cloths from the mudroom. If she could get one under each foot, she had high hopes she could slide it across the wood floor.

Still, the massive sucker didn't want to lift. Her arm strength wasn't one of her best features. The chamois was too thick, so, even though she could lift it a little, she couldn't get it high enough to jam the cloth under.

"Fuck," she said it out loud.

"So, you do know swear words," Finn's voice came through the air, almost making her jump. But her butt was on the floor and she was wrapped around the stubby leg of the sideboard. Jumping wasn't happening.

She couldn't see him, just a peek of his ratty, red sneakers under the edge of the tablecloth. She watched as they walked around the end of the table and Finn came fully into view—

broad shoulders, long lean legs in jeans that probably made his ass look good, and a half smile that told her he couldn't quite be trusted. Or maybe that was her: maybe she couldn't be trusted around him.

Then that half smile suddenly changed. "Bailey Ann, why are you crying?"

❧ 11 ❧

F inn frowned down at Bailey Ann crying. She looked up at
him, frowning back, asking, "What?"

"You're crying." He went for stating the obvious, but it
seemed to be necessary.

She hadn't known. Reaching up, she touched her face and felt
the tears. "Well, hells bells."

"What's it about? Sideboard too heavy?" He'd seen her trying
to lift it and hadn't wanted to startle her.

Bailey Ann started laughing. "Yes, it is. But . . ." She let her
voice trail off, seeming uncertain about continuing. He could see
when she made the decision to tell him. "I was just sitting here,
looking at all the colors and realizing that silly-booger green
color in the living room is from this too-dark and kind of ugly
wallpaper."

"That made you cry?" He was afraid he was looking at her in
that way that said *women are crazy*. Even though he knew women
weren't crazy. He just needed to hear more.

"No. What made me cry is that I ignored it and just thought
it was silly for over twenty-five years. And I only just now realized what she'd done right as I was erasing her from her own

home. That's what made me cry. By the time I saw it, it was too late, I'd already started to take it down."

He nodded then. "It is weird, dismantling what your parents built. Mine specifically told me to find a way to sell for as much as possible. That means remodeling."

Bailey Ann still sat on the floor, still looking up at him. "Why can't you just sell and walk with the money you get?"

"They wanted us to use it to pay off as much of our student loans as possible. It was something they regretted while they were alive—that they couldn't help us more with the programs we wanted to go to." He wished they hadn't thought that way. His parents had moved a continent away from home, away from everyone they knew, to make their kids' lives better. They'd fully succeeded and he wished they hadn't regretted that they hadn't been able to hand over college and advanced degrees without debt.

"What did Sioban do?" Bailey Ann's voice pulled him back to the present.

"Med school." He smiled. He was beyond proud of his little sister.

Bailey Ann's eyebrows rose up. "I remember her being shy. But then again when did I pay much attention to her?"

"You were always nice to her."

"I tried to be, but she wasn't around that much."

Finn smiled but was glad for the opportunity to change the topic from the finances of the Mayfairs compared to the Malloys. "You need a hand?"

"Yeah, a strong one." She proceeded to explain her idea to get the chamois cloths under the legs. At least that explained what the heck she'd been trying to do when he came in. Though he'd enjoyed the view. "I can't scratch the floor. That would cause more problems than it solves."

It was a great solution except for the sideboard being too heavy for her to lift. "Okay, I'll lift, you push the cloth under."

Just like that, they were working in tandem. They didn't talk, everything made sense and Finn tried to push away the feeling that she was the one person he'd ever really been able to do that with. In just a few moments, they had the chamois in place and the sideboard slid easily to the middle of the room. There wasn't a lot of space left to maneuver, but Bailey Ann could just fit in and get the spray onto the wall paper. Finn picked up the piercing tool and began running it over the wall, seeing easily where she'd left off and how she was planning to strip the wallpaper. She just made sense to him.

As she looked over, she seemed surprised that he was working alongside her, but he just motioned for her to keep going. They made a good team and, much faster than she'd likely been working alone, they had the whole room sprayed, pierced, and sprayed again.

"Thank you," she told him, looking oddly at him as though she didn't get it. Then her eyes flew wide. "Oh my gosh! I'm so sorry. You came to look at the wall."

"No worries. Let's get this wallpaper down. There's a window of time when it'll be easiest." He wasn't sure quite why he did it. He certainly had work waiting at his parents' house. But he wasn't ready to make this quite so cut-and-dried. He'd spent a long time chasing Bailey Ann Mayfair and when he'd lost her the first time, he hadn't fought back.

Though she tried hard to be perfect—and he saw that, maybe better than anyone—she wasn't. He knew. She'd screwed up royally when she'd broken things off with him. Though he'd tried, he'd never found anyone to really take her place. Given that she was here, unmarried, no kids, he wanted to believe that she hadn't found anyone to replace him either.

Right then, he made the decision to bank on that.

Picking up the scraping tool, he started removing wide strips of her mother's wallpaper. Though the system had worked, wetting the paper and loosening the glue that held it up, Bailey Ann looked as pained as if he was running the scraper on her skin.

His head turned suddenly at the sound. Was it almost strangled? He lowered the scraper and stepped back from where he was making great progress. "You don't really want to do this, do you?"

"It's too late. I can't leave it like this." She motioned to the half-undone wall, strips hanging, old and yellowed on the back, halfway down the wall. She sniffed and his heart hurt at the idea of her fighting off tears. She waved her hand angrily at the room. "And I probably can't find a wallpaper exactly this hideous to replace it with!"

He started laughing at her. "I'm sorry." Raising his hand to his mouth, he tried to stifle his giggles, but he almost poked himself in the eye with the scraper. And that made Bailey laugh, too.

When they got themselves together, he looked at her. "You want to keep going?"

She nodded, wondering if there was anything she could say.

Finn found the questions hard to ask. What if she said no? But he told himself that if her answer was "no," he needed to hear it now, before he got in too deep. "Do you really want to sell the house? Or might you stay here?"

She almost physically jolted, as though she hadn't considered staying before. He could see the clouds of dust that disturbance churned up in her brain. If she'd been straight with him before, then she was in a similar place to his own: sell the house, decide later what to do next with your life.

"So, you don't know?" Finn pushed and pulled at her thoughts. They'd both stopped scraping wallpaper until she found some kind of answer. He wanted her to say yes, she was staying here. Then he could say it, too.

For all he knew of her, she still managed to surprise him. "If I stay in Breathless, it won't be in this house. The problem is that I don't want anything to change! I want my Mama back, and I want my Daddy still alive, and I don't want to be the one responsible for this bad decision in wallpaper."

"Then you need to sell the house, and you need to find a way to be okay with that." He put his hands on his hips, the scraper still held firmly, but not in use. He paused as he wondered how to say it. How much to hand over to her. For all his bravado, all his belief that he could win her back, Finn hadn't forgotten getting his heart handed to him on a plate before. There was a reason he hadn't fought back the first time. He'd been far too wounded. But he went for halfway. "I think I understand. I got this massive knot in my chest when I hit one of the walls with the sledge hammer the first time. I couldn't take it back . . . I have a lot of good memories in that house. And some not-so-good ones. But I'm moving forward. That sledge hammer made going back almost impossible. And so does this wall. I like to think I'm turning their place into a home that will make another family happy there. Hopefully, even better than we were."

She absorbed the words like water into a sponge. She stared at the old wallpaper strips as though they held answers. "You're right. I can't keep the place. And if I do stay here, I don't want it to look like this. It would be like living in a museum. A museum with booger colored living room furniture."

"The house is just a shell. You don't need it to remember them."

"How do you do that?" She smiled and he wanted to believe she was asking how he knew her so well. "Thank you. Now I have to get this wallpaper off while it's still ready to come down."

"Then let's do it."

They worked side by side while Finn enjoyed having her close. Having no one else around. He worked steadily, but his brain made plans. If he could have Bailey Ann Mayfair back . . .

"Last piece!" He announced, motioning for her to do the honors.

He'd been getting the top pieces. Though he only needed a stool to reach the upper corner, Bailey Ann had to drag over a chair and climb up to get the scraper up under the last piece. At the top, it broke loose and fell like a wide ribbon to the floor. On the floor, it was no longer wallpaper, just trash to be picked up.

She hopped down with a smile and handed over her scraper as Finn held his hand out. Turning away, he set everything on one of the chairs she'd covered with plastic. Then he turned back to her.

She was opening her mouth—maybe to thank him—but the words never got out.

It happened so fast, they almost slammed into each other. He felt the breath jolt out of her. Her empty hands found his, and he pulled hers up by her head, and backed her against the wall as he pressed in closer.

His mouth found hers in a kiss both confident and needy.

Adrenaline bloomed sweetly in him, giving way to a rush he hadn't experienced since . . . When? Maybe the last time he had kissed her like this? No, that had been him kissing her. This time, she'd dove for him, too, and the feeling was heady.

They'd been kids the last time he'd pushed her up against a wall. The last time he'd pressed, full-body, against her and made it known that he wanted her. Only her.

Jesus, she'd wanted him, too.

Finn wasn't thinking. The scent and feel and taste of her washed over him like the tide and he hadn't felt this good the last time he'd kissed someone or even the last time he'd had sex.

With a mind of its own, his mouth pushed her own mouth open and his tongue sought hers. His hands trailed down her arms, leaving her with her hands up against the wall as though she was his prisoner. The description was wishful.

When his fingers threaded through her hair and tilted her head to deepen the kiss, he felt her reach out and grasp the front of his shirt as though she were drowning and he was her lifeline.

"*Finn*," she whispered it when they paused for just a gasp of air.

"You drive me crazy." The words came out somewhere

between growled and reverent. Where had the years without her gone? He could count them, but not find them in his memory.

He stepped back then, his hands falling away, stopping at his sides. He looked at her as she seemed to realize she was still gripping his shirt. She unclenched her hands and let them fall back. He watched as her eyes retained the heat of their kiss and she flattened her hands against the wall as though to anchor herself.

He sucked in a breath, his world spinning in ways he couldn't define or stop. "I think I should go."

❧ 12 ❧

Don't waste your time choosing a silver pattern. You don't choose your pattern, you inherit it.

THERE WAS NOWHERE FOR BAILEY ANN TO EAT DINNER THAT night. The table was covered in drawers of neatly aligned silver or linens. The silverware had begun to tarnish, but the various spoons and forks were nestled in the burgundy velvet trays designed specifically to hold sixteen of each piece, including dessert spoons, shrimp forks, serving ware, and tea spoons. The main pieces even had the Mayfair "M" engraved on the handles.

But that wasn't the real reason she couldn't eat there. Bailey Ann could have moved at least a few of the drawers aside and made a space. But she couldn't move the feeling that swamped her each time she entered her half-dismantled dining room.

Even now, her fingers rose to her lips as though to check that the buzz was just a leftover sensation. Or maybe to hold close the memory of that kiss. Her breath involuntarily sucked in each time she crossed the threshold.

Finn had said he would talk to her about taking out a wall. Which one?

She looked around and thought it must be the one between the kitchen and the dining room. It was pretty formal. There was an open pass through at the side of the kitchen, but it only looked at the short hallway connecting the mudroom to the living room at the front of the house.

Jesus, she couldn't breathe. She was standing here, looking at the wall, with her heart racing as though he was still kissing her. She held a plate in her hand. The same dinner she'd been eating last night, now cold as stone.

If she could get her shit together, she would heat it up.

Suddenly, she didn't want it. She wanted to get out of this house that she'd wandered for hours trying to deny that she'd been kissed senseless.

Wrapping the plate up again, she stuck it back in the fridge and turned for the door. Only, as she grabbed her keys she realized she hadn't showered yet. It took five minutes of debate to decide she was going to carry out her order anyway.

She did change clothes and scrub her face. She put on a bandana she'd rolled up that covered the worst of her hair and headed out. Punching the buttons from memory as she drove, she called the Magic Wok and placed her order. It would be too much food. She told herself she'd eat the leftovers for days. Then she could wander the house eating cheap Chinese food and remembering how she'd been kissed up against her freshly scraped wall.

The Magic Wok was tiny, and she was glad to see only a few people sitting at the tables far from the door as she headed to the counter. Her dinner was waiting for her in a brown paper bag, folded and stapled and then set inside a plastic one. It looked like she was picking up food for a whole family.

Bailey had handed over her credit card, signed the slip, and was turning to go when she bumped into a wall of man.

She smelled him before she saw him. Sensed him before her feet stopped moving.

"Finn!" She said it, happily, before she thought about it. Then she thought about it. "Are you following me?"

He only laughed a little at her. "Please." He raised an eyebrow, suggesting she was nuts. "It's a small town. There are only so many places I can go. And you know we both had pizza yesterday. Have a good evening, Bailey Ann."

With that, he dismissed her. And she let him! She didn't even say anything, just carried her too-big bag of food out the door.

Dammit, that man ruined everything.

No sooner had the thought crossed her mind than she rescinded it. The whole drive home, she remembered things he hadn't ruined. Peeling wallpaper. Prom. The letter he'd written her when he went off to college. Every time he said hello to her and her heart jumped.

She arrived home hardly aware of the drive and she could only hope she hadn't been dangerous. Heading in through the back door she bypassed the dining room, willing herself not to look in there and think about Finn Malloy. She marched herself right past the living room and headed down the half-staircase into the family room to set up a tray and watch TV while she ate.

As she silently tried to figure out who killed the most popular girl in high school while simultaneously not getting any sweet and sour sauce on her clothes, Bailey Ann thought it all felt familiar. In Nashville, if she wasn't dating anyone, she'd sit at home and eat her own dinner. She worked to cook for herself as much as possible, but she'd been known to grab take-out, too. She'd eat in front of the TV sometimes, root for her favorite characters, have a glass of wine.

This combination of being in a room in the house that was virtually unaltered since her childhood and eating alone was some kind of new normal. She felt adrift—her Daddy gone, her job gone, and no order to her days. Yet all the things she was doing were only further cutting her anchor. She was going to sell off Mama and Daddy's things, cut ties to what she remembered, paint over the old, haul in the new, sell off the valuable.

She looked down at the carpet under her feet, though she didn't know why. Her Daddy had called this room "the den" though it hardly was such a thing. Her Mama had wanted to paint it grey with touches of shell pink and Bailey Ann had been old enough to remember her father's quiet "no" when her mother had suggested that color combo. What they got instead was Mama's grey in the couch and furniture and a mottled blue in the carpet.

It wasn't quite shag, but it was still pretty plush and very out of date. This had to go. She wondered if it would feel like they were ripping out her heart when she had the carpet ripped up.

The problem, she realized, wasn't as much that she'd lost her parents. That hurt like hell, but she was coping. They'd seen Mama's death coming for months ahead and had been able to prepare. And even though Emma Kate had been shocked that Daddy had passed one night, Harper Rose had sensed it coming, and Bailey *knew*. She'd been taking Daddy to his doctors' visits. She knew his blood pressure wasn't good, that he had something up with his lungs beyond the lingering pneumonia, even though he wouldn't tell her.

The problem wasn't that her parents were gone.

She ate one of the pieces of beef-on-a-stick, sighing as it almost melted on her tongue. God it was good, and she had to stop eating it here in a minute. But she was interlacing her personal revelations with rich Chinese food.

The problem was that she wanted to have what her parents had.

Though Mama had stayed home and raised them, Bailey Ann had never gotten any sense of inequality in their house. Sure, Daddy had voted down the colors in the family room, but Mama got her own way in the living room. They'd divided everything, each lording over their own domain, meshing the two together to build a life and a family.

It had all worked fine until Mama had gotten sick and Bailey Ann realized her father couldn't feed himself, didn't know where the spare toilet paper was, or even the grocery store. She'd stepped up and taken care of all of it. She'd worried when he told her to leave him alone, but she'd done it. Then she'd come back at her own insistence when he'd gotten sicker.

She hadn't expected her father to die, but she couldn't say she was surprised either. He simply couldn't live without her mother. And no matter what else she had in life, Bailey Ann Mayfair wanted that.

❧ 13 ❧

In order to stay sane, Bailey Ann put herself on a strict schedule. She got herself a gym membership and went one morning a week. She also went one afternoon and one evening. Figuring if she changed up her times she'd see more people she knew.

She'd been shocked at the faces she didn't recognize.

So she picked up take-out food twice a week somewhere new. She would run out of restaurants in another month, but she told herself that was okay, too. So far she'd run into the Cotton brothers when she was out. Dane was nice, greeting her like an old friend, even though they'd been no such thing. But his younger brother Bobby was still an ass.

Bailey Ann could hear Mama's voice saying, *No class, those two.* So she smiled to herself and told Dane to have a good day. She didn't comment to Bobby, though in her head she told him he could go screw himself.

She'd run into her cousin Jax more than once, and promised to go visit his mother, her Aunt Gigi. He'd invited her to Sunday dinner and it made her heart clench hard enough that she knew she should go. Bailey Ann added that, and visits with Nana to her calendar.

She scoped out the whole house and made herself some massive to-do lists. From getting the outside painted and the shutters replaced, to polishing the silverware. She had some carpets to pull up, several rooms to paint herself, and—according to Finn Malloy—a wall to take down.

Beyond the house, she had her Daddy's affairs to get in order.

When she'd woken up that morning, she'd decided she couldn't handle calling another contractor for another bid. One had been nice, but exorbitant. The budget master in her didn't think they'd recoup the cost, so she'd said no. The other two had been misogynistic pricks. Apparently, little ladies couldn't make decisions about the house they'd called to get a quote about. Both had asked if her husband could make the decision for her. When she said she didn't have one, one of them had sat in her living room and looked up the stairs as he asked her if she could get her father.

Bailey Ann had put her hands on her thighs and pushed her way up to standing. She'd smiled sweetly. "Well, aren't you just a caveman in sheep's clothing?"

He hadn't known how to reply.

She'd smiled again. "Let me be more clear: don't let the door hit you in the ass on the way out."

His eyebrows had risen up under his hairline and she'd had to make a shooing motion with her hand to get him to leave. Jesus, she was an adult woman with a degree and a lucrative job.

She'd run into Jane Copeland at the gym and said hello as she noticed that Jane was running circles around Bailey. They'd known each other when they were younger, and it wasn't the first time she'd seen Jane at the gym. So she'd asked, "Are you running from something?"

"My ex-husband." Jane's feet kept pounding the treadmill beside the one Bailey Ann jogged on at a much more moderate pace.

"Well, shit," she replied. "What did he take?"

Jane had merely grinned and said, "My dignity, three-quarters of our savings, and a credit card which he used to buy Chinese hookers."

"What? No blow?" Bailey Ann had thrown out. Jane had always appreciated a good laugh.

It turned out she still did. Jane had laughed hard enough to *almost* fall off the treadmill. Bailey Ann would have. They'd met for lunch once, when Jane didn't have her kids with her. Turned out she'd had four in the intervening years. One very recently. She was working as an R.N. at the hospital and managed to keep the house. Bailey Ann invited her over for lunch.

Dear God, she needed a friend.

So this morning she polished the silver, deciding that they needed a fancy lunch and she'd set the kids up in the family room with frozen pizzas and a movie. She had some Disney stuff that Harper Rose's girls liked and figured it would be plenty successful.

She'd polished most of the batch, setting aside three pieces from Great-Grandma Brown's silver that had somehow managed to get mixed in. Harper Rose had inherited that set when she married. It had seemed serendipitous—the engraved "B" matching her new last name of Bass. Bailey wondered where she would be if she'd taken up either Todd Hooker or Ray Haley on their proposals. She might even be divorced or widowed by now. It was a strange thought. Jane was only a year or two older than her.

Jane had four children. Harper Rose had three.

Bailey polished her silverware. She had Great-Grandma Mayfair's silverware and, by God, she was going to serve her damned lunch with it.

A sharp knock had her looking up just in time to see Finn rounding the corner. Her heart skipped a beat even as she told herself she should lock that back door. "Look what the cat dragged in."

He smirked at her. "No cat. Just me. You ready to talk about that wall?"

"I'm having a friend and her children over for lunch in a bit, but you can try to talk me into it while I polish the silver."

"Some friend." He looked at her as though it was odd to serve children with the good silver. "Getting out the Spode?"

"Spode's for Christmas. Were you raised in a barn?" she shot back.

"Comparatively, yes."

Then she felt like crap. His parents had come over with not much more than they could carry. Their educations had gotten them decent jobs, then their ambition landed a better one that Mr. Malloy secured in Breathless. But they didn't have five generations of silver, or a gravy boat that great grandmama swore had been buried in the family yard during The Great War. Bailey dialed it back. "Actually, there's no good time to use the silver. I didn't want it out at Daddy's funeral, figured I might lose some pieces and I was in no place to be keeping track of spoons or knives. So I decided that I was getting it out for lunch today. Just for Jane and me though."

He nodded. "Let me know when I get to come over and use the silver and good china."

That hit her hard. Despite having dinner at her house a handful of times over the years, her mother had never served him on the good settings. Maybe because he'd just been a high school boy . . . Bailey Ann paused as she thought back, then she told him, "Whenever you want."

"Jeez, Bailey Ann, you should say that in answer to every question I ask."

She frowned at him, just as she had in high school when he'd been snarky to her then, too. Finn Malloy had changed a lot, and also he hadn't. "Dinner. I'm offering you dinner."

"I accept." Then he stepped out of the doorway and disappeared around the other side of the wall.

Though she fought the strong desire to keep him in her sight, Bailey lost and she hopped up to go see what he was doing. She found him with his hands on the wall, looking up at the corner where it met the ceiling. Then he walked around her, through the arch into the dining room and looked up in there, too. He came back and knocked on the wall in several spots.

Just when she was certain he was messing with her, he said, "We can take this right out." Then he looked down and pointed. "The problem is the floor. This is linoleum and that's wood."

Bailey Ann looked down at the floor, too. She shrugged. Another decision, another thing she hadn't been thinking about re-doing. So she asked him her new number one question. "Do you think it will get recouped in the sale?"

He thought for a moment and said, "Yes. One floor running all the way through this area and opening up the wall? It makes this house more modern with a more open feel in an older neighborhood. I would do it if I were flipping this place."

She nodded just as she heard the front doorbell ring. "Jane's here."

She was turning to head to the front—bad manners really, leaving Finn there alone, but he was just Finn. Still, she didn't make it.

His fingers encircled her wrist and tugged her back. She hadn't been prepared and in staying balanced, she swung right back to him. Right up against him. So close. Too close.

Her breath sucked in at the proximity, and she watched as his mouth opened.

"You think about that wall, Bailey Ann."

That's what he said? This close, that mouth? And he said—

He must have seen her thoughts, because he moved his head the short distance between them and captured her mouth.

The world disappeared around her, for one sweet second it was just her and Finn Malloy, kissing in her kitchen by the back door once again. Once, she'd seen no future other than this man. Only he'd just been barely more than a boy at the time. Now, she kissed him back, no longer the shy girl she'd been.

When he pulled away, her eyes stayed closed, and she could

have sworn she heard him whisper, "One of these days, you're going to marry me, Bailey Ann Mayfair."

❧ 14 ❧

"One glass of wine won't hurt. It will only help." Jane smiled as Bailey offered to get out a bottle of white that she had. "I can't believe you served me poached salmon on the good china."

"Please, when is the last time I used the good china? And when is the last time you had an adult meal?" She handed over the wine glass and retook her seat. She'd been refusing to let Jane get up.

Having hung around with Harper Rose's girls often enough, Bailey knew that parenting was exhausting—even with sweet, well-mannered kids. Jane's were, but the baby was . . . still a baby. At six months old she was starting to babble, and according to Jane, never stopped unless she was asleep.

"In fact," Bailey offered up, "let me keep them this weekend. Overnight, even." She smiled as Jane looked shocked. "I want my own kids someday. Someday soon! And you could use a break. I sit for Harper Rose's girls all the time."

Jane looked bewildered. "I want to warn you off, but then again I don't."

Bailey Ann laughed and took a drink from her wine.

"Were you drinking before I got here?" Jane looked at her askance.

"No!" Her confusion must have shown on her face.

"Well, what were you doing? You were all flushed like you were drinking or . . . Making out under the bleachers or—" Jane's breath sucked in on a rush as Bailey's face must have given it all away. "Don't you ever play poker, girl! You have zero skills. Who were you making out with?"

"I was not . . ." Bailey protested for all of three seconds before she realized that Jane wasn't buying any of that shit. Then she changed her tune. "It's nothing, really."

"Oh no, honey, *nothing* doesn't make your cheeks flush and your eyes glaze. I know. I haven't had that expression in quite some time." She leaned forward. "Please, please, tell me all about it."

Bailey Ann shook her head but said it anyway. "It's just Finn."

"Finn Malloy? Didn't you two used to go together in high school?"

She nodded and took another sip of her wine. She could not handle this conversation. Jane blinked at her and Bailey Ann had to wonder what the other woman was seeing.

Just then, she was saved by a toddler coming in and holding up her sippy cup.

"Are you out of juice, Stella?" Jane was starting to get up, but Bailey motioned to her to stay put. Grateful for the distraction, she hopped up and grabbed Stella's little hand and they happily headed into the kitchen to refill the sippy cup. Bailey even added water to the juice as Jane did. She'd thought it was a cost saving thing, but it was because the juice had so much sugar in it, Jane had said. So Bailey added water from the filter in the fridge.

Stella smiled at her and headed back into the family room without saying anything else to her mother. Bailey Ann sat back down with her wine and smiled at Jane. "She's very independent, isn't she?"

"Absolutely. I can only imagine that I cultivate it. All the kids are. But they're snuggly, too, so I hope I'm not screwing them up *too* badly."

"Nah, they're good, Jane. You're doing great." She ate more of the salmon and salad she'd made and said, "Next fall, you'll have two of them in school, right?"

Jane nodded. "I cannot wait. Daycare is expensive and hard to deal with. So far, Dylan really likes school. So Tyler is excited to get to go."

"That's some good parenting, right there." Bailey Ann clinked her glass against Jane's. She thought about refilling them, but it seemed like a poor decision given that there were small children about and they were the adults. She'd just relaxed when Jane looped back around.

"So, what's going on with you and Finn?"

She felt it this time—the blush that raced up her cheeks, the heat that somehow suffused her whole body at just the mention of his name, the way her breath clenched.

"Oh my God, you've got it bad." Jane was smiling though, enjoying Bailey's discomfort.

The problem was, she was right and there was nothing Bailey Ann could do about it. They were still just as bad a match as they'd been in high school. Only then, it hadn't mattered. Her mother had sat her down and asked her some hard questions, and it had taken a while for things to set in. But Bailey Ann had done it, she'd broken up with him at the end of her senior year.

He would have come home from college and spent the summer with her before they both went away to school, but she broke it off before the summer could happen. No reason to get in deeper with something that wasn't what she really wanted. Her mother knew. Mama had married well and it paid off for the rest of her life. Bailey Ann understood that even as a teenager. The only problem was her good decisions hadn't paid off at all yet.

"What are you thinking?" Jane asked her after letting the silence sit between them just for a minute.

She needed a sigh to get started, but why not tell an old friend? "I want what my parents had. Mama and Daddy met in high school, graduated together, went to college together and got married when they got their degrees. They stayed together ever since."

"Can I be honest?" Jane's eyes crinkled as though she wasn't quite sure this was the right way to go.

"Of course." At this point, Jane could tell her she was just an idiot, and it might be the right thing to hear.

"That hasn't worked out for you."

Bailey busted into laughter. For a moment it felt odd, laughing into a universe where she was floating and often afraid. Laughing into a universe without either of her parents in it. But it felt good to get back to herself. "I think you hit that nail on the head."

"I can't say I'm any more of a success story. I've never felt so stupid as finding out what Dipshit was doing behind my back. I didn't have a clue at all for the longest time." Jane drained her wine to punctuate that last statement.

"Getting taken by a con artist doesn't mean you're stupid. It just means you didn't already know that particular con. It might even mean that you didn't suspect the person who conned you."

Jane nodded softly, and Bailey was grateful the other woman didn't say, "But at least I have my kids" or something like that. It was understood. And Bailey knew it would be a dig in her soul. She was grateful her friend stayed quiet there.

"Well, I for one would take advantage if I had a hot guy like Finn Malloy kissing me." Jane grinned. "You could do so much worse and maybe things aren't the same as in high school. I mean, they *have* to be different, don't they? Maybe they'll work out this time. At least have yourself a steamy affair!"

"I cannot imagine that I spent the last fifteen years just to loop back around to the guy I kissed under the bleachers."

One side of Jane's mouth quirked up. "Rumors were you two were more involved than just kissing under the bleachers."

"My God! Really?" Bailey Ann couldn't believe it. Then she thought about what she'd heard about other couples. *Shit.* "But you graduated two years ahead of me. How would you have heard that?"

"Small town. Word travels. You know that."

Didn't she know exactly that?

Bailey Ann managed to get through the rest of the lunch without giving away her deepest secrets. Or she thought she did. She and Jane made plans for her to keep the kids overnight and Bailey saw sincere gratefulness in her friend's eyes. For herself, she thought it sounded like fun. Then she closed the front door behind them and leaned against it, finally letting that last kiss from Finn wash through her.

Holy hell, she was in trouble. Maybe it was everything going on in her life, and if things had been different, she wouldn't feel this way. But even she wasn't buying that crap. It was Finn. This was how she'd always felt with him. Last time, she'd given him up. Maybe this time, as an adult, she could try this on for size.

She decided to think it through for a few days.

✺ 15 ✺

She did not get to think it through for a few days.

That night she'd woken up, still half asleep and found him standing in the corner of her bedroom. She'd known it was him. She could smell him or sense him or something. It didn't matter what it was, it turned her on.

Bailey pushed aside the covers, revealing her short, slinky nightgown and bare feet. Her feet swung over the side of the bed and for a moment she dug her painted toenails into the plush carpet. She almost made it to standing before Finn was all over her.

He was all hands and mouth, touching her everywhere, making her head fall back and her breath catch. With a brush of his fingers, the small straps on her nightgown slipped away and she was laid bare under his touch. When she reached for him, she found that she, too, was touching bare skin.

He was hot under her fingers, his heat flowing into her and dragging her breath with it. Though it hadn't ever been difficult for this man to make her want him, in just a few moments, he had her begging him for more.

"Again," the whisper of his voice washed over her, both demanding and pleading at the same time.

She obliged him, "Finn, please. Please, now."

She felt him enter her, felt her own back arch beneath him, felt the rest of the world melt away as her breath escaped her. There was only her, him, and the slide of their skin against each other. Everything else faded. The room, the bed, even tomorrow.

So close to the peak that she could feel it, Bailey Ann blinked into the fuzz around her and saw her world come into a faint black and white focus. She blinked again and saw her room. Though her body buzzed with the feel of Finn Malloy making crazy, wild love to her, the man himself was nowhere to be found.

Seriously? That close and she freakin' woke up?

Sitting upright, Bailey Ann leaned against her pillows. She pulled her knees under her chin and put her head in her hands. It had been all wrong. Well, not the part where Finn was touching her, that had seemed real, but the rest?

She couldn't believe some man—any man, even Finn—could turn up in her bedroom in the middle of the night and not make her scream in absolute terror. And that slinky nightgown? She'd bought that thing several years ago when she'd been dating Ray. It slid around to the point that she couldn't sleep in it. It was purely decorative. Had she been sleeping in it and thrown the covers off, one strap would have been down and her boob hanging out, and the bottom would have been bunched up with the lace edge caught in her panties. Probably her hair would have been mushed on one side of her head.

Super sexy, she thought wryly.

No, she sat here in the middle of the night in the chill of the house wearing her button-up flannel pajamas. It was a classy pink plaid, but no one would mistake it for sexy. If they made that error, one look at her feet and the thick cotton, organic socks she couldn't sleep without would end that notion.

She sighed into the darkness and almost cried.

No wonder she was having sex dreams about Finn Malloy. The man kissed like a sinner and he hadn't seen her in her flannel jammies and fuzzy socks. She was hopeless.

It was four a.m., she was on fire for sex she'd started in her dream state and wasn't going to get to finish any time soon. And she sure wasn't going to be able to get back to sleep. If she got up, she'd . . .

What? There was no one to wake up, no one to answer to, and no reason she couldn't just take a nap when she felt like it later. So she threw off the covers, only this time it wasn't sexy at all.

Her mother and father were gone. There was nothing she could do about it. No way to bring them back. Despite tearing their house apart and telling herself she was moving on, she'd stayed stuck with all the old settings. She was still going to sleep and waking up on Daddy's schedule. She was still cold at night because Daddy was a stickler about the electric bill, but she wasn't.

She marched her thick sock clad feet into the hallway and punched the thermostat up five degrees. Damn, but her Daddy had liked the place cold. *No more.*

Fully awake now, Bailey Ann tromped into the bathroom and turned on the shower. If this day was getting started at four, then it was. She hoped by the time she got out, the air would be warmer. She hated stepping out of a hot shower in the dead of winter. Even so, she climbed in and scrubbed up. Then she shaved. She shaved everything she would shave if she knew Finn was coming over to fulfill her dream fantasy. *A girl could hope.*

She pulled on jeans and a sweater and combed out her wet hair. Normally, she'd put on make-up or at least sunscreen at that stage of the game, but it wasn't even five a.m. and she couldn't bring herself to do it. The fuzzy socks had to go back on. It was that or shoes until the house warmed up to where she'd set it.

Getting a bowl of cereal and gathering all the paint chips she'd collected, Bailey Ann headed into the dining room and was grateful she'd cleared things away to have lunch with Jane earlier. As she ate, she held up the color blocks against the wall and closed one eye to test each out.

She had colors that she liked. A rich blue, not quite a navy. A yellow, more creamy than bright. A peachy shade, if she wanted to throw away the classics and do something unique and beautiful. She liked them all. But her phone said to paint the whole house in white if she wanted to sell it faster.

No. She just couldn't.

At five a.m. before most of the rest of the street was awake, Bailey Ann Mayfair decided not to sell her family's house to anyone who wanted a fully white house. This was a house with history. She remembered the couple her parents had bought it from. They'd moved in with teenagers in tow, then moved out a few years later, when it was more house than they needed. Bailey's family had come in, another set of kids coming of age in this house. It was not for someone who needed a blank canvas. She picked the blue and the cream for the dining room.

Then realized that she would have to carry that color scheme into the kitchen with the wall gone. Taking her bowl to the sink, she held the color chips out at arm's length, thinking it would look good in here, too.

Next, she headed into the living area and picked out colors for there, too. Knowing she was erasing the green was a solidly good feeling. By six a.m., she knew the home store would be open, so she headed down to check out carpet samples. She knew what she was doing—filling her days with work on the house so she wouldn't go crazy and eat nothing but ice cream. Eventually, the house would go on the market and sell and then she'd need a real job. She'd have to decide whether to go back to Nashville or stay in Breathless.

In the meantime, she followed a tradition that went back to the days before the civil war—it was the women who got shit done. They wouldn't have said it that way, but it had always been the case. So she was going to get shit done.

Bailey Ann hit the hardware store again and then hauled her bags out to the car, carpet chosen, supplies to sand the dining room wall smooth, primer, plastic floor cloths . . . She'd just about bought the place out. She headed home—because that was what it was now, she'd decided, *her* home—with a sense of pride.

Hauling her things out of the car and into the back door, she was met with a puff of white dust. Then a noise like something tearing, cracking, giving in. Through the door of the mudroom, she could see Finn Malloy had already started on her project.

He lifted a claw end crowbar and drove it into the drywall, then hooked it and pulled a chunk of the wall off with it. All the noises were explained in that one economy of motion. He didn't see her, the sides on his safety goggles probably prevented it. She moved a little closer.

The man was not wearing a shirt. He was doing manual labor, in her kitchen, shirtless. She needed to take a breath.

For a moment, she got frustrated. She hated being so practical, but he was putting dust all over the kit—no, actually he wasn't. He'd tarped the counters and sink and fridge. He'd taped another over the door to the living room. Jesus, maybe he was her dream man.

Just then, he turned and saw her and smiled. "I'll get this out of here today."

That smile almost said he knew she'd woken in a hot blaze this morning after dreaming of slick, sweet, sweaty deeds with him last night. This was awesome. Maybe Jane had been right.

She was never going to lock that back door again.

❧ 16 ❧

Your home, even if it is just a small apartment, reflects you. You had better be reasonably neat and have lemonade on hand.

"You want something to drink?" Bailey Ann asked him as she crossed her arms and leaned against the wall. She looked like she was going for "casual" but she didn't quite make it.

He grinned at her and said, "Sure."

How in the hell did she manage to look sexy in a hair bandana and jeans with paint on them? But she did. He was smart enough to know that might be on him more than her. He'd always been attracted to her, and it hadn't mattered at all what she was wearing.

She slid past him and set her bags in the corner of the kitchen before getting into the fridge. Would she notice if he ducked past her and stuck his head in it for a minute just to cool off? He'd already peeled his shirt. He was starting to sweat from the work and the heat in the house—he didn't remember it being this warm—but having her close was putting him over the edge.

"Tea, lemonade, water?"

He almost missed the question, but said, "Water for now." Then he turned away from blatantly watching her ass before he got caught and pulled out another chunk of the old drywall.

Bailey filled two glasses with cold water and handed his over. He heard the crackle as she leaned against the counter and into the plastic sheeting he'd laid out. "Watch out for the dust there."

It was everywhere, and he was making it worse. But it was how the job got done. When she only shrugged, he turned and held the claw bar out toward her. "Want to try?"

She blinked and looked at him like she didn't understand. "Try what?"

"Taking out some of the wall."

"Oh, sure." She took it from him and it dropped a few inches, clearly heavier than she expected it to be. "No sledge hammer?"

He motioned back to the counter behind them, "No room for a good swing, so this thing will come out in small chunks."

He picked up a second set of goggles he'd brought with him because he was a fool and wanted to do this with her rather than just get the job done. He'd woken up last night thinking she was in bed beside him. No hot crazy dreams—he didn't need those, he had real memories of being with her—and it had devastated him when she wasn't there. Which was stupid. She wasn't his. Maybe he'd been thinking about Amanda, but that had always been the problem with Amanda—not what she was, but what she wasn't.

He watched as his dream-girl put on goggles and wondered what it said about him that he'd had the same dream-girl his whole life. When he'd first asked her out, he'd liked her. He'd wanted to fit in. He'd wanted a real girlfriend. She fit all those categories. But it turned out she was more than he'd bargained for, and he'd fallen. Hard. Finn told himself that she wasn't the same now. He told himself his feelings now didn't matter, because the last time they'd been together, she'd ripped his heart out and walked away with it. Though he'd understood that her mother wanted better for her than an immigrant kid with student loans and no real plans, after all she was right—he hadn't had any real plans for his life at the time, and he *was* an immigrant kid. Bailey Ann was stepping down to be with him. Still, it had stripped him to the bone when she'd chosen her mother's plans over him.

He would have done anything for her. And she'd picked a plan over what he'd always thought was the real thing. So maybe he was just as dumb now as he'd always been. Maybe this was a cycle he was doomed to repeat until he learned. But she looked adorable in her goggles and he still wanted her.

Chances were, she wasn't thinking sexy things about him in his goggles either. But the only thing less sexy than frog goggles was a grown man crying on the floor because his eyes were trying to expel massive quantities of drywall dust . . . irritating particles that could have been prevented with goggles. He grinned at her anyway.

Watching, he checked her form as she hauled back and struck the wall with the forked end and . . . nothing happened. It bounced off.

Finn didn't laugh at her though. "More force."

She offered up a sardonic "thanks" as though she hadn't figured that out for herself, but Finn scrambled. "Oh crap. I'm putting the water glasses in the fridge for later, otherwise they'll get dust in them."

Bailey just nodded and pulled back and this time let fly at the wall. He heard the thunk behind him and turned to see the claw had sunk into the wall. Lifting the end to catch as big a chunk of drywall as she could, she tugged back. This didn't work for her the first time either.

He stood back. He was *not* going to mansplain. She understood how the physics of it worked and if she wanted his advice she'd ask. But it was hard to watch anyone work their way around it the first time. Harder when he wanted to put his arms around her and show her what he wanted—how to use the claw . . . and maybe more.

Bailey Ann seemed unwilling to give her best yank on the first try as if she was afraid she'd pull too hard and ram the other end into the bar counter behind her. He smiled as she gave a harder tug the second time and managed to pull a small section off.

She handed the small crowbar back to him. "You do a lot of construction?"

He shook his head. "I've been at a desk doing design mostly. I like going on site and I'll do the occasional ten minutes of work, but nothing like this. It's pretty satisfying doing Mom and Pop's house with my own hands."

"I really appreciate you doing this."

He grinned again. "I don't mind." He paused, his brain racing. It told him he was an idiot, trying again for something that would blow up in his face. Almost guaranteed. The other side of him argued back, *But what if it doesn't?* He just shrugged, because he couldn't tell her what was in his head. It was enough that he greeted her by asking when she was going to marry him. He spoke to her as if he were confident. The twist in his chest reminded him it was all a show. So he aimed for the practical. Holding up the small crowbar, he asked, "Got one of these? You can join me."

"Yeah, give me a minute." She headed out the backdoor and he took out another two chunks of wall and was just getting worried when she returned with a slightly larger one. Holding his out, she understood he wanted to trade, taking the larger one for himself. It was still bitingly cold outside, and the metal felt harsh against his hand. "Gloves. You probably want some gloves."

She headed up the stairs this time, pushing past him, the mix of cold air and her soft shirt brushing his skin and turning him inside out. Had she done that on purpose? Brushed against him? Did she like it as much as he had?

God, he was a mess. If Sioban was here, she'd just laugh at

him. Or stare him down with her dark eyes and tell him she hated Bailey Ann and he shouldn't make that same mistake again. His sister was smart. Maybe too smart. And maybe he should listen.

Bailey Ann returned, tugging on old floral gardening gloves. Taking a reasonable hold on the smaller crowbar, she aimed at the pencil lines he'd marked between the studs. She sunk it on the first try. Then she just used it as it was intended and pried out the piece of wall.

"You're pretty handy with that," he commented, appreciating her speed at catching on.

"You think a woman like me is all about linens and shoes to match the bag, but we were raised to handle anything that came our way." She took another shot at the wall, getting into the swing of it. It felt good.

"I know that. It's why I handed you a crowbar."

Her smile killed him. It was unfiltered, pure Bailey Ann. That was why he was willing to crash himself on the rocks once again. If she would smile at him like that, no manners, no pretense, no guile, he would die a happy man. Instead, she frowned at the wall, narrowed her brows and gave it the what-for.

In no time, they'd pulled out the kitchen side of the wall and worked their way around to the dining room side. The loss of the wall would make a big difference. He could see it already.

When there was nothing left but studs and a few scraps of drywall clinging to their nails, Finn called it done and lifted his goggles off his head. Bailey headed back into the kitchen, carefully setting down her crowbar and pulling the water glasses out of the fridge. As she handed his glass to him, she looked at his face and laughed. "You have lovely goggle lines on your face."

He was opening his mouth when she added. "I know, I do too. It's sexy."

His mouth gaped like a fish, almost willing to tell her that he always found her sexy, but it didn't seem like the time.

She filled the gap with more words, not that it helped. "I'm wearing my oldest clothes and I'm covered in drywall dust, too. This may be the hottest I've ever looked."

She was laughing at herself, until she looked at his face.

He wasn't laughing. She might as well have tied him to a stake and lit a fire under him. Need shot through him. He looked at her old shirt and paint spattered jeans and thought she couldn't look sexier if she was in lingerie. He was looking at her as if she were actively trying to seduce him, and he couldn't stop it. Whatever was moving between them steamrollered him and before he knew it, he'd pulled the water glass from her fingers and set it on the counter behind her.

She was so close. Too close. *No*, he thought, *just right*.

She'd been leaning back, but her breath had been choppy. Not afraid, not wary, but responding to the heat in his eyes. In that moment, she must have decided.

So his hands came up and laced into her hair, and he didn't think about the dust, or the mess or the fact that she was up against the counter. He just reached for her. This time, instead of him kissing her and her reacting, she moved for him. Her mouth found his, the shock of it stronger than before. He wouldn't have thought it was possible.

Bailey Ann Mayfair was plastering herself to the front of him. Her arms gripped his bare biceps, holding him close, and he loved that her fingers were on his bare skin. His arms locked around her and he leaned in, tipping her back over the edge of the counter as she made another move and licked his lower lip.

He groaned, laughed a little, and sighed her name.

"Finn," she whispered back, her mouth moving against his. God, he loved his name when she said it.

He was well and truly fucked. He could leave town, leave the state, leave everything behind, but she seemed to follow him wherever he went. He'd tried things without her. Maybe now it was time to really convince her to try things *with him*.

❧ 17 ❧

Bailey Ann leaned into the feeling as Finn's hands slid down her back, along her hips and behind her thighs.

For half a second, she'd wondered what he was doing, but she remembered this move. He liked her up on the counter. *This counter.* They'd been here before, not covered in dust, not in their thirties, not thinking about a fling. She'd weighed less then, but he hadn't been built like this either.

She knew this. So she moved with him, and found her ass on the kitchen counter in one smooth lift.

Finn hardly stopped. He was standing between her legs, tall enough to hit in all the right places. She hooked her feet behind him, not letting him get away, though it was pretty clear he wasn't trying to go anywhere.

His mouth worked magic against hers and her entire body hummed as his fingers tucked under the hem at her waist to slide up under her shirt. It was a thermal, long-sleeved tee, about as un-sexy as she could get. But he was unwrapping her like it was Christmas morning. And she was letting him.

Lord, this was the oldest, ugliest bra she owned. And as it was a sports bra, it was going to be hell to get out of. She looked up at him to ask forgiveness, but he was looking at her as though she was in red lace. Bless that man.

Taking his face in her hands, she pulled him forward and kissed the daylights out of them both. She didn't stop until his hands found her breasts and made her gasp. They were both breathing heavy when they pulled back.

Finn found enough voice to whisper, "Take it off."

Shit. Also not pretty, but she was not getting off this train. Leaning back for space, she crossed her arms, grabbed the elastic at the base and peeled it upward. She had to twist and pull, and she could hardly do it because she felt his mouth on her collar bone, licking and sucking at her skin. She wondered for a second if he'd leave a mark, then all thought fled as she felt his lips on her breast and she tried to keep enough of her brain active to untangle her hands from the bra holding her wrists in a knot over her head.

He pressed into her, into the seam of her jeans, the thickness of him pressing through his jeans, the feel of him between her legs was driving her crazy. Crazy enough to sit on her kitchen counter, dirty, sweaty, with goggle marks on her face, and having some of the most mind-blowing sex she'd had in too damn long.

Tossing the wadded-up sports bra to the side, she plunged her fingers into his hair. For a moment she held him to her skin, where his lips and tongue worked their magic. Then she tugged him up to her mouth, pushed her chest forward so they fused, skin to skin, and hooked her heels behind his knees.

She would have said she had him stuck, but she could tell, even if she let him go, he wasn't going anywhere. He was in as deep as she was.

Her fingers traced the indentation of his spine. Followed the waistband on his jeans. Walked over the denim into his pockets where she plunged her fingers to tug him closer—as if that was possible.

His hands were on her ass—large, capable hands that

spanned a good part of her butt and held her as he ground against her. Her legs moved involuntarily, adding to the sensation. Her fingers dug in, clenching of their own accord.

His mouth traced her lips, then her jaw, and finally her earlobe, before he whispered, "You know, there's nothing in those pockets."

Confused, she looked at him a little oddly.

He grinned. "Everything good is inside the jeans."

She laughed then, her fingers still in his pockets.

He was looking at her, his expression a sexy combination of amusement and heat. Without breaking eye contact, she pulled her hands out of his back pockets and traced her way around to the front of his jeans where she undid the top button.

A sudden flashback hit her. It had taken them a while to get good together. Their first time had been the first for both of them. It had been awkward and sweet and eye opening. They'd tried again. And again. Even as a teenager, Finn had been eager to please her, and she him. Though she was pretty sure he'd been reading up and doing actual research. He would whisper, "Let me touch you like this. Let me try."

She remembered gasping at the sensations. She remembered him smiling each time he figured out something new she liked. She remembered him guiding her hand to touch him and watching his eyes roll back. She'd loved that she could do that to him. And they'd gotten to where they both almost went over the edge just reaching for the front of the other's jeans.

She remembered he favored these button fly jeans, and she could run her finger down behind the buttons, popping them open and touching him at the same time. She remembered doing that while reaching into his back pocket for the condom he carried tucked in behind a folded piece of paper. He did that so it was handy, but so it didn't show in his pocket. No one needed to know what they did together. Given what Jane said, people had guessed or figured it out, but she was still certain that he'd never gone bragging about it.

The button fly on his jeans took her back, and brought her to now. Now with her finger behind the row of buttons, her knuckle grazing his erect form as she slid it down. Bailey reached into his back pocket, just like she used to and . . .

Nothing.

She frowned. "Finn?"

"*Whah . . .*"

His hands were flat on the counter on either side of her hips. He was leaning over her, broad chest brushing the tips of her breasts as he breathed heavily. His head was tipped back, his eyes closed as though the feel of her touching him again after all these years was as wild and sacred to him as it was to her.

"Finn. Condom?"

"*What . . . ?*" This time he opened those blue eyes at her. Dark with need, he still looked confused.

"Condom?"

He shook his head. "I don't have one. Not on me." Then she watched as realization dawned on him. She felt it herself. *Noooo.* He looked to her. "You?"

She shook her head slowly.

His eyes squeezed shut and she watched as pleasure turned to frustration.

"You didn't bring one?" She looked at him incredulously.

Suddenly, he grinned, though his frustration showed he was almost exasperated at her. "Bailey Ann Mayfair, I came over here to take out a wall. I didn't even bring my wallet. I was wearing my goggles. I did not intend to take you on the kitchen counter."

"You took off your shirt."

"I got hot."

"You started off hot," she countered.

He grinned back at her, kissed her, deeply, with tongue, but lacking some of the heat of earlier. It was hard to dive into that gusto when there was no condom to let it go any further. She ground her teeth.

He nipped at her ear. "You do it to me."

That goes both ways, she thought as she tried to get her breathing under control. *Crap.* Her bra was on the floor across the room and she was topless on the kitchen counter with the hottest guy she'd ever known still standing between her legs. Good thing they still had their jeans on or she would have decided to throw caution to the wind then worried about it for the next two to four weeks.

He leaned back, took a deep breath, and pushed away. Without a word, he leaned over and picked up her bra and handed it back. Then her long sleeved shirt, for which she was grateful. It had been hard enough getting out of that bra, getting back into it? With him watching? No, she wasn't going to do that. She slid the shirt on without the bra and hopped off the counter. Absentmindedly, looking for some conversation to start up with the man she'd almost banged on her kitchen counter, she said, "I need a shower."

Behind her, Finn groaned. "Jesus, Bailey Ann. Unless you have a condom in your shower, then don't say things like that when I'm standing here like this."

Usually she'd be watching the clock and listening for the door to click open. There'd been more than one time they'd rushed to put clothing back on. She'd always thought she fooled her parents, but looking back, she wondered. Now, as an adult, she could stand in the kitchen with her bra wadded up in her hand and half grin at him. "I'm sorry, it was a statement of fact."

He sighed heavily, the weary resignation of his state clear in the sound. "I'm going home. I will also shower. Alone. But when you're done, come over and help me lay out my parents house for show. It's payment for taking out this wall. I just want another set of eyes on colors and options before I commit. Can you do that?"

"Of course." Small potatoes, and it would get her out of this house. Being here was hard. Changing this place was harder. She was still grieving the loss of both her parents. Every opportunity to be out and useful was welcome. "I'll be over in a bit."

Then she watched that very fine ass walk out her back door as she realized she'd been left wanting for the second time in twenty four hours.

❧ 18 ❧

Bailey Ann wondered what she must look like to the neighbors.

She was walking along the border wall between their houses, carrying Finn's short crowbar and goggles. He'd left both behind, going out the door without looking back, clearly sexually frustrated. She understood.

She was surprised he didn't leave his shirt, but at least he managed that. So, while the neighbors might notice the traffic—first Finn, then her—at least it hopefully didn't look like a straight up booty call.

And it wasn't. It *wasn't* a booty call. She was going to help him pick out tiles or paint colors or something like that. She didn't have a condom with her because she didn't own any. She'd been single for a while and was still on the pill but the last guy she'd been with had been serious enough to ditch the condoms, just not serious enough to get engaged and be a family.

She was in jeans again, though these were clean. This time she had on a nice sweater that could be seen in public places other than the local hardware store. And if she happened to have on some really smoking lingerie, well that was between her and her conscience, wasn't it?

Watching for loose stones, she picked her way across the distance. She looked up to see if either the Millers or the Johnsons were watching and even waved once, though she wasn't sure if she was seeing someone in the rec room or just catching an odd reflection. Looking at her feet until she hit the edge of Finn's back yard, she didn't see him until the last moment, standing on his back deck, coffee mug in hand, watching her.

She hopped down and saw him there, smiling at her. Another flashback hit her. A younger Finn waiting here for her when his parents were out. She would carry her backpack and books and tell her parents they were doing homework—and sometimes they did, so it was somewhat true. But now, she was only returning his things, and now, Finn had broader shoulders to fill out the flannel shirt he'd thrown over the black t-shirt for warmth.

She should have worn a jacket, but a jacket wasn't sexy.

"You left these," she hollered up to him, picking her way across a backyard that wasn't as well tended as it used to be. She said it loud enough that neighbors with big ears might hear. Let them see goggles and a pry bar, that would likely stop them from thinking Bailey Ann Mayfair and Finn Malloy had picked back up where they left off in high school.

She started up the stairs as he came down to meet her. Halfway there, he paused, blocking her way up. "Can I kiss you?"

"Now you ask?" She was grinning, but she could see she'd missed his point.

"Someone might see." It was all he said, and he didn't move out of her way, just left them hanging there in the space between until she answered.

She hadn't thought about it. Good girls didn't flaunt their affairs, but this wasn't the street either. This was Finn's property. Either way, anyone seeing anything would set tongues wagging. She wasn't arrogant about it, but she was a Mayfair, and the Mayfairs had run this town since it was defined by a dirt road.

Sure, the Zemps and the Cottons had moved in with more

money, but the town had once been called Mayfair. The county was still Mayfair County. And her last name was still Mayfair. She'd had that decorum drilled into her from childhood.

Then all those thoughts and rules blew away. Finn Malloy was a good man. Any tongues that had anything bad to say about it could be put to rest by her own. Or maybe by a sharp word from her Nana or Aunt Gigi.

Bailey didn't say yes. It seemed too small for a man who was smart enough to ask. Ray Haley hadn't asked. He'd just assumed that, since the Haleys had people in Atlanta and Nashville and Mobile, there was no need for her to worry about what the public might think. With Finn she didn't believe it meant he thought any less of himself, just more that he knew she worried about what others thought about her. Well, that had to get thrown out the window, because look where it had gotten her.

She grabbed the front of his shirt with the hand holding the goggles in it and pulled him down to her. She caught the slightest glimpse of his grin before it disappeared under the curve of her mouth.

It wasn't a deep kiss, or a rough one. It was small, but big in its own way.

He turned around, not having spilled a drop of his coffee, and walked back up the steps. Looking back over his shoulder, he asked her, "Are you looking at my ass?"

"Yes, sir. I am."

But that was the end of it. Finn Malloy became the perfect gentleman, leading her in through the back door again. Setting down his mug, he took the tools from her and placed them off to the side. Then he took her hand and started pulling her through the house.

"I got tile samples for the kitchen and the bathrooms." In his excitement, she could hear a little bit of Ireland creeping through. In high school it had bothered her, separating him from the other students. It had bothered him then, too. But now, with a new ear, she found she liked it.

Having no choice but to follow him, she watched as he flipped on lights and held up tiles. He showed her squares in various shades of cream with a variety of textures. Just when she said she couldn't pick, and he commiserated, he then held up three different pieces for her.

"What's this?"

"Accent tile."

"Jesus." She shook her head.

"I know."

"Wait. It's family economics 101." She smiled.

"What are you talking about?"

"It's not about what you like. They all look good, but this cream tile, it's all equal, visually. It's the accent stuff that's different. So pick that piece first—spend your visual currency there, and pick the other to match."

He nodded. "This. It's the prettiest that doesn't break the budget."

"Good point. What's the cheapest, good quality square that goes with that?"

He pointed.

Bailey Ann grinned. "Done. Who knew a business degree would help me pick out tile?"

"College is useful for more than they tell you about," he added, then tugged her down the hall to the bathroom. "Do it again."

He laid aside what they picked and dragged her upstairs where they picked another set of bathroom tile using her method.

"You are a lifesaver." He was grinning as he twirled her around, guiding her in closer, bringing her mouth to his.

As their lips touched, they went up in flames. All the banked heat from earlier burst back into life and she found herself shoving his flannel shirt off his shoulders and tugging up the black t-shirt before she even realized what she was doing.

He'd backed her against the sink, all hands and mouth, and

he was groaning in admiration and peeling her bra before she even realized her sweater was gone.

His hips found hers and she could feel him through the jeans, once again ready for her. She moved against him, eliciting her own gasps as she held his head while he kissed his way down her chest. He had his fingers working the snap of her jeans before she'd even thought that far ahead, but she wasn't thinking well as it was.

Then she sucked in a breath. "You'd better have a condom, Finn Malloy."

"In here," he whispered it as he lifted her, guiding her legs to wrap around him. Like that, he carried her down the hallway, dropping her on a queen-sized bed in his old room.

She hadn't been in here since he'd re-done it, but her brain didn't have time to examine the place. The mattress was at her back, and her shoes and jeans were disappearing rapidly and she was getting behind. Finn still had pants on.

Bailey remedied that within the minute and wound up trying to strip him even as he was reaching into the bedside drawer and ripping open a brand new box of condoms. For a second, her brain caught that—he'd just bought them, these weren't from a stash, they were for *her*. She was grinning as he covered himself and pushed her back on the bed again.

"Bailey Ann, I've been waiting for this. For you."

There was no time to respond as he was fully over her and her breath was sucking in in anticipation of the feel of him. She didn't have long to wait. Though he'd learned to tease her as they went along, he didn't seem to have that in him now. Good thing, because neither did she.

"Finn," she set his name loose on a breathy sigh. "Please."

He obliged her. The feel of him pushing inside her was both new and old. Both exciting and like coming home. She heard a noise and discovered it was her own voice, but she didn't care. She didn't have to be quiet, didn't have to lock the door, didn't have to hold back. So she didn't.

As he moved inside her, he said her name, over and over. She begged him for more. And he delivered.

He was almost shouting by the time he pushed her over the edge and she discovered she could moan with the best of them. She held onto him, fingernails digging in, legs wrapping around him, while the world burst and swirled around her, while he came as she still swooned in half-consciousness.

Then, at last, he calmed to a stage of heavy breathing, as though he'd run a marathon, but she realized it only matched her own. She felt the weight of him as he slowly lowered himself and curled around her. Her world was settling back into place, but it was a different place than before. It took a while for her breathing to even out, for her to accept that she'd changed everything.

Just then, the weird clicking she heard started to make sense. It was a door.

"Finn?" she asked, but before he could answer her, they both heard a louder female voice yelling through the house.

"Finn! It's me!"

❧ 19 ☙

Bailey stared at Finn with wide eyes even as she put the sound together. For a moment, he seemed frozen, and Bailey was struggling to recognize the voice. She couldn't place it, but there was another woman in the house, calling for Finn. "Are you married?"

That, at least, got his attention. "It's Sioban."

Bailey Ann blinked. His little sister?

Then it hit her. *Holy shit.* He had family *inside* his house. And she was naked. *Nay-ked.* Her Mama would roll over in her grave. And she'd just been thinking that they didn't have to worry about people barging in. That would show her.

Bailey could not remember the last time she'd gone from zero to sixty as fast as she did right then. Her underwear was on faster than record time, even though she was hopping as though the floor was on fire. Her jeans were harder to work, but she got them. She was putting her shoes on before her bra because she could see them. Her brain was functioning enough to know that Sioban would figure it out if Bailey Mayfair came downstairs barefoot.

Her bra?

Shit.

In the bathroom. Across the hallway. Finn could pull another shirt from his closet, but she had to go after that sweater . . . and the bra. There was no way around it with this layout, she had to walk the hallway. She just took a moment to thank God that she hadn't worn anything with buttons. A mid-afternoon walk of shame across the backyard wall with her clothes crooked was not what she wanted.

Glancing out the open bedroom door, she prayed that the noises she'd heard were Sioban coming in the door and not from knocking around after being in the house *while* Bailey had screamed the woman's older brother's name. Bailey made a break for it and dashed across the hall.

Safe!

Just then, the voice came again, only this time it was louder but more uncertain. "*Finn?*"

Unwinding her arms from over her breasts, she picked up the bra and spent far too long untangling it. When she got it on, she was pretty sure she'd put a twist in the center, but at this point, she couldn't afford to care. She slid the sweater on just before catching a glimpse of herself in the old mirror.

Finn said he was going to replace it. Too bad he couldn't replace the hairstyle that now said, "just got laid." She finger-combed it and came out into the hallway to find Finn putting the final touches on his own *no, I wasn't just banging Bailey Ann Mayfair. Why do you ask?* outfit.

He yelled down the stairs as he looked Bailey over and nodded at her, deeming her at least well enough put together.

She took a deep breath and decided to let Finn do the talking.

As Finn hit the bottom of the steps, she watched as Sioban lit up and threw herself into his arms. He swung his younger sister around, his voice happy.

Bailey understood, even if her own reunions with her sisters weren't quite as exuberant. Then, it happened. Sioban caught sight of her, and she shoved out of her brother's arms to stop and look at the woman still standing on the top step.

Her voice changed. Lower now, wary, she offered a greeting that was anything but warm. "Bailey Ann."

Trying for a kinder response than the one she'd gotten, Bailey smiled. "Sioban."

"It's Sha-vaughn."

Which was exactly what Bailey Ann was pretty sure she'd said. So she didn't reply. Finn did it for her.

"Sioban." His tone was scolding, though to Bailey it still sounded exactly like what she'd said. "She said it fine."

Sioban dropped it and went a different direction. "What are you doing here?"

"She helped pick out the tile for the kitchen and bathrooms," Finn interjected.

"Did she now?" Sioban was still looking at Bailey Ann.

Finn's face was a play in exasperation, though Bailey was pretty sure Sioban understood exactly what they'd been up to. She hadn't interacted with his sister much when they were together, simply because Sioban hadn't even been in high school with them. A handful of years younger, she'd barely been in middle school when they'd been dating. So Bailey wasn't sure where this attitude was coming from now. Still, she refused to play into it.

"I didn't know you were coming. What prompted this?" Finn could play the change-the-topic game, too, it seemed.

Sioban lit up again. "I got the job in Atlanta. It went down fast, but I've got some time before I start."

"That's amazing!"

They spoke for a few moments, with Bailey offering some congratulations but not otherwise participating. She was just getting ready to make her goodbyes, when Sioban sighed.

"I drove straight through from Oklahoma. Finn, do you mind getting my bag out of the car?"

"Sure." He tossed a quick look of apology to Bailey and

headed out the back to where Sioban must have pulled around in the drive.

Bailey was opening her mouth to leave when Sioban beat her to it.

"If you hurt him, I will gut you with the precision skill of the surgeon that I am."

Bailey jerked back as though she'd been slapped, but she pulled herself together the way she'd been taught. "I don't know what you're concerned about."

Sioban leaned in, the happy woman who'd hugged her brother with abandon a few moments ago was gone, replaced by a fury. "That letter you wrote him, I know about it. You had no right to screw him over like that, and I won't let you do it again. I don't know what he's doing with you, but I hope like hell he's going to fuck you and throw you away just like you did to him last time. Don't worry, I'll be right here, laughing when he does."

Sioban paused, her glare holding steady, even though Bailey was struggling to place everything the woman had said. That letter had been that they'd grown apart and wanted different things. That it wasn't wise to get back together for a summer and get closer when they both knew things weren't going to work out. Clearly, his sister had no idea what she was talking about, but she was more than capable of spewing venom.

Bailey Ann took a breath, but she didn't let it show. Instead, she pasted on her best friendly smile and didn't let it go to her eyes. "You go right ahead and do that, honey. But I'm going to show some class here and end this little conversation. You have a real nice reunion with your brother now, and don't you worry about me." She turned to head out, then as she hit the door, she saw Finn at the bottom of the deck stairs, two bags in his hands. *Shit*, Sioban was staying for a while. Bailey Ann turned back and called over her shoulder. "You just watch where you step now."

She waved and closed the door before anything further could come out of his sister's mouth. The last thing she wanted was a war with Finn's last remaining family, but she was not capable of just taking shit like that.

He kissed her briefly as he passed on the stairs, but it was quick and awkward. He was hauling suitcases for the woman who'd just insulted her, carefully and out of his earshot.

For a second, he looked at her as though to ask what was wrong.

What was wrong was that she was trying not to shake from her anger and shock. She shook her head softly and said, "Go have a good time with your sister." Then she headed down the steps and across the backyard.

She didn't even have anything in her hands. No purse. Nothing to carry, not even the goggles and crowbar she'd brought on the way over. Though it was probably a good thing she didn't have access to the small, heavy, metal tool right now.

She waved at the Millers' house again as she went by, more certain this time that someone was home. They waved back, though she couldn't quite tell if it was Mr. Miller or Mrs. Miller. At least they weren't yelling at her to get off the wall.

By the time she hit the corner of her own backyard she'd managed to calm down a bit and was just angry. Sioban had no idea what the hell she was talking about. It took some balls to be that bitchy when you didn't even have your facts straight.

She let herself into her back door and looked around her own home. Somehow it was only two in the afternoon. She was starving, Finn having highjacked her day in the best way possible. But she was too worked up to do any real work in the house.

At times like this, a girl needed her Nana, and she bet Nana would love to get out for a meal. But first, she brushed the tangles out of her hair. No point in having Nana ask if she'd just been "tumbled." Nana was hard to lie to.

F inn set the suitcases down just inside the door. He was opening his mouth to say something to his sister, but she was gone.

Bailey Ann had looked angry, and he couldn't blame her. They'd spent their entire teenage years getting interrupted and scrambling to put themselves back together. They'd had to sneak away and lie to their parents to get a night together, and even then there was always the possibility of getting caught.

Tumbling Bailey Ann in his own bed with no one to interrupt them had been a hallmark of finally being with her as an adult. And then, boom, someone coming in the door. He loved his sister, he wanted to see her, but now was not the time.

For whatever reason, Sioban didn't like Bailey Ann much. Most likely she'd been jealous of the girl who'd taken all her big brother's time, but she was an adult now and should have put that behind her. He headed up the stairs and found her looking into the rooms.

She pointed at her old room and just raised her eyebrows at him. It was gutted, down to the drywall, carpet ripped up, the wall between the two rooms starting to come down. "So, don't sleep in there."

"Where do I go?"

"The master." He was at the top of the steps, leaning against the wall, trying to figure out his little sister. Always shyer than most, always keeping to herself, she was smart, stubborn, and wily when she wanted to be.

"It's gutted, too." She turned back to him in the doorway.

"I'll get you an inflatable mattress and some sheets." He shrugged. It wasn't as if she hadn't known this was happening. She'd signed off on it. This was going to make a sizable payment to her medical school loans once he sold it. "I wasn't expecting you."

"Yeah. I could tell." She waved her fingers at him. "Sorry if I interrupted anything."

He only shook his head. Technically, no, she hadn't. But he'd been three heartbeats away from pulling Bailey Ann into his arms and falling asleep. Something he'd never been able to do with any certainty that he wasn't going to get ripped away from her. Sioban had some crappy timing. Still, he didn't want to hold it against her. "Do you want to go out and celebrate the new job? Catch me up on what's happening?"

"Sure. Bobby's?"

He started to nod. He'd never been certain if the pizza place really was her favorite, or if she'd just always been used to skimping on everything. When they'd been kids, pizza once a month was their outing. He knew other kids who ate fast food each day at lunch and went out several times a week with their families, but he and Sioban hadn't. The money hadn't been there.

Then she'd been in medical school, and it was most certainly more of the same. He thought for a moment. "Do you want to go somewhere like Zeal? Really celebrate."

"Nah." She waved him away. "Bobby's is good. But I'm starving, can we go now?"

"Yeah, me too." He was grabbing for his coat when he heard her.

"Let's not talk about what you did to get that hungry."

He frowned and set his coat down. "What's the issue? I'm an adult."

"Are you?"

God, he hated when she did that. She was so smart but she liked to pull things on him when she could. He didn't rise to the bait. Damn, this day should have been wonderful, amazing, and parts of it were. But it had also been harsh and exhausting. He'd walked away from Bailey Ann wrapped around him on her kitchen counter. Then he'd gotten a second chance. Then Sioban had showed up and now she was pulling crap on him. He'd really like to not have to work so hard at the rest of the day, but that wasn't in the cards. He stared at her.

She finally conceded to talk to him, as though he was the one who'd started it. "I don't like that look in your eyes."

"What look?"

"The moony one. Over *her*." She pointed out the back door, the last place he'd seen Bailey Ann and he wondered now about the expression on her face as he'd passed by. But Sioban was talking again. "She never treated you well when you were together—"

"What do you know about it?"

"I know what I saw!"

"You were twelve!" He was yelling now, angry, frustrated and hungry. And happy. All mixed together. He was a mess.

"How old did I need to be to know she broke your heart?"

Fuck! He thought it but managed not to say it. Just barely. Sioban wasn't wrong about that. But she was wrong to question him now. To question this. And he had zero evidence to back that up. Just a little worse, she was right. He clenched his jaw. If Bailey Ann gutted him again, it would be awful. He'd be done. He'd give up and crawl into some little shell and design houses and live out his life with three cats.

Though he didn't know why, he was willing to try again.

"You're acting like an addict." She said. Only she wasn't yelling. She might as well put on her white lab coat. The one she was so proud of, with Dr. Malloy stitched in blue letters. She was pulling out her bedside manner.

"I'm not your patient. I'm not an addict."

"Then walk away."

Oh, fuck. She did not just play that card. "Sioban, when was the last time I told you who to date?"

She frowned.

"Never. The answer is that I never did. Now it's time that you adopt that policy." He grabbed his coat and her elbow and steered her out the door and down the back deck stairs. "Let's get pizza."

He wanted to ask what she'd said to Bailey Ann, but he still wasn't certain that she had said anything. And at least now they weren't yelling. "So, tell me about Atlanta and the job. You have a place yet?"

Sioban saw what he was doing, but she only frowned at him once more. He didn't ask how long she was staying, not yet. Because he wanted her here. He didn't get to see her much. But he also wanted the house back to himself. He had work to do.

🌿 2 1 🌿

M*ost true belles are small town royalty. Being a belle in a small town is no hardship as long as you get a nice come-out.*

BAILEY ANN WAS STARVING BY THE TIME SHE ARRIVED IN THE complex where her Nana lived. It was an assisted living home she'd moved into almost ten years earlier after GrandDaddy had died.

It seemed she'd known she'd outlive the man. She'd just made plans with her friends. Nana's unit was a little five-hundred square foot house just like all the others in her little cul-de-sac, and it was the place to be. As she pulled up, Bailey Ann could see that it was hopping and Nana was saying goodbye to two friends so she could go out to lunch with her granddaughter.

When Nana had moved in here, she'd gifted Bailey with the family silver in anticipation of her marriage. That now seemed premature on several counts. The silver remained at Mama and Daddy's and Bailey Ann Mayfair had remained single. Hell, Emma Kate was going to get married before her.

Pointing her car into the short driveway, Bailey popped the car in park and hopped out to get the door for her grandmother. She wasn't sure how the woman was holding up. It was one thing to lose her husband, another thing entirely to lose her son.

"Bailey Ann!" She smiled and held her arms out as though she handled the grieving process with more class than the rest of them. As she hugged her Nana back, Bailey Ann thought it was probably true.

They passed the sign to label the entrance to the unit and Bailey gave up and asked, "Nana, you know you live in a section called 'Cluster F'?"

"Of course, I do. Why do you think I picked it? It's funny." She put her purse in her lap and turned to Bailey. "Where are we going? Please don't say anywhere with a buffet."

"Want to head down toward Atlanta? Not all the way in, but close enough to get some good seafood?"

"Oh girl, you are really my granddaughter." Nana sat back and smiled.

"Well, then, I have to have a snack to get us there." Bailey rummaged through her purse and pulled out the granola bar she'd crammed in there in case Nana was up for the drive. Then she peeled it and offered a bite to her grandmother.

They weren't fifteen minutes past the edge of town when her grandmother let fly. "Tell me about that Malloy boy you've been seeing."

Bailey almost stomped the brakes she was so surprised, but she shouldn't have been. Nana had become that crazy relative. Raised a pure Southern Belle, she'd taken care of GrandDaddy, raised her kids, and now had zero time for crap of any kind. Though Bailey would never have talked to her about boys—or anything really—when she was a kid, Nana was now her last parental-type unit and she was at least less strict than Mama had been.

"Word gets around, does it?" she asked sardonically as she took a turn off the freeway.

"Oh please, we don't have anything to do except rewrite our

wills and cook and gossip. I can do all three at the same time." In her seat, Nana smiled. "Now talk."

"Well, just for clarity's sake, Nana, that *boy* is a thirty-four year old man. He's an architect and he's home for a few months to flip his parents' house and sell it for the proceeds. They're going to use the money to pay off some of his and Sioban's student loans."

"That's a good idea," Nana was saying as they pulled up to Woodlands. The name didn't inspire trust in great seafood, but they had good everything. Pricey for a mid-afternoon lunch, but Bailey Ann needed this. She needed to get beyond the borders of Breathless and know she wasn't stuck there. She sometimes had visions that it was like a sci-fi show and she would bump against an invisible barrier and she would be stuck in the small town forever. As they parked, Nana opened her door and popped out, her spry nature always made Bailey Ann relieved after watching her Mama get so sick. Fingers crossed, she'd have her Nana for a while.

They headed in the door and put their names on the list, and Nana asked her, "Flipped means he's redoing it differently, right?"

"Yes. He's changing it from a three bedroom to a two. Linking the upstairs bath into the newer, bigger bedroom, like a master, and expanding the downstairs bath a bit. He's modernizing the kitchen, too. Opening up the front windows."

"You sure know a lot about this. I assume you're sleeping with him."

"Nana!" Bailey Ann had to swallow her shock as they were called to the table right then. Her face must be fifty shades of red as she tried to get her heart under control. How had Nana asked that? And within hours of it coming to be true? *Dammit.* If the old woman had asked her that this morning, she could have honestly said no.

They were brought menus and waters and Bailey Ann hoped the topic had passed.

It had not. "You are sleeping with him, right?"

"Is that any of your business, Nana?" Bailey tried to keep her voice low but feared she couldn't do a good enough job of it.

"No, not at all. But everyone says it, anyway. So I thought I'd ask."

"People are talking about me and Finn?" She almost put her hand to her heart. But then who would the old woman at this table be?

Just then, the server arrived, and they put in their orders. Her hopes that this would stop the topic were much smaller this time and just as useless.

"You two were like a fireworks show, back when you were in high school. I always thought you belonged together."

Bailey Ann frowned at her. Mama had thought differently, and Nana had said nothing of the sort at the time. But Nana kept talking as though no one was making any sort of facial expression at her. "So now is a good time to pick up where you messed up."

"Oh, I messed up, did I?"

"You know you did." Nana looked up and then pulled her hands back to accept the hot plate the server brought with the utmost grace. Bailey Ann hadn't even noticed. Now she was just as likely to choke on her food as not.

She let them set her plate down, then said, "I know nothing of the sort."

"Well, I do. And you should, too."

Bailey waited her out, but Nana didn't explain. She started a new tack that made Bailey wonder if she could take Nana out in public anymore.

"I only ever slept with your grandfather. In my day, we waited."

"Nana!"

"Hear me out!" She waved her fork at Bailey even though it had an asparagus speared on it. "I wouldn't change it. Things were different, and I loved that man, but you have a lot more options. You get to test drive your cars, if you know what I mean."

Oh, dear God. Her Nana had just said, "If you know what I mean." At least she wasn't loud? Bailey told herself to take what she could get. Otherwise she would be crawling under the table. Instead she nodded politely and ate her shrimp pasta, waiting for whatever shoe was coming flying at her next. The other shoe simply "dropping" would be far too easy.

"If you work together in bed, if you have that spark and you also genuinely like spending time with that man—I mean time when you're not naked—"

Okay, she was ready to crawl under the table now.

"Then you consider cutting slack on everything else. Anything else can be worked around. But that kind of compatibility is rare."

She finally paused, and Bailey Ann prayed for a break. It didn't quite come.

"And he's hot. You could do a lot worse."

Her face must have flushed to a full red, because Nana frowned at her.

"Well, you could."

It took ten minutes of calmly eating her food to get back to where she could talk. This was certainly not the same as listening to Jane Copeland telling her to go for it with Finn. But apparently, in spite of referring to Finn as "that Malloy boy," Nana had deemed her an adult and that meant full scale gossip talk. For a moment she wondered if Nana was going to go back to Cluster F and tell all her little old biddy friends about Bailey Ann and Finn Malloy boning. *Oh, good lord.*

"Nana, I do really like him—as a person! I'm not answering the rest of it."

"Oh honey, you don't have to. Your red face answered for you." Nana smiled sincerely as she delivered her line, a true Southern Belle.

"I just don't know that we're right for each other. I think we come from different worlds."

"What? Because he grew up poor and you're the Princess of Breathless?"

"No! Nana, nothing like that." *Right? Nothing like that* . . . She changed the topic. "And his sister hates me."

"Oh? Do tell!" Nana leaned forward. "Tell me we're getting the chocolate cake. This deserves chocolate cake."

❧ 22 ❧

I t had been evening before she made it home. When she'd dropped Nana off, her grandmother had insisted on showing Bailey off to her friends. Mrs. Winters even commented on Finn Malloy being back in town. If she'd thought she was being subtle, Bailey Ann had missed her mark.

"He's doing well, Mrs. Winters," was all she was willing to give up.

It took a while to extract herself from the clutches of little old ladies on a mission. By the time she'd made it home, she was ready for a glass of wine and a good TV show. When she started falling asleep on the couch, she packed it in and called it a night. Luckily, she was too tired to recount her day. It had been a doozy.

The next morning, she'd slept in a little, gotten up and scrambled eggs and made toast. She was starving, since her lunch had been late, and she'd not eaten dinner the night before. As she stood at the plastic covered kitchen counter, eating her breakfast, she tried not to stare at the wall of stripped studs in front of her.

The upside was that she could see into the dining room, imperfectly, mind you, but well enough to start to get an idea of

Finn's vision. She found she liked it. What she didn't like was that she could almost see him there, with no shirt on, pulling out her drywall. And that got her hot. There she was, getting all turned on looking at exposed two-by-fours.

When she'd finished eating, she considered getting to work on the walls in the dining room, but when she checked her to-do list, she found out she had a lot more to do first.

Sitting in the living room, she went to stack the pages on the coffee table but found that there wasn't enough room. Mama had back issues of Southern Living lined up on one end of the table. Looking at the dates, it appeared her Daddy had kept the subscription and just put the magazines on the table as they came in. He certainly wasn't reading them himself.

She tossed all but the most recent one, thinking of it as cleaning up. Still, little heartbreaks hit her along the way. It was yet another method of erasing her mother. It was impossible to keep things the way they had been. The house shouldn't be a museum to a woman who was gone. Finn's idea was right, the house deserved to be a good place for a new family. So, though it was hard to do, she watched all the magazines go into the trash can.

Then she pulled them all out and stacked them on the floor and made a note to get a recycling bin. Mama hadn't believed in recycling. She bought into every argument against it that could be made—it cost more to make old stuff into something else than just buy something new, no one wanted her old magazines, sorting it was such a hassle.

Bailey Ann had loved her Mama. They'd disagreed on things, but she hadn't been able to hold onto any of that while her mother was sick. She was the daughter who'd come home, taken her to chemo, opened the door to the hospice nurse and then repeated to her Daddy that Mama had a couple more days at most. Her Mama had died the next morning, with Bailey Ann by her side. Arguing the value of a recycling bin was hardly appropriate at the time.

She must be coming out the other side of some of her grief at least, because she looked at the magazines on the floor and said out loud, "Mama, you were wrong."

Then she trekked back out to the living room and started into Daddy's papers.

She found the deed for the car and set it aside. She was about to file the next one when she realized she should just do each thing as it came up. So she pulled out her laptop and turned it on.

That was another thing her Mama would have a conniption about—a computer in her living room. Living rooms were for tea and company, not technology. Then again, Mama hadn't grown up with computers in the house. Bailey Ann had saved up for her own laptop, even though her parents made sure the family had a good system set up in the basement, they had never really seen the need for each girl to have her own. It was Nana who'd eventually gotten them all iPads one Christmas.

Finding a place to advertise it, she started filling in information about Daddy's car. Luckily, he was meticulous about it. He also bought new, which meant that, despite being a Cadillac sedan that looked like an older gentleman's car—exactly what it was, no pizzazz or anything—it was in great shape. She checked it against the blue book value and hoped it would sell well.

That done, she marked a satisfying cross through the "list daddy's car" line on the massive to-do list. Now if she could just mark the "sold" line, she'd be happier.

Next, she started into other papers.

Three timeshares to take care of. Did she want to keep one? Two were co-owned with other families. That sucked. Daddy should have sold them himself. He had some kind of agreement with these people and Bailey Ann didn't know specifically how that worked. No time like the present though.

She called the Duckworths about the one on the Alabama coast. Ron Duckworth answered on the first ring. That was impressive since she'd called the home line and she was pretty sure their phone was still mounted on the wall and maybe a shade of mustard yellow to boot.

"Hi, Mr. Duckworth—" she didn't get a chance to finish.

"I'm sorry I didn't get back in touch with you sooner, Bailey Ann. I talked to Harper Rose but didn't see you much at the funeral service. I got the feeling you were busy handling everything. It was just beautiful. I know your Mama would be proud."

She thanked him for the compliments, despite the fact that he'd interrupted her. Elders and all. Then she leaned back on the couch. This call was going to take a while.

In fact, it took five full minutes of reminiscing, discussing her plans, and checking up on the Duckworths' health, before she could even bring up the timeshare. If she hadn't been raised on this, she might have gotten impatient.

Bailey Ann knew what she was doing and her phone didn't have a cord. So she headed into the kitchen while they chatted and poured herself a glass of white wine. Back on the couch, she sipped at it while they talked.

"Well, I reckon we should sell the thing and just split the profits. It's all owned—your daddy and I paid it off about seven years ago." That was good. It was the first timeshare her family had gotten a stake in. When they found out they loved it—she'd taken a ton of vacations there over the years—her Daddy had gotten another. Then Mr. Duckworth broke into her reminiscing. "Have you been out there recently?"

"No, not in about . . . nine years." She'd not had as much vacation time as her retired parents, or Emma Kate who still had spring break long after she did. Or even Harper Rose, who didn't work outside her home and had Thad raking in the dough. Or so they'd thought.

"Well, it's not been kept up. The company did a great job for a long time, but the whole complex was sold. I don't think we're gonna see that much out of it. The value's definitely down. Not a ton, but a handful of the units are on the market."

That was going to devalue theirs quite a bit. "I see." She told herself they didn't need the money. Even a few grand would be a bonus. They talked about the timing and she agreed they could likely wait for a better price, which seemed to make Mr. Duckworth breathe a sigh of relief he couldn't quite hide. So that was one good deed for the day.

"Before we sell it, we'll have to go out and get our things out of the closet."

Her eyebrows popped up. He was referring to the locked family closet. She hadn't even thought of that. She'd have to go to each of the timeshares and get their things. Then Mr. Duckworth popped back in.

"Tell you what, if you or your sisters want a last trip out, you should take the whole two weeks." Usually the families split the time. It was a generous offer. "If you don't want to go, Wendy and I will go and take care of it. I think you'll have other units to deal with, if I remember correctly."

"Yes, we do, and it would be wonderful if you could do it. Our other options are in Arizona and South Carolina." She was getting a headache thinking she'd have to travel.

She hung up the phone and looked at her list. How had it gotten longer?

❧ 23 ❧

By afternoon, Bailey Ann had spoken to the other family her parents had owned a timeshare with. They wanted to buy her out, which sounded like not the best deal money-wise, but the best option sanity-wise. Plus, she'd already fielded a lowball offer on Daddy's car. Turning it down, she politely waited through taking the man's number in case she changed her mind. She wouldn't. The glass of wine had turned into a second one; lunch had come and gone with a microwaved plate of funeral leftovers she'd thawed the night before; and she'd not heard from Finn.

Twenty-four hours since they'd been together in such heat and doused with such a cold interruption. She told herself he was busy with his sister, and she shouldn't expect to hear from him. She told herself it was okay, but the way her heart knotted, she knew it wasn't.

Hardly the fling you considered, huh, Bailey Ann? She could hear her own voice mocking her in her head. Nana's lunch conversation hadn't been any help either, and Bailey could hear some of those words knocking around in her brain, too.

At almost five p.m. she was still on the couch, still sorting papers. She should have quit hours ago. Once, she would have gotten up and gone to sit on the swings at the elementary school across the street. After hours, it would be taken over by locals and families. Looking back, she'd liked that. Now, however, there was a chain link fence around it. It wasn't locked, she could open the fence and go in, but it was good deterrent. A reminder that the playground belonged to the school and creepy adults were not welcomed.

Telling herself she'd get up and hit the gym soon, she flipped through more papers. The bank wanted Daddy's death certificate to release the account. Among other things, they also wanted cause of death, which she didn't really have handy. Since several more medical bills had come in the mail, she decided to open those and maybe kill two birds with one stone. Maybe they would have that diagnosis she needed.

One of the letters was addressed to her mother, from a prominent banking company. Opening it, expecting it to be an advertisement of some kind, Bailey Ann was shocked to discover her mother had a stock account in her own name. Jesus, she should never have gotten a business degree, then she never would have realized how screwed up her parents' finances were.

It was good for individual family members to have their own accounts. Especially someone like her mother, who'd worked part time for a few years after college then again when Bailey Ann was in high school. That was the sum total of her mother's paid work experience. So the account was a good thing, but the mess was not.

Calling in, she told the account manager her Mama had passed away over a year ago. She drained her wine. After taking down the list of things he needed to release the account, Bailey Ann thanked him though she wanted to throttle him. She understood the need for all the work. God forbid someone could just say you'd passed and sell all your stock. But here was yet another thing she couldn't liquidate. She wanted to get some of the money out to her sisters. Harper Rose could use it. Emma Kate was still in school. Though she wasn't up to her eyeballs—there had been college funds for all three girls—she wasn't rolling in it either. This would make her life easier.

Only first, it would make Bailey Ann's life infinitely harder.

She poured another glass of wine and finally admitted that she wasn't going to the gym tonight. Maybe tomorrow. She'd been itching to call her sisters and tell them she had good news. But what she had was a damn mess.

Bailey sat back on the couch and thought about her younger sister. It had all come so easily to Harper Rose. Even now, with her world crumbling around her, her little sister stood tall and serene, sheltering her girls with a cool Southern smile.

Bailey didn't know if she could do that. She'd always worked so hard to be perfect. Sure, she'd had a rebellious teenage streak —see one Finn Malloy for evidence—but the rest she'd done exactly as she'd been told.

Both times she'd had a man get down on one knee, her heart had soared. She'd done it! She'd gotten the proposal, from the right kind of guy, with the big diamond ring. Bailey had opened her mouth in awe each time. Each time thinking, "This is it!"

And each time, her heart had taken a sudden, sharp turn and dived toward the Earth with a fiery crash. Each time it had suddenly become painfully obvious in that last minute that she loved dating, and she loved wearing her little black dress out on the town with him. She loved chatting with the other women about him. And she loved the proposal. But she didn't love the *man*.

She'd wanted what her parents had. Her mother lit up every day when Daddy came in the door. Bailey Ann would not have done that for Todd Hooker or Ray Haley. She saw a future with kids and minivans, but without that spark. And, though she'd dated, she'd been basically single ever since.

The problem was Finn Malloy. He was exactly the opposite of the others. The boxes didn't check right. Her mother had warned her about marrying a man she was crazy about but didn't fit with. It wouldn't work out, and no one wanted a divorce.

Trying to get out of her melancholy, Bailey dove back into the paperwork and told herself again that she wasn't disappointed she hadn't heard from Finn. When night had completely fallen, and Bailey Ann had made piles of documents to take to the bank, and to copy and send to the stock company, and the timeshare paperwork to show the Peeveys and the Duckworths, and so on, she finally opened the last of the mail.

As she'd guessed from the outside of the envelope, it was a bill for Daddy's medical visits. It included a note from the staff that they were sorry about her loss, though it was addressed to "The Mayfair Family" and not her directly.

The bill said that her father had been diagnosed with congestive heart failure. *A year ago.*

Bailey Ann almost dropped the paper. She'd known his blood pressure was a problem, and that he sometimes had trouble breathing, but . . . congestive heart failure? She scrambled her attention back to the pages in front of her.

He'd been billed for oxygen he didn't use. There was a treatment plan—he was supposed to be taking other medications. Bailey Ann hadn't filled prescriptions for any of these.

She ran into the bathroom and sorted frantically through the brown bottles. Two thirds were Mama's that he hadn't thrown away. She tossed them over her shoulder as her anger grew.

At last the shelves were empty. The medication wasn't there.

❧ 24 ❧

Bailey Ann woke up on the couch late the next morning. It took a moment to orient herself. To feel that her face was puffy, to feel the anger seeping back into her skin as she came around.

In her hand, she clutched a medicine bottle. At the back of her jaw, her teeth clenched. The light coming into the room was too bright and her eyes hadn't fully adjusted. As her fist clenched, too, her arm shook just a little and the pills rattled.

She knew what they were—Mama's pain meds. Like most people they hadn't flushed her old prescriptions. Too much of what was in the cabinets was leftover from a year ago. Well, it wasn't in the cabinets anymore. She'd made a mess in her fit of organizing what she'd already looked at—on the floor—and what she hadn't—still in the cabinet.

Stuck with the nagging idea of the pain meds, she'd gathered all the bottles and brought them downstairs. She'd learned most of the names and purposes while caring for her mother, even though her medications would often get filled, her condition— and therefore her prescription—often changed before anything ran out.

Bailey had made a second trip upstairs, scouring the little

brown bottles on the floor for any she didn't recognize. She knew Daddy's Lipitor, and she knew which one was for his breathing, so she left those. But the ones she didn't know, she lined up on the coffee table.

It was a morbid scene and she'd grabbed the bottle of her Daddy's whiskey she'd found in the liquor cabinet. It turned out she and her sisters had only polished off the bottle he'd decanted. Inside the cabinet, in the back, were four more bottles, enough to make Bailey wonder if he'd been buying in bulk. Still, she'd pulled one out, decanted it, grabbed one of the crystal glasses and made room for that on the coffee table, too.

Then she hopped online and, one by one, learned what each medication did. She found two generics that matched some of the prescriptions her father had been given. That had made her feel better until she'd knocked one of them over and heard it rattle.

Tipping it out, she lined up the pills and counted. They were all there. The bastard had filled the prescription but never taken one, and Bailey Ann felt her anger growing. She wasn't ready to condemn him yet, but she had a feeling she would be in a bit.

She'd looked up the others and found out exactly what they did. Though she'd known Mama was on serious, high-end painkillers there at the end, Bailey Ann hadn't felt the need to monitor them.

Her stomach churned as she realized her mistake. In contrast to Daddy's unused medications for his heart, the number of pills in her momma's most serious pain medication were very, very low. Given the date the prescription was filled and the date her mother had died, it was impossible to have needed all of them. Bailey could only assume—especially given the other evidence she had amassed—that her father had been helping himself.

When she had sat on the couch, the little white pills counted out on the coffee table in front of her and not adding up to anywhere near enough, she'd blinked away the tears and sunk back into the cushion.

Her father had killed himself. There wasn't any evidence on his death certificate of any kind of an overdose, but he'd clearly been ignoring medications that would save his life. Medications for a diagnosis of congestive heart failure that he hadn't told her or any of her sisters about.

Five pill bottles later, she stopped looking up what the medication did and counting how many pills were in the bottle. The problem was far too obvious. Momma's medications for chemo, for her cancer, the hormone supplements she was taking, those all came out right, down to the last pill from the date they were prescribed to the date she died. But her pain medications were all suspiciously low . . . or empty.

Bailey Ann hadn't been taking them herself, and that left only the person who lived in that bedroom and used that medicine cabinet. Livid, she'd clutched the pill bottle in her hand and fallen into a very worrisome and unstable sleep. Later when she'd woken up on the couch, she'd had to look at it all again. Not only did she have to live with knowing what Daddy had done, but she had to decide whether to tell her sisters.

Honestly, she was relatively certain he hadn't overdosed, so it didn't seem like a quick suicide but a long, slow one. However, did she really want Harper Rose and Emma Kate to know this? She'd known her father had given up, but she hadn't realized that he had actively pursued his own death.

She didn't get up and eat breakfast and she didn't get dressed or take a shower. She simply sat there, staring at the medications, and she didn't know how long she did it until she noticed the pair of men's shoes square in front of her. Finn had apparently let himself in the back door, and as she followed the line from those shoes up the jeans to the T-shirt that clung to Finn's chest, she saw the expression on his face. He was horrified.

"Bailey Ann, tell me you didn't take these!" he demanded. Then softening his voice, he tried again. "Bailey Ann, did you take any of these?"

He seemed to be trying to make it okay to tell him that she

had swallowed the pills, to admit that something was wrong. And she probably looked like she'd done it, too, since she'd clearly cried herself to sleep here in a heap on the couch. But the only thing wrong was her father, and her father was already gone. She shook her head at Finn.

He didn't believe her, and though she wanted to explain, she realized she had a tough road ahead of her. She wasn't sure how to make him understand that she had fifteen pill bottles on the table in front of her, three different kinds of schedule three pain killers, loose pills counted out across the coffee table, and she hadn't taken one of them. Or even thought about it.

Finn paused for a moment, seeming to try to find the right words, but in the end, there were no right words. He simply crouched down in front of her, placed his hands on her knees, and asked, "How can I help?"

That was a question she could answer. Unfortunately, it wasn't a good answer. "You can bring my father back."

Knowing he couldn't accomplish that, he tried yet another attack. "What is all this?"

She explained what she'd been doing, that she'd looked up all the medications, counted the pills. She didn't tell him she concluded her father had killed himself. That wasn't information she needed out in the world. Though she trusted Finn not to share it, she'd have to flat out say, "Don't tell anyone." And that would make it a secret and she didn't want or need a secret.

She didn't even want to admit it was real. By the time she finished recounting everything she'd figured out, she remembered. She was sitting on her couch in last night's clothes, her eyes puffy, her hair a mess, not having even brushed her teeth, and here was Finn, now sitting on the couch beside her, arm around her, pressing a kiss to her cheek, and telling her it would be okay. She didn't know that it would be, though.

❦ 25 ❦

Finn hauled the sledgehammer back to whack at the wall again. This house was taking the brunt of anger aimed other directions. Everything was making him mad. His sister's poor sense of timing, and his own desire to both spend time with her and shove her out the door. Bailey Ann's father, too. He'd had no love lost for the man, but Con Mayfair was gone and he was still putting his oldest through the wringer.

Sinking the head of the hammer into the wall felt good, at least. But it wasn't accomplishing any of the things Finn wished he could actually do. Though he'd helped Bailey Ann put away and throw away the medications she had out yesterday, he wanted to go back over and check on her. But he was torn. What else was new?

She'd told him she was fine and he should spend time with his sister. But she didn't seem all that fond of Sioban, and that was mutual as far as Finn could tell. He sunk the sledgehammer into the wall again and imagined a disastrous meal with both of them. That was almost as much fun as when Bailey Ann had pushed him to leave her alone yesterday. He hauled back on the handle, the weight at least satisfying, and got ready for another shot at the wall.

"Hey, watch where you swing that thing." Despite her outburst at his movements, Sioban stood calmly behind him, not even having sloshed her cup of coffee.

"Can you get me one of those?" he asked her and was grateful when she just nodded.

He reminded himself he loved her, and he was glad she was here. He did. He was. But her timing could not have been worse. It didn't help that she was inviting him down to Atlanta to see her new apartment. Asking how far it was from his. And making sure he was paid up on his unit. He was. He wished he wasn't.

The fact was, he didn't know if he was staying here in Breathless, didn't know if he had a reason to. He didn't know if Bailey Ann really wanted him or if they'd had a boff for old times sakes and that was all she needed . . . just someone to get her off. Sioban's questions were like a blade, constantly re-injuring an already open cut. And Finn thought she might be doing it on purpose.

He'd been whacking at the wall, each swing another thing he couldn't fix in his life. He hit it once because he'd had Bailey Ann in his bed and been interrupted. He hit it again because he'd found her with enough medication to overdose an army and looking like she'd been through hell, but he hadn't been able to stay. It had been three days, and Sioban was staying for three more. Her apartment wasn't ready yet. And Finn was about to do the most uncharitable thing and throw the keys to his place in Atlanta at her and tell her to get out.

"Here."

He turned and saw her holding out another mug of coffee. Looking down into the cup, he saw she'd gotten the color exactly right, and his heart softened a little. He did not get enough time with his sister. The last year had been spent worried they'd drift apart with their separate careers now that their parents were gone. He should be grateful for this time with her.

"Are you still up for heading out to the outlet mall in

Alpharetta today?" She innocently sipped at her own mug, her pajamas hanging loose on her small frame.

"Sure. I just thought you'd sleep in later and we'd go then."

"How was I supposed to sleep when you're banging the house up?"

He shrugged. He didn't know how he was supposed to fix the house if he was supposed to be quiet for a whole week. But she had just come off a round-the-clock type residency and was heading into another. Sioban should sleep as much as she could this week, and he wasn't helping. Telling himself the house could wait, he leaned on the sledgehammer and took a sip. Yes, the coffee was perfect.

He also told himself that Bailey Ann could wait, too. He'd waited more than a decade, so a week wouldn't make a difference. But she wasn't a house. She wasn't just something he could fix or change to suit a new era. And she certainly wasn't waiting on him.

"How about we go earlier and meet up with my friend Rachel for lunch?"

Oh, hell no. The thought shot through his brain like a bullet. "I'll go help you pick out furniture. I'll gladly haul it back here. And I will help you put it in a truck to get to your apartment. But I will not sit through another of your thinly veiled matchmaking attempts. I'm not your project."

She tipped her head as if to disagree. "But you need someone, and Rachel is—"

"Rachel is not going to happen. I have someone." *Shit.* He'd said it out loud. He knew his sister, she was going to make him defend it. But he'd said it.

Sioban didn't even ask who it was. "Really? If I ask her, she'll say she was your girlfriend? That you're on the track to something bigger? Is that what it is?"

When he didn't answer, she pressed harder. "So, she's not seeing anyone else?"

Fuck. He couldn't answer that either. He didn't believe Bailey

Ann was, but they'd not had that conversation. Damn, couldn't he just get a chance to see where it was going?

Apparently not.

Sioban pushed again. "Please understand, I come at this with the best of intentions. She hurt you last time. She had no right to say those things—"

"How do you know what she said?" It hit him just then, that Sioban had seemed to know things she shouldn't. He was staring at her. "Did you read that letter?"

Sioban looked away. "I—"

"You had no right!" Finn felt the top of his head blow. "That wasn't yours!"

"It doesn't matter. I know what she did and—"

"It does matter!" He was yelling. Hell, Bailey Ann could probably hear him. All the neighbors probably could. His chest was heaving, and it felt like his sister had stabbed him with some old, rusty knife she'd found.

"But I just want you to be happy."

"*She* makes me happy!" He was angry. God, that was not the thing to yell. He still had a sledgehammer in his hand and probably shouldn't. Not when he was this mad.

"Clearly." It was all Sioban said, one eyebrow up. Still questioning him.

"Sioban, stop. Stop setting me up, stop baiting me, stop questioning my decisions. You're driving a wedge just like you want, but you've got it wedged between you and me."

With that, Finn watched his little sister suck in a stunned breath and turn away.

It broke his heart, but he was angry, too. She was an adult now, and she'd been a kid then, but she should never have read that letter. Hell, he wished he never had. But he'd never wanted anyone to see just how truly broken he'd been.

The worst part of the fight was that he couldn't defend his feelings for Bailey Ann. He was petrified Sioban was right.

❦ 26 ❦

Cooking is an art handed down through generations, and usually involves opening a handful of cans and mixes. All this is fine, but you'd better use real mayonnaise.

BAILEY ANN SPENT THE NEXT SEVERAL DAYS IGNORING WHAT she'd learned and sorting through her parents' finances. Her father hadn't transferred much of anything over to his name. He hadn't dealt with the finances much—or at all?—when her mother had been alive, and it seemed there was no reason for him to start doing it once her mother was dead. As long as nothing bounced, Daddy probably hadn't cared.

She hadn't seen Finn since he told her she would be okay and made sure that she actually was. He'd helped her put the pills back in the right bottles or flush them and told her he probably wouldn't be available with his sister in town. It figured, Bailey thought. Though he kissed her once—hard—before letting himself out the back door, and though he checked in by text over the past few days, she hadn't seen him at all.

It felt weird. She'd been in his bed screaming his name, and then his sister had shown up . . . and *nothing*. It left her hanging.

Were they a thing? Were they a fling? She had no idea. Maybe they were nothing. Maybe he was just a really great guy who got laid the other day.

Finn or no Finn, she had work to do. She had to find money for her sisters. She had to clean up her parents' estate. And while there was no set timeline to do it, she would run out of her own savings soon enough if she didn't get busy. She had decisions to make. Stay in Breathless? Move back to Nashville? Move somewhere entirely new? Without her parents here, once the house sold, there wouldn't be anywhere to come back to town and stay and see old friends unless she got her own place here. Sure, she could stay with Uncle Dex and Aunt Gigi, or with Aunt Wes and Uncle Dawson but she would be imposing on someone else. That wasn't anything she'd ever had to deal with here in Breathless. She'd always simply come home before. But she was selling more than a house now. She'd be selling "home."

Harper was out in the west, out where wonderful Thad Bass had dragged her and abandoned her with no money. And Emma Kate was still at UCLA. Bailey found herself wondering again if selling was the right thing. They'd left the decision up to her, and now she was wishing they hadn't.

Three days later, she sat at her table eating yet another take-out meal from the Magic Wok, only this time she hadn't run into Finn. Her phone lit up just as she bit into a wonton. Though it wasn't Finn, like she'd found herself hoping, her cousin Lennon's face popped up on the screen. Her wide smile showing off even white teeth from the orthodontics Uncle Dex and Aunt Gigi had paid for years ago.

Bailey Ann blinked. Though she and Lennon had each others' numbers, and though they texted occasionally, she didn't expect Lennon to call her much. Concerned that something was wrong, she snatched the phone off the table, swallowed her wonton quickly, and answered.

"Hi, Lennon. How are you doing?" Bailey Ann Mayfair had been raised never to say, "What's up?"

There was a short pause and a sweet voice. "Bailey, it's so good to talk to you. I was calling because I have a little favor to ask." Another pause. "Actually, I take that back. It's a huge favor."

"No problem," Bailey Ann said, but then she paused and wanted to make sure that was all it was. After her own night a couple nights ago, figuring out what was going on with Daddy, she found herself wondering now if it was right when people said everything was good or they just needed a favor. It usually meant something was up. "Is everything okay, Lennon?"

"It is," Lennon said. But the tone in her voice said it wasn't all good to go. "So, it's a bit of a long story if you can bear with me."

"You know I can, Lennon. I've been sorting my Daddy's messed up financial information all week and I could use a break. Tell me all about it."

Lennon did. There was a burial mound just on the edge of town. Bailey Ann knew about it, the whole town did. It was on community property, and Lennon had been talking with the mayor and the town council about doing an archeological dig there. She was getting her master's degree and considering going on for a doctorate in her combined field of anthropology/archeology.

"The burial ground should yield some very interesting information about the history of the local area. Basically, what it means is I would come back for at least a semester and live in Breathless and do the work. The town council gave me my approval yesterday. Mama and Daddy are really excited, and they want me to come home." Another pause. "But Bailey Ann, I don't want to live in their house again. They think I'm their little girl and they want to impose rules, like high school, and I can't deal. I need a place I can be an adult."

And didn't Bailey Ann understand that?

But she wasn't sure she fully thought of Lennon as an adult yet herself. After all, Lennon and Emma Kate had been thick as thieves, and Emma Kate was so much younger than she was. But that was Bailey Ann's problem. Lennon was certainly old enough to take care of herself. That's when Lennon proposed something that Bailey Ann had not expected.

"Is it possible I could stay at your house? It will be another month before I get there, but I could pay rent and I know the area. You know I'll take good care of it. I won't throw wild, crazy, drinking parties. But it would be nice to have a familiar place. And rather than getting an apartment, it would allow me something I can tell my Mama and Daddy that doesn't look like I'm just skipping out on them, which I am."

Bailey Ann experienced the second time in three days where she sat back on the couch, stunned at what she discovered.

"You know, Lennon, I hadn't even thought about renting the place out."

"It's okay. I mean, if it doesn't work, it was just something I wanted to ask since you had the house."

Bailey Ann interrupted. "No worries. It's actually a really good idea. You may have me for a roommate for a while, and right now I've got a wall between the kitchen and the dining room that's down to bare studs because Finn Malloy was knocking it out and then his sister showed up, and now I'm stuck halfway. I can't paint in there until he finishes."

Now she was just laying her own problems at Lennon's feet. Lennon had plenty going on. She had a master's thesis committee breathing down her neck, a project to start *and finish* over the course of the next year and more.

"Well," Bailey Ann amended, "at least the wall should be fixed by the time you get here. I may be painting or rearranging things, just so you know. And certainly if I'm here, I can't imagine charging you any rent. I do have to run the idea by Harper Rose and Emma Kate first. We had been talking about selling the house."

"Well if you need to sell it, you sell it, Bailey Ann. I understand."

But the more she thought about it, the more Bailey Ann thought it was a good idea. She would likely still be here a month from now. The house needed plenty of work. Her savings would last longer than that. She wasn't paying any rent herself. And to be honest, it'd be nice to have a roommate. The fact of the matter was, Lennon was an adult. She might just save Bailey Ann from Finn.

❊ 27 ❊

Bailey slept in late the next day and woke up to a series of strange noises coming from downstairs. Pulling her jacket on and tucking it around her, she snuck down the stairs and peered through the hallway into the kitchen area, only to find Finn testing the studs and wearing his jeans and goggles, and not much else again.

She considered going down and talking to him, but the fact of the matter was he'd just let himself in her backdoor and started making noise in her home while she was asleep. He could wait while she turned around, went upstairs, and brushed her teeth this time. She certainly hadn't made a very good impression the last time he'd come in on her.

Bailey headed downstairs a few minutes later wearing jeans and a t-shirt and an actual bra, with her hair and teeth brushed and her face washed. He wasn't getting any makeup, but that was as much as she was willing to concede.

"So," she asked, "did you just come in my house and start pounding on my walls?"

Turning around to face her, he grinned, and it bothered her how devastating that smile was. How it made it okay that he'd done exactly as she asked. "Pretty much," he said. "I've got to get this wall out and I left you hanging for almost a week. I know you couldn't paint. But Sioban was in town and I don't get to see her that much anymore. Also, I got the feeling you two never really knew each other."

Bailey Ann only nodded. She didn't mention that Sioban had threatened her with death in the only three minutes they'd interacted. She also refrained from mentioning that she'd made it very clear that she was not putting up with Sioban's shit. So, "didn't know each other very well" was something she could accept from Finn as his belief for her and his sister's relationship.

He turned back to the wall, but looked over his shoulder again—those broad, bare shoulders that made her want to drool and made her tuck her arms a little closer around herself so she didn't reach out to touch him.

"Now that you're awake," he said, "I can start taking the studs out. It's gonna be a little noisier. I was just double checking everything, making sure this wall isn't load bearing."

Good God, she thought. He was an architect. He had to know what he was doing, but she was suddenly worried that he might break her house. He seemed to understand her sudden onset of nerves.

"Don't worry, Bailey Ann. I'm good. This will look great when I'm done."

So she stood and watched while he took his sledgehammer to one of the studs, whacking it sideways, and then grabbing the wood, twisting it back and forth until it came loose in his hands. He made a pile on the linoleum. Two pieces. Three. Four.

Then he turned and looked at her and said, "Shit. I didn't ask. Are you removing this linoleum? I thought that was agreed upon."

"It is. It's got to go. I mean, it's linoleum," she said, counting in her head the expense of all the little pieces of the house that needed to be redone, not just repaired.

"Thank God," he said. "Because if not, I was throwing old

wood directly on a floor you were keeping. Would've needed a towel. I mean, I can get one anyway."

"No, it's good," she said. Then she sighed and started talking to him while he took out her boards. "I need to re-do the countertop, too. Maybe you can recommend something. What kind of surface is nice but at a good price? This tile is too old and I'm not sure sunshine yellow was ever a popular color."

He nodded. "You could clean it up, you know. Bleach the grout. Even repaint the tile. You can glaze it a different color."

But Bailey Ann shook her head. "All that and it would still be tile. It doesn't make the best kitchen counter. There are a lot of better options these days, and I know Mama loved the yellow, but nobody else does."

He asked her about the paint she picked for the dining room, questioning her about the chips she had left on the table for her color swatches. And then when she said he was right, he volunteered to come help paint with her and asked her to do the same at his place. She said yes, but she didn't really know why. This man was going to be the death of her, seeming to want to work with his shirt off, and seeming to want to have sex at least sometimes. And there she was, saying *yes* all the time. Standing here watching him flex his muscles wasn't helping her libido any.

"Can I help?" she asked.

"Unless you want to swing a sledgehammer carefully in a confined space, I don't think so."

"I can take the boards out to the trash."

"Nah, I got it."

Maybe he wanted to flex his muscles for her. *Oh, well.* She turned away and went back to the living room, tried to continue sorting through the papers while he worked. Tried not looking through the archway to watch him as he swung the sledgehammer back and forth, twisted the boards, adjusted his goggles, and occasionally leaned over to set something on the floor. Yeah, that fine ass was a distraction. She did not need a distraction.

"What you got over there?" he asked. He didn't look. Kept swinging, taking out studs.

"The same damn thing I was working on last week. I keep getting mail from this account or that account. My mother seemed to think that money should be put into savings when the opportunity arose. However, I don't think she ever put money into the same account twice."

"Seriously?" He asked.

"Yeah. She was the financial master of our household, so even if I had thought to ask Daddy, I don't think he would have known where everything was. It turns out she made *another* college savings for Emma Kate that still has some money in it. So I at least managed to get that sent over to my sister. That was a win. But I didn't find it until two days ago. We had no idea it even existed. Mama had automatic withdrawals going from their bank account into this college fund for Emma Kate, and no one knew it."

"Well, it's a good thing you found it, then. Isn't Emma Kate supposed to graduate soon?"

Bailey Ann could not help the indelicate snort she made. "Well, she's *supposed* to. But you know Emma Kate. Emma Kate and *supposed to* don't get along that well. She's already balking at her thesis, isn't going to finish it this year. Maybe next. Well, she *says* next year."

"Isn't this already her second senior year?" Finn asked.

"Don't you know it," Bailey Ann said. But then again, she'd done everything right, and look where she was. Maybe she should've taken three senior years herself.

"What's she getting her degree in?" He asked.

"Hell, that's a million-dollar question," Bailey Ann said, then tried to reign herself back in. She didn't want to be mean about her little sister. Emma Kate was just Emma Kate. Actually, she was just Em, if you listened to her. "Well, she started out undecided. And then she spent a year trying to pursue anthropology, following in Lennon's footsteps, but she dropped that pretty quickly. She has taken a handful of science classes. She likes them, she's really good at them, but she doesn't follow through. So then she went into sociology and economics, and God, I don't even know that she's picked one as her major now. She's supposed to have a thesis idea, and I haven't even asked her what it is."

Finn grinned over his shoulder. "Afraid of the answer?"

"I may be," Bailey Ann conceded.

Then he turned serious. "Did you get all those pills flushed?"

"Yeah. I didn't want to. I wanted to keep them around, so I could count them again."

"You counted them," he said. "*We* counted them. We know what was there and what wasn't. Better that they're gone. Some of them are close to expiring anyway."

"It's true." But she felt like she had brushed her father's problems aside or flushed them down the toilet. She still hadn't decided what to tell her sisters, and she hadn't said anything to Finn about her need to do so. Maybe she should. Lennon was going to show up. What if he said something then?

❦ 28 ❦

F inn finished pulling the wall out just after noon, leaving her with an opening and some raw, exposed wall. Grinning, he pointed at the worst of it, hoping to smooth the small frown on her face. "No worries, we'll cover that, then do the floor, then paint."

She almost smiled, then startled a bit. "*We're* doing the floor?"

"Sure, why not?" He hoped she'd say yes. He couldn't say it was a fun project, and he couldn't admit that he was maybe just asking so he had an excuse to be in her pocket every day. "I'm going to do mine. This space isn't even that big." He pointed from the corner of the dining area—now an area and not a room —to where the kitchen butted up against the steps leading up to the bedrooms.

"I'm not a contractor, Finn. Or even an architect." She was shaking her head. He had no idea if that meant she didn't want to lay floor, or she didn't want him to lay floor, or she didn't want to spend time with him.

"You can do it. It's not that hard. Just some labor."

Expressions played across her face, as though she was thinking first about something good, then bad, then confusing. "I don't know about that."

Accepting that for now—it was all he could do—he changed the subject. "Can I take you out to Bobby's for pizza?"

Bailey took a breath in but didn't answer. Once again he watched her expressions play out one after another, but not landing on anything.

"Is it that difficult of a decision?" What was going on in her head? He had too many different scenarios playing out in his own brain to decipher hers.

"Yes," she conceded with a smile. "I told myself I was going to eat better, and Bobby's is not that." Before he could say anything else, she added, "If you're done here, I can make us lunch."

"I need to shower."

She shrugged at him. "You're in exactly the same shape as the dining room."

Both he and the room were coated in a light layer of drywall dust, and that wasn't the impression he wanted to make. "Let me shower, I'll be right back."

He almost leaned in for a kiss but didn't. As he headed back across the wall he felt like a teenager again, not sure if it was the right time to kiss the girl or if he should hold back. The feelings were like a punch into his history. Even the girl was the same.

He made it back as quickly as he could. Turning the door-knob and entering without asking felt as though he finally belonged here. With her. He had a good career. He had income. He didn't have a house, but he could. He had a path and he had drive. He now had all the things her mother had warned her he was missing. Would it be enough?

She looked up from chopping something on a cutting board, and he saw she'd shoved the plastic back to get to the clean counter underneath.

"That smells good. What is it?" He'd moved inside the small kitchen space, inside the arc of the wraparound counter when he should have been standing on the other side of it. But the two of them never really had that concept of personal space down. For a flash of thought, he remembered the first time they'd studied for Algebra 2 together. They'd opened the book between them and sat with their shoulders, hips, knees and elbows touching. They'd known each other for five days.

"It's chicken and rice." She opened the pot and used the stirring spoon to serve him up a bite.

"Oh, my God, that's good." He stood there with his mouth open. "More."

Which was how she wound up feeding him as they laughed at her cramped kitchen counter. After several spoonfuls, she shoved the salad plate at him.

He shook his head. "Green peppers? Really, Bailey Ann?" Finn picked the curved pieces off his small plate and fed them to her.

She knew he didn't like them, if she remembered. But it was a good excuse for him to feed her this time, and as he did the look in her eyes changed from laughter to heat.

His fingers grazed her lips and he felt it like a butterfly in his stomach. He watched her do something as simple as chewing and swallowing a strip of crisp green pepper and she had to see the smolder in his eyes. Her return half-smile made the twist in his heart sharper. By the time he ran out of peppers, he'd pinned her to the counter, and as soon as she swallowed the last one, he kissed her.

In less than two brushes of his mouth across hers, her arms were around his neck. She smelled of that same perfume, of hope and heat. And need. Though whether that was his or hers, he couldn't tell. He couldn't untangle the threads between them.

Grasping at first her hips, then her ass, he lifted her onto the edge of the sink as her legs wrapped around his waist. *Thank God*, he thought, she wanted him, too. She was just above him now, his face turned up to hers as though he was asking her permission.

With a smile, and a soft brush of her lips, she gave it. The only defense he'd ever had against Bailey Ann Mayfair was distance, and there was none between them now.

Leaning in, she pulled tighter, pressed harder, wanted more. He indulged her every touch.

"Finn." It slipped out on a whisper of want and it was enough.

His hands came under her again, and he lifted her off the counter, but he didn't set her down. She knew this dance. It was old, from high school, from when they'd been left alone and would make out with her up on the counter until they couldn't stand it anymore. He carried her up the stairs, just as he had back then, to the room at the end of the hall. Her room.

It had been hers then, before it was Harper Rose's. And now it was hers again. And she was his again, if only for this moment. He felt the punch of that heat only she had ever generated in him.

He didn't tumble her back onto the mattress as he had when they'd been younger. This time he was a man who knew what he wanted and knew what he was doing. His mouth didn't leave hers until he peeled the shirt he'd just put on a while ago.

She was trying to run her hands over his chest when he whipped her shirt off nearly as fast. His mouth was on hers again, tasting, testing as his hands reached to snap her bra open and she was arching into his touch.

Together, they kicked off shoes, peeled jeans and shoved at underwear. He fumbled in his pocket—now abandoned on the floor—for a condom but managed to produce it quickly. Then he was over her, and inside her, and he was home. Everything fell into place in these moments. This was what made him believe they stood a chance. That he did.

They moved together, pushing toward the headboard until she braced her hands on it to push back against his thrusts, both of them wanting him deeper, both of them needing the release they felt building.

When it finally hit, he felt the rush rolling up through her system, as her legs came around him like a vice she cried out his name. The sound tangled with hers coming from his lips and somewhere in the air between them, they blended perfectly.

As he sank back to Earth, he told himself Sioban would not interrupt this time. But, though he tried to shove them aside, her questions lingered in the back of his head.

❧ 29 ❧

B ailey lay there in her room, staring at the ceiling. Naked, she had Finn's arm draped around her. He'd fallen immediately asleep. No wonder, he'd been working all morning. He was probably exhausted. She didn't even know when he'd started, only that he'd already been working before she'd woken up.

So, it wasn't just once. It was at least twice. Was it a fling? Was it a thing? She still didn't know, but she knew it wasn't nothing. She had to consider the idea that this man kept asking her to marry him and that she knew—no matter what she wanted—what was right for her and what wasn't.

The problem was she wanted two completely separate things. She wanted what her Mama and Daddy had. Maybe not the end of it, maybe not the way her Mama had gone or the way her Daddy had gone, it turned out, but she wanted that kind of love.

She wanted a man whose eyes lit up every time he talked about her. While she couldn't quite yet bring herself to forgive her Daddy for the way he'd chosen to go, she understood, at least in her soul, that he'd done it because he couldn't live without her mother.

On the other hand, she wanted Finn. Finn was the only one who'd ever made her feel truly alive, but she knew if she went down that road, she was going to wind up not where she wanted. They came from two different worlds.

The two of them had always burned bright and hot. She'd known, even as a senior in high school, that *bright and hot* burned out. Mama and Daddy had been slow and steady. Thad and Harper Rose? Bright and hot. And though they'd made it till death do us part, man, had Thad fucked things up. Bailey Ann didn't want that either, so she lay there breathing shallowly and thinking, no decisions yet made.

Did she throw herself at Finn? Burn bright and hot, burnout, enjoy it while she had it? Or should she do the hard thing and push them aside now before *bright and hot* got too bright and too hot? That was a very hard decision to make when *bright and hot* had his big sexy arm thrown across her waist and both of them were naked in her bed in the middle of the afternoon. It was a hard decision to make when *bright and hot* made her feel alive, when everything around her felt like it was grinding to a halt. At least he hadn't asked her to marry him again, because the answer to that question got harder and harder the closer they got.

She lay there, unable to pass out and sleep away the afternoon like he did. It was another hour before he finally shifted, breathed heavier, and then roused and looked at her.

"What do you want to do, Bailey Ann?" He asked, that sleepy bedroom voice calling to her in a way nothing else had. And she had no idea if he meant "did she want to get up and take a shower" or "did she want to stay together forever"? She had no idea if it was a practical question or a seriously philosophical one, so she only raised her eyebrow. She'd learned young from her Mama not to answer a question she didn't know the answer to. That only got you in trouble. Sure enough, it worked. Finn filled in the pieces for her.

"I'd like to take you out tonight. I understand you didn't want pizza. You want to do better, so we'll do better, but I'd like to take you out on a real date. It feels like we got the cart a little before the horse on this one." His eyebrows quirked though, so did his mouth. "Then again, we've never had our cart and horse straight."

She had to laugh along with him at that. That was true. Sharing all their classes in high school as they had, having alphabetically close last names, they'd wound up sitting next to each other often. They'd shared homework assignments and kisses long before they'd had a date. Here she was at thirty-four doing it backwards all over again with the same man. A moment later, she realized she still hadn't answered him because he asked again.

"So, can I? Take you out tonight?"

She thought for a moment. What else did she have to do? Even the things she had to do seemed to have no definitive timeline. The only anchor she had was the touch of Finn's hand, so she said yes. Then she wondered if she'd made the right decision. He kissed her hard again in that way that he had and left her. She watched him get dressed, and leave her lying there in bed, naked, admiring those jeans as he went.

He said, "I'm going to go home, and I'm going to probably shower again and change. Then I'll be back. Is five good?"

She nodded. They'd only eaten half their lunch, might as well have an early dinner. He mentioned that the Breathless two-screen Cineplex managed to get a new feature in that he wanted to see, and did she want to go with him? He even knew what time it was playing. Bailey Ann said yes, thinking how interesting it was that he'd clearly planned this out much further ahead than his casual offer sounded like.

It was only after she heard his footsteps traipse down the steps and out the back door, followed by the closing of the screen as he went off to her backyard, that she rolled over. Putting her head down onto the pillow, she wondered what in God's name she was doing, because she surely didn't know.

At least Lennon was coming at the end of the month. She'd have a roommate then and while she wasn't beholden to Lennon —and Lennon certainly wasn't beholden to her, which was the point—having someone else in the house would be good. Having another set of eyes watching her comings and goings, watching Finn just let himself in and out the back door, well, it might make Bailey Ann act a little less insane, and that had to be a good thing.

In that moment, Bailey told herself she could do whatever she wanted until Lennon arrived. So, she got up and showered and was ready when Finn showed up.

He shocked her. He brought flowers—a bouquet clutched in his hands, handed over sweetly and softly without much fanfare, but she knew. She understood he'd gone to the trouble. He waited while she cut the stems and put them in the vase that her mother had left for her in the upper kitchen cabinet. Bailey Ann had known it was hers. Mama had told her, but she hadn't had the heart to take it, and now here she was having come to Mama's things, rather than them coming to her.

So she looked at the flowers, sweetly sitting in the glass with the ribbons still tied around them, then she followed him out to the car. He'd taken her that night to Zeal, the restaurant high on the hill that overlooked the city and charged more than she would've thought appropriate for this level of date. Though she had decided she was having a fling, she had to wonder what Finn had decided they were doing.

By the end of the date, he'd picked up a tab to rival her senior prom. Next they missed most of the movie, because they were making out like teenagers. Bailey Ann knew that was going to get around town tomorrow. No matter how dark the theater was, or how discreet they thought they were being in the back row, word on the street would be about Bailey Ann Mayfair and Finn Malloy.

Everyone would know what they were doing.

Everyone except Bailey Ann.

❧ 30 ❧

W hat surprised Bailey Ann was that she slept in well past ten a.m. Normally, she was an early riser, but not lately. Maybe she just wasn't what she'd always thought she was.

She'd been out again with Finn the night before. Three dates in three days. In the morning, they'd work together on her house. Then he would take her out in the evening. Each time he brought her home, he'd pulled into the driveway and walked her around to the back door. Though they'd often touched or kissed during the date, he would still press her up against the door, all tongue and hands, and make her melt.

Each time, she'd invited him inside, and each time he'd said, "No, that's not what this is about."

So, for three dates, she had more Finn than she could handle, yet still not enough. Each evening, he'd left her at her back door, making sure that she made it safely inside, like the true Southern gentleman he was—despite the fact that he wasn't southern at all. Each night, Bailey Ann had lain awake, staring at her bedroom ceiling again, wondering what was really going on with him.

What didn't surprise Bailey Ann was that before eleven a.m., she'd gotten a message from her Aunt Gigi inviting her over to lunch. While her own mama had always known what was going on with her girls, Aunt Gigi was positively psychic. Bailey Ann had no idea how that woman knew everything she knew, she wasn't surprised by the invitation.

She'd shot off quick emails to her sisters about Lennon's question about renting. Both quickly responded, saying it was perfectly fine for Lennon to stay in the house, and that no, she should not be charged rent. Although Bailey Ann had written back to both and pressed about the need for money from selling the house, they all agreed that there were plenty of other assets to sort out and sell off, and no one was hurting right at this moment.

Harper Rose had given her the good news that she and her girls had just been granted legal permission to stay in the house while a lawsuit played out to determine who might actually own it, and whether it would be repossessed. They would have been considered squatters up to that point, but Harper Rose had banked on the other side not being able to toss a widow and three small children out of their own home. She'd won that round. So at least for now, they had a place to stay, and they didn't need the money as desperately as they might have.

As for Emma Kate, Bailey Ann wasn't sure if the money ever came into it. Bailey Ann had a degree in finance. Emma Kate seemed to let money simply sift through her fingers, not keeping track of it and never quite knowing where it went. She never ended up with anything to show for it either, at least by Bailey's accounting. So, she hadn't expected Emma Kate to consider the finances of the house sale much at all. Her littlest sister, being Lennon's best friend, had jumped all over the idea of making sure her bestie got a room. So, that was decided. And Bailey Ann had immediately shot off a happy note to Lennon letting her know that the house was hers.

Aunt Gigi most definitely wanted to talk about the new arrangements for when her baby girl was back in town and doing her research. What Bailey Ann was uncertain of was whether Aunt Gigi also wanted to talk about "that Malloy boy."

When she'd finally gone downstairs it was to a surprisingly quiet house. No Finn, no wall, and no work being done. With a deep breath in, she picked up her phone and called him.

"Oh, no," he said when she asked, "I thought I told you. The flooring isn't in for your place yet, so I was working on mine. Are you going to come over and help?" The last was said with such a wonderfully low tone that Bailey Ann was quite certain she was not being invited to help lay flooring. Though that was exactly what the words said, the tone suggested something else might be getting laid. Unfortunately, it wouldn't be her.

"Actually, my Aunt Gigi invited me out for lunch."

He seemed to harbor no ill feelings that he'd come over and done all this work at her house and the first chance she had to repay him, she'd rapidly tapped out. "You enjoy your lunch with your aunt, then."

"Oh, I don't know," she replied, "I think I'd better order fish, so at least I'm not the only one getting grilled."

He'd laughed at her and said, "Maybe come over when you're done."

Bailey Ann had thought about it. Disturbingly, even in her thoughts about what to do after being interrogated by her Aunt Gigi, hanging out with Finn sounded like it would be soothing. Though there wasn't much about that man that soothed her nerves.

So, she'd showered, and for the first day in the last week or so, instead of either staying in her pajamas or climbing into clothing for painting or tearing out walls, Bailey Ann dressed up. Her Aunt Gigi was her mama's contemporary, and Mama had believed in noon dresses, heels, and the occasional hat. Aunt Gigi, a belle to her core, may have been the only one who outdid Mama on that scale. Furthermore, Bailey Ann had known when she'd come back to Breathless, sooner or later this occasion was going to happen, so she had dresses at the ready. While she had matching shoes, she opted out of the hat. Bailey Ann considered herself a new generation of belle. No hat. However, that was about as far as she could distance herself from the women before her.

Rain was coming down in sheets, and she looked out the window, grateful for her carport. There was one at Aunt Gigi and Uncle Dex's house, too, though she'd probably wind up running to the front door. Sure enough, she pulled up to more cars than fit in the driveway and was grateful for her umbrella.

Dashing along the walkway and up the front steps in her heels was an art, and she arrived at a door thrown open by her uncle. Stepping inside, and not wanting to get him wet, she smiled at him. "Uncle Dex," she exclaimed, her happiness real, but she didn't offer a hug until she had her jacket off.

"Hey, baby girl." He welcomed her into the house with that Southern accent dripping from every word. Just behind him stood his son, Jackson, and Jackson's two little girls.

"Hey, cuties!" Bailey Ann grinned, leaning down to hug each of them, "Are y'all here for Aunt Gigi's lunch?"

"Oh, hell no," said Jackson, and Uncle Dex laughed behind them. "We're going out for pizza. Mama put those finger sandwiches on the table, and we knew this was not for us."

Bailey Ann laughed, but inside she wondered. Finger sandwiches indicated conversations not for the faint of heart. In fact, the finger sandwiches so scared off the men and tiny children that they went out the door before it even closed behind Bailey Ann, and she was suddenly left alone in the living room.

Within moments, Aunt Gigi came around the corner with a snap to her step. Her health and ease of mobility both made Bailey Ann incredibly grateful that she still had family that was going to hang around for a good, long time. However, it also made her incredibly jealous. But it was what it was, and Bailey Ann embraced her gratefulness and her Aunt Gigi. The return hug she got was warm and tight and something Bailey Ann hadn't even realized yet she'd needed.

Grabbing her hand, Aunt Gigi dragged her into the dining room where the good china was already set out, steam coming from the hand-painted teapot, tiers of plates on racks filled with tiny foods that Aunt Gigi had made for their little luncheon. What Bailey Ann didn't see was anyone else, and that worried her again.

"Sit down, honey, and tell me how you've been. I've only seen you the one time since your daddy's funeral," Aunt Gigi told her, and Bailey Ann did exactly that.

She mentioned tearing out the wall, painting the house, even Lennon coming to stay. This time, she framed that more as a conversation she and Lennon had and a mutually beneficial idea they'd arrived at, rather than a favor her cousin had requested. She'd also left out the part of the housework that involved Finn being shirtless most of the time. Aunt Gigi probably knew all that anyway.

They talked for a good while about Lennon's thesis and how excited Aunt Gigi was to have her baby girl back in town. Somewhere in those exchanges, Aunt Gigi had worked in the idea that she was okay with Lennon staying with Bailey Ann, and Bailey Ann found herself breathing a little easier.

But then, of course, it happened.

"Tell me you're going to marry that Malloy boy this time." Aunt Gigi looked her in the eyes and demanded agreement.

Bailey Ann shook her head. "I can't do that, Aunt Gigi. You know he's not right for me."

"I know nothing of the sort," her Aunt replied firmly.

Bailey Ann replied by listing all her reasons, finding they were the same ones she'd had since her senior year of high school. How it wouldn't last. How they didn't come from the same place, and so on.

Then Aunt Gigi rocked her world. "Please tell me you are not still holding onto these ideas from that racist mother of yours."

31

Bailey Ann wasn't certain how long she sat there with her mouth hanging open before she finally managed to close it. Then she told her Aunt Gigi, in the most polite words she could find, that she was wrong.

"Mama wasn't racist, Aunt Gigi, she loved you."

"Oh, Honey, I know she loved me, but that doesn't change anything. You and I both know better these days. We know that having a black friend doesn't make you not racist."

That much was true, but Bailey Ann couldn't see how that applied to her mother.

She'd never seen her mother have a single racist tendency toward Aunt Gigi. Jackson and Lennon were mixed race, but honestly Aunt Gigi's DNA seemed to have played a bigger role in them than Uncle Dex's had. And Bailey Ann had seen her mama stand up for her cousins on more than one occasion. Even times when maybe Jackson and Lennon hadn't known things occurred. Things had been said at their house sometimes about Uncle Dex "going across the tracks." Horrible things, but her mama had stood up fierce and proud defending Uncle Dex's choices and, of course, Aunt Gigi.

Bailey Ann had learned to stand alongside her. So what Aunt Gigi was saying simply didn't make sense.

"Think about it," Aunt Gigi cajoled her, trying to make the acceptance a little easier, though Bailey Ann wasn't having it. None of this was going down very smoothly at all.

"Think back," Aunt Gigi told her again. "Think how many of your friends are white."

Bailey Ann did think about it, but she thought about the town, too. "Aunt Gigi, Breathless is relatively white."

"No, it's not, Honey. Just the parts you know of it are."

Bailey Ann had to sit back in her seat, stunned, to think about it. Who did she pass on the street? Did she say hello? She'd never doubted her own willingness to accept people regardless of class, or creed, or color, and she always thought of that as a stark Southern trait.

She'd been raised, *she thought,* that "y'all meant all." She said so to her Aunt Gigi though it sounded like she was pushing back against her elder. That wasn't how she was raised, but she couldn't have her Mama's good name maligned. Still, this wasn't a fight, though it was definitely a *disagreement.*

"All of that is true," Aunt Gigi told her, "And I appreciate it. I think your mother had the right idea in her heart and I think she raised you girls better than she herself was raised. If you asked her, she would tell you—like most people will—that she was not racist. But if we drove through my section of town, you could see her cringing. Honey, we weren't poor. It wasn't ghetto. You can't claim that. It was just different. People were still segregating themselves and it made your mother nervous."

This time, Bailey Ann was listening a little bit more and trying to think back on her mother's life. She asked Aunt Gigi in all sincerity, "Does that really make her racist?"

"It's more than just that," Aunt Gigi said, "But yes, it was in the way she reacted, the way she spoke to people. I watched. I was there, I *know.* I've been on the receiving end of that and I'm glad I never got it from your mama. I was a special case, I'm well aware, maybe because I was a relative, I don't know. But I do remember when they arrested the Timmons' boy, she jumped in claiming what a bad seed he was and all that."

Bailey shrugged, wondering what the point was.

"The fact of the matter was, the Timmons' boy got straight A's in school. He went on to become an actual rocket scientist. There was never anything wrong with him, except being in the wrong place on the wrong side of town. The police kept trying to arrest him and he's just one example. That's the problem." She sighed but kept going. "Do you remember she fired that black maid you had?"

"She was stealing."

"Do you remember what was missing?" Aunt Gigi had that look on her face and Bailey Ann didn't know the answer. Her aunt filled her in. "Little Debbie cakes. That was it. One or two oatmeal crème pies or something. I told her I thought you girls were sneaking them."

"We always did," Bailey Ann admitted. Someone had gotten fired over that?

Aunt Gigi wasn't finished. "She replaced the first maid with a white maid who was never fired. But guess what? The Little Debbies still went missing all the time. It's stuff like that. She would tell you it's because the woman was stealing, but really? All that jewelry your mama left out . . . and what was missing were the treats she'd told her kids not to eat."

Aunt Gigi let that one sit for a minute. Bailey had been stealing the Little Debbies. She'd take one for her and one for Finn. Though it was entirely possible her sisters were filching them, too. She'd never realized the maid had been fired over that. She felt tears pressing at the back of her eyes as she finally was forced to accept what her Aunt Gigi was saying. She didn't like the way it made her remember her mama.

"Why are you telling me this, Aunt Gigi? She's dead and gone. I thought we don't speak ill of the dead."

"No, baby, we don't," Aunt Gigi replied with a conciliatory

nod. "And I do want you to know how very much I loved your mama. I still do. I miss her every day. It wasn't conscious, and she worked to be better, but she only went so far. She was one of my dearest friends, but I also want you to understand that I saw her flaws. I saw her as she really was, not the way you see her."

"But she was my Mama," Bailey Ann whispered, not liking the use of the past tense that had finally settled on her tongue after a year or so.

"She was, and you should go on loving her just as fiercely as you always have, but I cannot hold my tongue when I see her prejudices interfering with your life right now. Her old beliefs are stopping you from having something wonderful."

Still reeling from all the things that had been said, Bailey Ann wasn't ready for one more blow. So she ignored the last statement and sat there in her chair, no longer eating finger sandwiches or sipping at tea that suddenly seemed so very cold, and she just blinked at her Aunt.

Aunt Gigi let her sit like that for a while to absorb what had been said. She rearranged the silverware, refilled the teapot, and let Bailey Ann have her moment. Aunt Gigi had always been good at that, though Bailey Ann couldn't remember the last time she'd felt so scolded by the woman.

Just when Bailey Ann thought she might be able to get herself together and head home with some dignity intact, Aunt Gigi spoke again. "Your mama is working from beyond the grave on you, little girl, and she is ruining your relationship with that Finn Malloy."

Now Bailey Ann was confused as all get-out. Was Aunt Gigi going senile? Was this early onset dementia? Maybe. Despite the things she could see and the truth she felt in Aunt Gigi's words even though she didn't like it, she almost wanted it to be a senility problem. Then she could chalk it all up to make believe and put it away, write it off as the same problem Aunt Gigi had.

She pointed out the massive flaw in her aunt's logic. "Aunt Gigi, he's not black."

"No," Aunt Gigi said. "But he's Irish and that may be just as bad. He's an immigrant. Not just his parents but Finn himself."

Bailey Ann, once again, thought about how Aunt Gigi knew all the goings-on in town. Apparently Aunt Gigi also knew all the goings on in parts of town that Bailey Ann had never really paid much attention to. So she just admitted defeat. "Aunt Gigi, I don't even understand what you're talking about. What is wrong with Finn being an immigrant?"

"Nothing, and that's exactly the problem."

"You're acting like there's something wrong with it," Bailey chided, then thought better of it. In a softer tone she added, "I don't think there's anything wrong with it. My decisions have nothing to do with Finn Malloy having immigrated from Ireland as a child."

"Really?" Aunt Gigi pressed. "Do you remember when you were teenagers and you used to correct him when he would say something with that wonderful Irish brogue he had? That boy had the coolest accent and you worked it out of him."

"Aunt Gigi, he asked me for help."

"He probably asked you for help, Honey, because your Mama acted like it was a horrible thing when he talked that way."

That couldn't be true, Bailey thought. Finn had specifically asked her to help him lose his accent, but just as she'd begun to open her mouth to protest her Aunt Gigi's ideas once more, she came up against a few memories that made the problem seem more real in hindsight. She thought about the times she'd seen her mother ever-so-politely cringe when Finn would use the phrasing from the old country, or roll an R. Bailey Ann, too, had sometimes reacted the same way. It made her boyfriend different and "other," and she hadn't liked it. She'd liked Finn plenty, but she'd wanted him not to be different.

"It was bad enough," Aunt Gigi went on, "that your mama didn't know who his people were. Then he came in with that out-of-place accent and those hand-me-down clothes and strange foods, and your mama couldn't deal."

"Mama dealt just fine," Bailey Ann told her. "Finn and I dated for years and my mama didn't stop us from being together. We broke up on our own."

"She let you *think* it was you. She talked you around to believing it, too. That what you felt was just some teenage crush. Then, when he stayed with you through his first year of college, she got worried it wasn't going to end on its own. That's when she really went to work on you, little girl."

"What are you even talking about, Aunt Gigi?"

"You wrote that boy a letter breaking up with him because you knew it would never work out. But you were barely eighteen years old, not even an adult. How would you even know something like that?"

"I just knew, Aunt Gigi. We didn't come from the same place. We were so on fire, and that kind of relationship doesn't last. I know that. Mama and Daddy were slow and steady, not bright and hot. It's why their love didn't burn out." She finally put voice to the words that had been bouncing around in her brain all week.

"Oh, baby girl, you don't know anything. Your mama and daddy were bright and hot right from the start, and they stayed that way until the day she died. They had what you and Finn have. But for whatever reason, your mama decided he wasn't good enough for you and she *worked* on pushing you guys apart."

"She did not."

"Baby, she did." Aunt Gigi paused a moment. "I know it, because she told me."

F urniture should be upholstered to match the décor. And it's not a 'couch,' it's a 'sofa.'

LATER, BAILEY ANN DIDN'T REMEMBER ANY OF THE DRIVE between Aunt Gigi's and home. By the time she was lucid, it was hours later and she was sitting on that booger-colored sofa staring into space. She still wasn't sure that Aunt Gigi was right, but she was coming around a little bit more that maybe Aunt Gigi wasn't wrong.

Despite the fact that it was a Southern Girl no-no, Bailey Ann had fought back. Finn's parents hadn't liked him dating her any more than her parents had been in favor of her dating Finn. She thought it was in part about how close the two of them had grown and the fact that they were just kids. But Aunt Gigi set her on the straight and narrow over that by saying, if Bailey Ann had dated one of the Zemp boys, her mama would have let it fly.

"Brodie Zemp was a misogynistic asshole," Bailey Ann said.

Then her hands had flown to her mouth, having said the "A" word at Aunt Gigi's luncheon—with the good china out. Not only that, but Lennon had dated Brodie for a while.

Luckily, Aunt Gigi had laughed. "That, my little dear, is true, and that's exactly the problem. Your mama would have been happy if you had dated Brodie Zemp—or even one of the Cotton boys."

The Cotton boys weren't a-holes; they just had more money than sense.

Aunt Gigi was still going. "Your Daddy kept your Mama in good money. She didn't have to work, and she wanted that for you girls. She thought Finn couldn't provide that. In part, because his parents were poor, and he had too much to do to climb the social ladder. He didn't know what he wanted, besides you. And he was 'other.' It was too much for your Mama to imagine for her oldest."

"But his parents did so much!" Bailey could still hear her protest. "They moved to another country. They completely changed their social status."

"Your Mama never saw it that way. She believed in history and that people are where they come from."

Bailey Ann was still sitting on the couch thinking about all the things Aunt Gigi had laid at her feet. When she thought back, she did remember her mama pushing her toward the Zemps and the Cottons. They were local families. The cottons had lived in Breathless almost as long as the Mayfairs. That meant they were good people. The Zemps had enough money to make up for the roots they lacked. Finn's family had neither.

She told Aunt Gigi that it wasn't because Finn's family were immigrants, but because they were strange, that her momma had protested. And Aunt Gigi had shot that one down, too. She'd talked Bailey Ann through what it must be like to be an immigrant and leave a home that you left because it was unsafe. And she talked about it as though she knew what it was like to try to be that new immigrant, clinging to "home"—a home you loved and hadn't wanted to leave—and yet also assimilate into the country that had supposedly welcomed you, even though in many ways it hadn't.

When Bailey Ann had pressed, Aunt Gigi opened up and told stories about being a young girl and leaving Mississippi with her family. It hadn't been safe for them there. She hadn't come from another country, but she felt she understood. Her father and several friends had spoken out against one of the local Mississippi companies that was dramatically underpaying just the black workers. When they'd protested, one of the men had ended up murdered. It was never tied back to the company, but they'd all known it was a warning.

Bailey Ann was stunned. She thought she'd known her Aunt Gigi, the genteel woman who always wore dresses and hats, who believed in Good Southern Etiquette. That woman had hugged her momma tight every time she saw her, and always said what a good woman she was and what a good friend. Bailey Ann found herself pressing for still more answers. "Were you lying when you told Mama what a good friend she was? Because I remember you two as great friends. You took care of her when she was sick."

"No, Bailey Ann. I never lied. She was a wonderful woman, and I loved her with all my heart. But like I said, I'm not blind to her faults. She wasn't blind to mine either. So it was fair, you should know that."

"Your faults?" Bailey Ann had laughed, and Aunt Gigi had rattled a handful off.

"Well, I'm far too controlling. I've almost ruined my marriage to your Uncle Dex a couple of times before he managed to get some patience on and talk me down."

"You cannot be serious," Bailey Ann said.

"Oh, yes, honey. I am. And on that respect, you're right. Bright and hot has its bad moments, everything does, but I'll take bright and hot over slow and steady any day."

It had taken hours to get through the lunch. Aunt Gigi had shifted over, telling Bailey Ann happy stories about when her Mama and Daddy had been dating—things Aunt Gigi had been there for and seen. Things Bailey Ann had either only heard in stories or never heard at all. Like the time her mother got caught sneaking out her window to meet Con Mayfair; or the time the police officer had brought them home, found them in the back of Con's car up at Lover's Leap. Aunt Gigi made it very clear that the officer had *not* caught them making out, but actually having sex, and Bailey Ann had laughed so hard she'd cried.

Aunt Gigi had hugged her tight and let her cry it out, whispering sweet words to the girl and saying, "Honey, I think I've filled you up with enough tiny sandwiches and big ideas for one day."

So she found herself here, sitting on the stupid couch staring into space, not seeing the old color on the walls in the living room and not seeing the torn out pieces of the dining area or the kitchen. What Aunt Gigi had said had smacked her in the face, and she had a lot to think about.

Finn called later and asked if she was coming over. The buzzing of her phone in her purse sitting next to her on the couch where she'd dropped it was the only thing that brought her out of the stupor she was in.

"Oh, no, my lunch with Aunt Gigi went on way too long. And I woke up late. I think . . ."

He didn't even let her finish. "No worries. You get some rest and I'll see you tomorrow," almost as though he understood what she was dealing with. Yet, surely, he couldn't.

Bailey Ann ate her dinner by rote, not even tasting the food she'd made. Then she went to bed, sleeping only fitfully until late into the morning again. This time when she woke, she didn't answer a summons for lunch but created one of her own, calling her grandmother.

"Nana, can I come talk to you?"

"Well, I'm here with my ladies." But Nana Rue seemed to sense something in Bailey Ann's voice. "Do you need me to carve out a little time, honey?"

"If you could, it'd mean a lot."

Nana Rue didn't drive. So Bailey Ann once again got dressed, not in work clothes, and headed out. This time it wasn't a dress.

Nana Rue didn't quite stand on ceremony the way Mama and Aunt Gigi had, but Bailey Ann still made sure she looked nice to show up at Cluster F, and at least the name still made her laugh. She didn't realize that, by the time she knocked on her Nana's door, she already had tears rolling down her face. She didn't like this. Her Mama was dead and gone, but Aunt Gigi hadn't let it rest. She said so to Nana.

"What did that woman tell you?" Nana asked as she held her tight.

"She said momma was a racist, Nana Rue."

The silence that greeted her statement made Bailey Ann pause. It hit her even harder than yesterday's conversation had. When she looked up from the hug Nana Rue had enveloped her in, she saw the straight line of Nana Rue's clenched lips.

"Are you serious? You think so too?"

"Well, honey, I'd love to tell you no but I'm not going to lie to you."

"What in God's name is this? The woman is dead and gone. Why can't people leave it be?"

Bailey Ann could have gone to her own grave not knowing any of this, and she'd have been much happier for it. She said exactly that to Nana Rue, and then Nana Rue asked, "Why did Aunt Gigi tell you this?"

"Well she said I was ruining my own life with momma's problems."

"Oh. Well, she's right," Nana Rue said matter-of-factly, leaving Bailey Ann as stunned as she had been the first time she'd heard it. Nana Rue continued, "She sees it, and I see it too, honey. You are ruining your own life with things that your momma handed down to you."

Bailey almost fled right then, almost grabbed her jacket and walked out on her Nana, even thought that would have been the epitome of rudeness. She was getting ready to flee. Nana, however, circled her bony little hand around Bailey Ann's wrist and kept her pinned on the couch beside her.

"You will stay, and you will listen. This can of worms has been opened and it cannot be closed."

She was not ready for this. Then Nana Rue started in, "I raised my boys one way. And I will admit that your grandpa and I screwed up a lot. My sons grew up believing that if you were afraid of the police it was because you had cause to be afraid—that it meant you'd done something wrong. It's what I taught them. And while I'm grateful they could grow up that way, and that they had faith in a police force that would protect them, after meeting your Aunt Gigi I realized I missed some pieces. The problem was, after meeting your Aunt Gigi your mama didn't make that same realization. I knew her all her life, and the good news is she was much less bigoted than her parents. Her parents believed that anyone who was not the same color, class, or creed was of no value to them. They had more money than God, and they disowned Della for marrying your daddy."

"*What?*" Bailey Ann asked, stunned yet again. Her grandparents had always been around and been friendly.

"Yeah, baby," Nana Rue said. "There's so much you don't know."

🌿 33 🌿

Bailey Ann cried herself to sleep that night. She tossed and turned and woke back up several times. She stared at the shadows on her ceiling from the faint light around the edge of the windows. It was from the streetlights beyond the houses and maybe a little from the moon, too. She listened to another rain storm pass through, pounding on her roof, and she comforted herself by thinking normal things, like how old the roof was and that maybe she should replace it.

For a moment, she thought she should ask Finn, and then she shut that down as quickly as it had come. She couldn't ask Finn anything right now. She didn't know where to start. It had been two whole days since she'd headed out to Gigi's and she'd barely spoken to him in that time.

She was left afloat again, in another way. Before, it had just been her life. Now, she had no idea if she was a terrible person or a decent one, and she'd always believed she was a good person. She wanted to know that what she thought about her relationship with Finn was not that tied to some deep-seated prejudice. She still believed she didn't belong with him. She wasn't sure any of that had changed. But Bailey Ann was no longer sure that idea was her own. And if it wasn't? She didn't know what to do with it.

Hell, she'd barely made it around to thinking about her own life. She was still neck deep in her Mama and Daddy's. It turned out her maternal grandparents hadn't spoken to her Mama until after Harper Rose was born. Bailey Ann had still been a toddler at the time and hadn't realized that she'd had no contact with her grandparents on her mother's side up until that point.

She remembered seeing them when she was very young. Now, she knew that might have been the first time. Maybe that's why it was stuck in her memory, one of her earliest ones. But according to Nana Rue, she'd never met them before that day. Bailey's brain was churning with the things her parents had never seen fit to tell her.

Nana Rue had asked her, "Where do you think the money for all those timeshares came from?"

Bailey Ann had replied, well, her parents had always told her Daddy worked hard, stayed in the same job, collected his pension, and they'd saved. But as she'd looked at their finances again that evening, she saw it in a new light. She was right that they'd never spent all the money they'd earned. They'd stayed in a smaller house than what they could have afforded later and bought cars that weren't flashy and only when they truly needed one. They socked their money away and they'd invested it wisely.

"All that may be true," Nana Rue had told her, "but it doesn't add up. She inherited money from her parents."

"Well, the way you talk, it should be much more. You said they were loaded. I'd hardly say Mama and Daddy were loaded, just well off."

"And that's true too." Nana Rue went on to tell her about when her grandparents had died and at the reading of the will, to no one's surprise, Della Mayfair had been left only a small portion of the money. The two boys had gotten far bigger chunks—four or five times as much as Della had been left.

In the will, it had been claimed the small amount was

because the boys were part of the business, but Nana Rue suspected it was payment—or payback—for Della having married someone they didn't approve. Bailey Ann knew her Mama had come from Atlanta society but she hadn't realized—given the Mayfair name was such a big fish, though in a small pond—that her Mama had married down with Daddy.

Awake and unable to even fake trying to sleep, she found herself online at four a.m. researching segregation in Atlanta and where her Mama might have gotten these ideas. Unfortunately, nothing she found out about her mother's time growing up there made her feel any better. If anything, it only confirmed what Aunt Gigi had intimated and Nana Rue had told her outright.

Bailey Ann stopped and looked at her computer and felt the sands shifting under her feet. What she had believed was solid bedrock was nothing of the sort. Nana Rue had loved Della Mayfair. But Nana Rue also finally told Bailey Ann outright that "She is not who I would have picked for your father. They defied her parents to get married and they defied me. Your Grandpa was okay with it. Said they were just crazy kids in love and they'd make it work. I thought more like you do, that they were burning bright and it was going to burn out. I was very afraid that when it did, it was going to get ugly.

"In those days, remember, divorce wasn't something you just did and got over it. If your marriage didn't work out, especially in our world, it was a life sentence. I did not want to see Con unhappy for the rest of his life or saddled with the bad choice he'd made when he was too young to know better. I told him that."

It seemed the blows kept coming. "But they worked out Nana Rue. They were fine."

"I know," her grandmother said with a smile. "I was *wrong*. I was wrong about my own child. I was wrong about your mother. I was wrong about their marriage and their resilience. That inheritance your mamma got was a pittance compared to what she should have had and she never regretted it.

"She had her faults, but she had her good points too. She loved your daddy till the moment she died and they're probably somewhere in the afterlife together. I console myself with that every day because it hurt like hell losing him. Truth be told, it hurt like hell losing her too, because I loved her. She brought me you girls, and she raised you better than she'd been raised herself. That takes a strong woman."

Bailey Ann was smiling at the praise for her Mama. It felt like sunshine after rain. She'd heard enough bad things about a woman she adored. A woman she'd always looked up to and felt so very lucky to have as her mother. But Nana Rue wasn't quite finished.

"But I see you, I see you trying to be like her. The problem is, you're more like her than you know. She didn't let you see who she really was. Though she ran off and married the boy that her parents told her she couldn't marry, and though it worked out, she was not about to let you girls do the same thing. All that society was still bred into her. And I guess she saw some kind of Mayfair-Breathless society in Con that her parents didn't see, but she did not see it in Finn Malloy."

Nana Rue took a deep breath. "Think about it. That boy Emma Kate dated in high school—DeSean—that drove your mamma batshit crazy. While those two were together, she was over here daily asking me if she should tell Emma Kate to break up with him or let her ride it out. It was the same with you and Finn. Your mamma let the two of you slide until your senior year. That boy had left for college and she caught you writing *Mrs. Bailey Ann Mayfair Malloy* in your notebooks and she decided she had to do something. She did some work on you, little girl, made you believe that you and Finn Malloy didn't belong together, and she was pleased that she had saved you.

"I told her she should stay out of it, but your Mama never really listened to me. When it came to her and your Daddy, I have to guess in the end it was a good thing she didn't listen to me, but when it comes to you and that Finn, I don't think the same holds true. I was wrong about her and Con. And she was wrong about you and Finn."

So Bailey Ann laid back down in her bed in the dark of her lonely house and cried and cried. She cried until her eyes were puffy and her head hurt. She got up, took a shower at five a.m., then took a couple of Tylenol, hoping that might ease the headache, but it didn't. Maybe the headache wasn't really in her head. Maybe it was in her heart and every other bone. She felt like she was coming down with something. An hour later, she was sure of it.

Somewhere around nine, she finally managed to get some real sleep despite the light coming in through the window and the fact that she'd cried so hard, she could no longer breathe through her nose. At eleven, she'd woken up slowly seeing the clock in front of her and felt warmth for the first time. She thought about rolling over and going back to sleep, but she wasn't able to, her limbs heavy as sandbags.

As she shifted a little, she realized it wasn't her limbs that were heavy, and it wasn't her that was warm. Finn had come over and crawled into bed behind her. He'd probably seen her puffy face. He'd probably worried about her. She tried not to act like she was awake and thought maybe she could fake it and go back to sleep, but that wasn't like Finn. He wouldn't let her get away with much of anything, for sure.

"Hey, Bailey Ann," he whispered softly, stroking her hair. "Are you okay?"

She wanted to say *no*, she wanted to tell him everything she'd learned, but how could she? So she nodded *yes* and lied to Finn Malloy.

34

Bailey Ann managed to convince Finn that she was sick. Then she managed to stay in bed, mostly, for the next two days. Though she got up and got around a little bit, she didn't travel into town or do anything where people might see her. She couldn't have word getting back to Finn that she was faking it, and she wasn't faking it, per se. She really did feel like crap.

She'd always heard that one day children discovered their parents were human beings and not gods, and that that day would come as a shock. Bailey had slowly discovered her parents were human, but she'd never lost the vision of them. It just figured, her epiphany had been shoved at her at thirty-something, and not simply realized before.

Maybe it was because she hadn't yet gotten married or had children of her own. Or maybe it was because she'd been such good friends with her mother. She'd actually genuinely enjoyed spending time with her, and she knew that wasn't always the normal mother/daughter relationship. It was certainly one Mama hadn't had with Emma Kate, and Harper Rose had been too far away to become friends with their parents. Bailey Ann had always felt like the favorite daughter, though Mama had never said anything of the sort.

With her brain as jumbled as it was, she'd had two hard days of Tylenol, chicken soup, and hard introspection. When it came down to it, she decided of course she was her Mama's favorite. She did everything her Mama wanted, including dumping the boy she loved because her Mama thought it was a good idea. She was also old enough and smart enough now to know that making a full one-eighty reversal on what had been a solid decision—and doing it in two days when she was upset—was not a smart move. So she was holding out and holing up and staying away from everybody while she tried to work things out in her own mind.

It felt like everything she knew or believed was up in the air now. Now she wondered if Daddy had died without Mama not because he couldn't live without the person, but maybe because he couldn't live without the one who ran the house. Bailey Ann had come in the last couple of months and taken care of things for him, but she'd noticed before then that he hadn't been eating very well. He hadn't been going to the bank. He hadn't been monitoring their finances and didn't even know that Emma Kate had a savings account she could be using for the past year or so. Now, Bailey Ann wondered if maybe he hadn't wanted to go on simply because he didn't have the ability to do so.

He and Mama had divided the household up so cleanly. Neither had ever crossed that line that she could remember. Bailey, as a child, had thought that made perfect sense. It worked for her and her sisters. It didn't matter what happened—you always knew which parent to go to. If you needed a Band-Aid, you went to Mama. She knew exactly where they were and whether you needed a cloth or waterproof one. If you needed decisions about what classes to take in school, you went to Daddy. He was the one who gave that kind of career advice. Money? Talk to Mama. Need a new car? Trouble with your lawn service? Daddy.

Looking back, she realized he'd also told her to find a job, stay in it, set up a 401K and give her loyalty to one company for her whole life. She'd had a very hard time convincing him that the job market simply didn't work that way anymore. He never believed her and thought she was crazy when she moved from the company she started with to a new company only three years later. She'd spent hours, days even, trying to convince him that she'd done a good thing. She'd negotiated a salary increase and that this was simply the way the market worked now.

She'd moved again another three years later to another excellent salary bump—and another lecture on company loyalty from her father. That move landed her in Nashville, and she'd loved it there, but she'd left it, and now, coming home, fixing the house, dealing with Aunt Gigi and Nana Rue? She was past her eyeballs in craziness, far more than she'd ever been when Mama was dying and she thought the world was caving in.

Maybe it was also something else. As the oldest, she'd become the anchor of the family. Harper Rose should have been. She was the most settled with three children, a house, and a husband. But that had fallen out from under her and she was in no position to be the head of their little family. She was up to her neck in lawsuits, apparently.

Bailey Ann was hopeful her sister would call if she needed advice, but Harper Rose hadn't dialed her up yet. And Emma Kate? Emma Kate had always been the one Mama had to corral. Now Emma Kate was on the other side of the country and Mama was gone and Bailey Ann was trying to figure out if it was her job to sit on her little sister or just let Emma Kate be.

It had to be harder on Emma, losing Mama when she was so young. Bailey Ann had an extra decade with her parents and had gotten along better with them the whole time. She wondered what her little sister was going through, wondered if she should tell her sisters what Aunt Gigi and Nana Rue had laid on her. But she was thinking better of it, at least for right now. She laid in bed with the electric blanket turned up to a nice, warm temperature and spent her days staring at the wall and thinking.

She was trying to remember, to put together all her childhood memories, and look at them with new, adult eyes. It wasn't anything she'd tried before. Now she was carefully combing through all her cherished memories to see if Aunt Gigi was right.

Bailey had no reason to doubt the woman. The problem was it didn't make her Mama look very good, despite all the times Aunt Gigi had said that she loved the woman and that her mama was one of her dearest friends. Bailey Ann was starting to think Aunt Gigi and Nana Rue were right.

And if she accepted that and decided that her Mama hadn't liked Finn Malloy because he was Irish, because his accent made him sound strange, because he had no roots and no income to speak of, at least at the time, what did that make of her? She was still convinced that she and Finn weren't meant to be, but she had no idea now where that was coming from.

One voice told her to stay the course with Finn, that it didn't matter what Aunt Gigi said or what Mama's motivations had been. The woman had been right. The other voice told her Mama hadn't been right. All that "good advice" had landed Bailey Ann right here: thirty-four and single, having the best sex of her life with the man two houses over, the same man she'd been with in high school when she had loved him with every single fiber of her being and she'd known it. If he'd asked her to run away back then, Bailey would have readily ditched her high school diploma and climbed on the back of any bike he bought and gone off with him. Her mama was just lucky he hadn't asked.

Interestingly enough, he was too much of a gentleman to do it, and they'd missed their chance. She tried to imagine where they'd be right now if they had been that crazy. She could envision herself almost like Harper Rose: three little children clinging to her legs. She could see Finn in her life, as he looked now. And that was the thing—she couldn't see anything more about this imaginary Finn that she had married in high school and run off with. Aside from his face, she couldn't tell anything about him. Certainly, she wouldn't have a degree. He might not be an architect. Would he resent that they'd thrown things away to be together? Would she? What if she'd gotten pregnant right away? There were so many *what ifs* she couldn't even begin to imagine the future that she would have if she'd changed her past.

Being the practical sort and having too much finance training under her belt to make sunk cost decisions—to bet on things she couldn't change and money she'd already lost—she decided to look forward. What if she stayed the course? What if she had this fling with Finn and let it go as soon as Lennon arrived and she needed to become an adult? Or, what if she threw all caution to the wind?

35

"**P**lease tell me you're feeling better. I really hope that you are." Finn hoped his sincerity came through the phone line. It was the third day, and he was torn between wanting her to actually be better and wanting her back for himself. It was selfish, he knew, but he wasn't above some selfishness. Sioban had come and stolen a few days from him, then this.

"You know what?" she said, "I feel okay. It's time for me to get out of bed and get back to work. We have a wall to finish."

His ears perked along with his heart. Pesky heart. It either needed to get over this woman once and for all or he needed to convince her that he was the one. "Do you want me to come over? I can get started on the wall in the dining room."

He was thinking it through. Patch the places left by the wall removal. Kiss Bailey Ann. Take off some pieces of clothing. Do some work . . . then . . .

"You know what?" she broke into his increasingly dirty thoughts. "I owe you some work. You've been doing so much on my house. Just tell me what you need. Are we laying tile? Laying flooring? Painting?"

He laughed at her. "I tell you what, I'll get pizza if you're up for it and you can help me paint the bathrooms."

"Well, that sounds exciting," she replied.

In his mind, it was. But he didn't say so.

She told him she'd show up shortly and he hung up before looking around. Was he a mess? Was his hair sticking up? He'd been getting ready to paint the bathrooms himself. Looking around the place, he spotted the coffee pot and turned it on, thinking the smell would be welcoming when she got there. He poured out the last of the first half-pot he'd made and headed to the back window. He told himself he was just looking out over his half-dead lawn and not watching for her.

But he saw the first flicker of movement as she hopped up onto the wall at the corner of her own backyard. It was as though she was magnetic to him and there was nothing he could do about it. She had on her old work-clothes again—tight jeans with paint splatters and a t-shirt under a sweatshirt. Her hair was tied up in a ponytail and the whole thing took him back to high school. To his parents shaking their heads at him as he watched for her. Would he always be watching for her?

How long had it been since he'd seen her coming over? Almost two weeks. The last time had been when Sioban had showed up.

Finn had been walking back and forth plenty, but Bailey Ann hadn't. He watched as she almost tripped but righted herself. Something about that movement, about the stutter in his heart that he was too far away to catch her, made him realize it had *always* been that way. Though Finn hadn't had a great relationship with her parents, her relationship with his parents may have been worse.

He wondered if they shut her out because they were embarrassed about the threadbare carpets and the older home that hadn't been renovated. Or had he done that? The house had been a huge achievement for his parents. It didn't matter as much to them what anyone else had.

But to Finn, fitting in had been everything. Bailey Ann Mayfair was captain of the cheerleading squad and homecoming queen. She was the ultimate ticket up the scale. Though he'd truly loved her—and probably still did—he'd been conscious that he didn't have as much and that the Malloys' house had always needed repairs. His mother was always cleaning, while Mrs. Mayfair had luncheons with her friends at "the club." It stood out in stark contrast in his mind as he watched Bailey Ann hop off the wall and come through the back yard.

Now, she climbed up the back deck and Finn noticed the lumber he'd set outside to season in the air. He was going to rebuild that deck and the rickety third step on the way up would be repaired. Hell, she might even help do it. Inside, the carpets weren't threadbare anymore—they were completely missing.

He'd never had anything nice to show her. Had he pushed her away because he felt inferior? Or had he simply let her go? She'd written that letter, but he'd never fought back.

Well, it was fifteen years later, but in that moment—as he reached for the old, round, steel knob on the back door—he decided. This time, he wouldn't go down without a fight.

"Finn!" she smiled up at him. She looked healthy and happy and his heart swelled at the sight. He didn't know why, but she was *the one*.

"You look good." He held back everything else that wanted to pour out of him, and settled for, "Coffee?"

She accepted the old mug he pulled down from the cupboard and startled him with her question. "Did your parents bring these with them from Ireland? I've never seen this design."

"Yes. There were four. And now there are three." Something in him swelled at the old, chipped mugs.

"You should hold onto these. Keep them safe."

He smiled. Maybe there was something he brought that she didn't have. Maybe he had old world roots, too. He just hadn't seen them.

"I was painting up here, before you came," he offered and led her into the bathroom he was painting a soothing shade of green. They worked in silence together, occasionally bumping in the small space and only speaking of the work. When he wiped his face with his shirt for the third time, Finn gave up and peeled it.

"You look like you have a green pox," she said, noting the flecks he'd earned when he'd been painting earlier. Then she tilted her head. "So you're not just taking your shirt off for me."

"Disappointed?" He looked at her, "You know, you should take your shirt off too, just so we're even."

She laughed at him but didn't comply. "That's okay. I don't really need a green pox myself, but I will happily appreciate the view from here."

With a grin, Finn handed her a roller to start on the one big wall. Three minutes later he had to critique her paint rolling technique. "No, you can't do it that way. It's getting built up. See? It's going to drip."

Looking between her work and his, she frowned at it. "Yours looks like glass and mine is thick and bubbly. I thought I was doing what you're doing. Clearly there's a skill here."

"You bet there is," he said. "There's a skill to everything."

"Well, I'm missing this one." She changed the topic before he could wrap himself around her and give a painting technique class. "Okay, so if you're an architect, don't you spend your time making drafts and doing blueprints? You don't do house painting."

"Well, not normally, but I did do it to put myself through school. Worked the whole five years. I did construction a lot, thinking that it was best to have both sides of the job, so I'd know what I was doing. I saw a lot of my classmates not have a clue how to put up a wall in reality. They understood the theory, but never having done it, they didn't have an idea of what load bearing meant, other than that they shouldn't knock it out."

"That makes a lot of sense," she told him, as she tried once again to roll the paint in a nice W-shape then smooth it outward from there. The walls here weren't big enough for her to get a lot of practice and he pointed out that they were going to wind up doing more edging than painting. Finally, he decided it didn't matter and told her if she goofed it up a little bit, well, it was the bathroom. She seemed grateful that he was being so forgiving. Truthfully, she was doing good work for an amateur, but he'd wanted to hold her and show her how to do it. Oh, well.

Instead, he kept talking. "That history in construction saved my hide as an architect more than once."

"Can I ask you a question?" she stopped rolling the paint for just a second, then looked at the wall again as though she were avoiding his gaze.

"Sure," he replied, suddenly very curious where this was going.

"Okay, first, I'm going to paint this wall and then I want you to come over and fix it. And two, Finn, I should tell you, it's a pretty personal question."

He stopped and looked at her for a moment, serious now. "Okay, I'll bite. But I reserve the right to tap out."

"Fair enough," she said. "I was wondering about your father. I went over and had lunch with my Aunt Gigi and she told me stories I hadn't heard before." Bailey Ann paused as though there was something more to it that she was editing out. Finn waited until she started talking again, now wondering where this was going. "She told me about when she was a little girl in Mississippi and how the family felt they had been driven out. That they weren't safe there anymore, and I wondered if that was what it was like for y'all, coming from Ireland the way you did. Why did you leave?"

Interesting. Was she psychic? Or maybe, just maybe, thinking the same things he was? "There were no jobs. My father had a job that paid just enough to keep food on the table. We had a small house and I had a room, but it was more the size of a closet. That small closet in your bedroom? Double that. That was the size of my room."

"That's hardly big enough for a twin bed, Finn!"

"I don't think the bed I had was an American Twin," he told

her. He tried to focus on rolling paint on the wall as though it wasn't such a big deal to be telling her this.

"Go on."

"When he lost that job, my parents thought we'd be okay for a while. The house was so small, I remember hearing that conversation. We owned the home outright—it belonged to the family for a while—but even with that, there wasn't enough money to keep everybody fed. I didn't realize it at the time, but they were really struggling. So they borrowed money from my grandfather to come here. Grandfather didn't really have it either. I found out only years later that they scraped it up from about fifteen different places and sold the little house for far less than it was worth because the economy had tanked. We arrived in the States with almost nothing left over. We lived in Texas for a few years then just outside of Chicago for a while before we came here."

"What?" Bailey Ann's paint roller stopped moving and she turned to stare at him.

"I was little when we first arrived. I remember Chicago, though I don't remember Texas much. There are a few family pictures of us in this very small apartment that we rented."

Now he had her full attention as he described his father getting the job offer in Breathless and how excited the family had been. Siobhan had been born right before they left Ireland and his mother had often lamented that the cost of travel would have been cheaper without the baby—had she still been pregnant, had they managed to leave just a few months earlier.

Bailey Ann heard that a different way from the way Finn told it. "That does sound a lot like what my Aunt GiGi was talking about. Your mother was desperate enough and scared enough to leave home that she would do so within the few months after having given birth to her second child."

Finn had never really thought of it that way.

But she asked another question, "How did he do once he got here?"

"What do you mean? My dad had the same job for years."

"I know," she said. "I just wonder if you felt he was treated badly, or maybe just differently, because he was an immigrant. Do you think that he got passed over for promotion or anything?"

"Definitely," Finn said.

❧ 36 ❧

Southern Drawls come in 157 varieties, but you'd better have one of them. And it can't have any twang.

BAILEY ANN LISTENED WITH AWE AS FINN TALKED ABOUT HIS parents and their struggles for the first time. She'd never thought to even ask before, but now she was learning.

"They did better here than they'd done at home. But it was harder than it should have been." Her heart sank as he went on. "I don't think people took my mother's degree all that seriously."

"She had a degree? In what?" Bailey hadn't known that.

"Education. But it was from a university in Dublin and since it was foreign, I don't think anyone around here really valued it. And who would want someone with that thick of an accent teaching small children? She was a phone operator at the plant for a while. She tried customer service, but it didn't work out. She learned all the products, but she never really got the hang of the Southern phrases well enough to communicate by phone. She was a secretary for one of the managers, but never moved up the ranks." He shrugged. "I have no idea if that was because she was female, foreign, or what. I always thought my mom was amazing, but I was her kid, so my judgment was definitely clouded."

"Your mom was amazing," Bailey filled in. "I remember she would organize school stuff and she could get all of it to line up." She thought back. The other mothers should have loved Mrs. Malloy, but they'd always been a bit standoffish. Even her own mother. "And your father?"

"I mean, he was in sales, and he had that thick accent, so it was hard to get promoted that way. You can't sell to people who can't understand you. He worked at it, but it was ingrained. They were older when they had us, and older still by the time we got here." He shook his head as though he couldn't quite make the pieces fall into place. "It's the same thing like with my mom. There might have been other reasons. It might have been straight up age-ism and had nothing to do with them being immigrants. But they went to church and made a few friends and never fully fit in here. Not the way your family did. Or the Zemps, or the Basses."

He'd listed off two of the town's most respected—or at least well known—names. All white upper- and middle-class families who went to the Baptist church or the Methodist one. All families who fit in to the standard mold.

"We had friends from the local town center. We met other families in similar situations. There's a big Indian population— well not big, but decent for a town this size." He grinned at her surprised look. "We have good friends who taught Sioban Hindi. And there's a Muslim community, here, too . . . I have to say they were nicer to us than the upright citizens ever were."

Bailey felt that sitting like a weight in her chest. She hadn't been one of the nicer people back then. Hell, she still wasn't one now. She realized he'd stopped painting and was looking at her, the edger he was now using held out to one side. The tarp he'd put down crinkled as he shifted his feet.

"Did your Aunt Gigi bring all this up?"

Bailey just nodded at him, trying to keep her outsides calm while her insides swirled.

Finn stared at her for a moment. "My parents did fine. We did better here than if we'd stayed in Ireland. They had friends—just not anyone you would know. Probably not anyone your mama would have counted as 'acceptable' but that's not why they worked so hard. They wanted a better life—more opportunities—for me and for Sioban. They achieved what they wanted."

Bailey nodded, her head moving rotely as her brain absorbed what he'd said. "You're an architect. Sioban is a surgeon."

"Not yet, but almost," he laughed. "But it's about more than that. It's about the fact that we haven't worried if we can pay our bills in a long time. We haven't worried if we would have enough food since the early days in Texas. It kept getting better the whole time we were here."

"That's good." She still wasn't paying attention.

"Hey, get some paint on this last piece here before your roller dries out." He pointed to the small area to the left of the sink. At least one of them was still paying attention to the job.

It was barely big enough for her to get the roller in without hitting the trim around the door. It actually looked pretty good when she was done, though she was certain that was because he'd already taped it off and edged it.

She smiled at the wall and sucked in a breath when she felt his arms come around her waist. His mouth found the sensitive spot at the nape of her neck and she felt her shoulders relax into him, as she always did.

"Whoa." He pulled the roller from her hand just a split second before she let it drop onto the edge of the sink and paint what she wasn't supposed to paint. Finn laughed and set it in the tray next to his own tools before wrapping his arms around her again. "I missed you."

"I missed you, too." The words were out before she even realized they were true. Her hands covered his, feeling the tiny paint flecks along his skin. She sank back into him and heard the hum of his voice as a vibration along her skin.

"I want you."

This time she only sighed her response as his hands snuck up under the front of her shirt. Hers snuck around behind him, reaching for the back of his jeans, wondering if she'd find the folded paper and the condom there. She laughed when she did.

Finn took it as a signal and began peeling her like a banana. Shirt, jeans, hair tie. The bathroom mirror was missing and the tarp crunched under their feet. Bailey Ann helped him shuck his jeans and watched him shiver as she traced the line where the green flecks stopped.

He tugged her behind him and into his room where he threw back the covers on his queen-sized bed. It had been a twin, back in the day. The room had been American-boy blue back then, too. Now it was cream and had the faint odor of fresh paint.

"Finn, I'm so dirty and you're worse. What about the sheets?"

"I can wash the sheets. I want this moment now. I missed you."

"You said that." She grinned as she tugged up against him, his mouth coming to hers, his tongue seeking something more. She was leaning into him hard, when she jerked up straight. "The condom."

He leaned over and pulled out the drawer of the small bedside table. Inside was a smattering of square wrapped condoms, almost like a college dorm. She'd never made it to his college dorm. She'd believed at the time that he'd been faithful to her, but looking at everything with adult eyes, she didn't know. Still, she was here now, and he didn't care if they got green paint on the sheets.

She pushed him, tumbling him back onto the bed, his surprise and delight at her bold move showing on his face. Bailey moved over him then, kissing and sucking and even lightly nipping him in all the fun places she found. With each flick of her tongue, his breath sucked in or sped up and she felt powerful, having that control over this man.

Then he was tearing open the condom and rolling it on, grabbing her hips and with his motions begging her to ride him. She did. It wasn't like her, or it wasn't like what she thought of herself, but it was glorious. She threw her head back and cried out his name. She loved the way his fingers clenched into her hips. He'd leave marks. He'd be upset that he did it. But she liked it.

When the world burst into stars behind her eyes, she stayed where she was, riding out the storm inside her. It was Finn who sat up after a few moments, kissed her and rolled them over. This time, it was Bailey Ann who fell asleep first.

It was somewhere around five in the evening, getting dark and colder outside, but inside was bright and hot. She wasn't sure, but she thought she heard him speak right at that moment she slipped under the veil of sleep.

"I missed you a lot longer than just these past few days."

❧ 37 ❧

Finn watched as Bailey Ann woke up. It had grown fully dark outside, and the clock said it was well after seven p.m. She rolled over, turning toward him. He'd been there the whole time, behind her with his arms around her, and it was about time she faced him.

She managed to get one arm wrapped around his side before she looked up at him.

"So, you decided to wake up," he teased her.

"Oh, did I sleep too late?" She smiled, the slow easy grin looking right at home on her face. "I don't know what it is, but I've been sleeping weird lately."

He shrugged at her, the only way a man could when he was warm and naked in his own bed next to a warm, naked woman. "Everything's been out of whack," he said. "You know. With your dad . . ."

He didn't say, "Your dad died," but he didn't have to. Finn let it hang there, softly for a moment, before he continued. "But that's what had happened. Now you're changing the house, getting everything in gear to sell. You don't have your regular job. I know, it's been the same way for me."

She nodded absently, and looked as though she was drifting away. He could only assume that's what she'd been doing—thinking through everything, like she always did—while she'd been sick. He wanted to tug her back out of it. "I asked you about pizza. I know you said you were trying to eat better, but you want pizza, right?"

Bailey Ann laughed at him, her focus turning to him again. "I can do a pizza."

"Okay, so here's the thing." He tucked her hands into his and offered the words up like a secret. "Let's get it delivered and find a movie on TV, and you stay over here tonight."

That gave her pause, and once again, Finn tried to see what was going on in her head. "Don't think too hard about it, and don't worry about what other people think."

"You're suggesting a walk of shame down the rock wall between the back yards tomorrow morning."

"Well, no. I mean, how much of a walk of shame is it if I go with you? And if we wait until ten or eleven, it's hardly a walk of shame. For all they know you came over and had breakfast with me."

"What normal single woman goes over to the neighbor's houses for breakfast?"

"Sometimes people do that, Bailey Ann." Then it was his turn to turn more serious, "I won't push if you don't want to. Do you *want* to stay?"

She nodded quickly. He tried to hide his sigh of relief that wanting to stay, at least, was a no-brainer. He figured not much else in her life was. "Then stay. Curl up on my couch. Watch a movie with me, and actually spend the night."

"Okay," she whispered, and right at that moment her stomach decided to punctuate her words with a nice growl.

Finn laughed at her, "I'd better get on ordering that pizza."

Before she could change her mind, he popped out of bed, headed down the stairs, and was on his phone. Of course, he remembered what she liked and hoped it was all the same. But he remembered what she'd had at Bobby's the other day. He could do this.

Later, when she was on the couch with him, curled up under his arms, while explosions rocked across his wide screen TV, he realized they'd never spent the night together before, not once. When he'd been in college, she'd driven out to see him twice. But she hadn't stayed over. Her mama would not have let her, and Bailey Ann wouldn't either. It simply wasn't proper. So, she'd stayed all day and driven home at the end, as he'd only been a few hours away. They'd broken up just before she graduated. So there had been no overnights between them.

While they'd been dating, her parents had never been foolish enough to leave her alone when he might have come over and stayed. Sure, they'd traveled a bit without the girls, but Bailey had always been saddled with her two little sisters and that did not make an opening for Finn to climb in a window or just stay. Finn had come over, of course, but those times, *absolutely nothing* had happened because Emma Kate was barely eight years old and the biggest blabbermouth in the history of the world.

After the movie ended, Bailey followed him up the stairs to his room, where she curled into his arms. Finn slept the best night he had slept in a long, long time. He hadn't pushed her for sex, and she hadn't pushed either. Though he wanted her—it seemed he always did—he wasn't after sex. He was playing a long game.

That didn't dampen any heat between them the next morning, though, as he'd woken up hard, with her hand around him. He'd laughed as she'd wound up checking her hair three times before heading down the brick wall between the houses.

The tightness in his chest had slowly loosened as they settled into a rhythm like that, though Bailey Ann had insisted that they simply couldn't spend *every* single night together. But, between Finn's soft pressure and her own easy acquiescence, they managed to be together about two out of every three nights. She said she was trying to keep some sanity regarding the two of them, but for Finn it wasn't working very well at all.

Side by side, they'd sanded and spackled the ripped-up patches in the dining room where the wall had been torn out. She went out to buy paint and Finn accompanied her. They'd been spending most of their days together. She talked him into helping her paint rooms she said she originally hadn't had the intention of painting.

He helped her haul furniture to donate or deliver to new homes.

"It's been hard," she told him, "selling it all off. But I don't need it and other people do. Mama would have wanted her dresser to be loved. And I am not the person to do it."

Though she talked him into helping her paint more, and Finn asked her all the standard questions he'd learned house painting in college, and she wound up choosing richer colors. She and Finn painted the beautiful peachy color on the wall and it looked gorgeous. "You're much better at this than just a few weeks ago!"

She grinned at him and threatened him with the roller. "I had a good teacher."

Three days later, she'd shelled out for new carpet. He almost felt as though he let her down when he told her that was a skill not in his repertoire. As soon as the carpet installers left, the two of them began putting together the new queen bed in the master bedroom for Bailey Ann.

She had completely taken the place over. Gone were the dingy powder blues and greens of her mother's choosing. Instead, the carpet was a deep but bright blue and the walls a dusty orangey-red, the bright coloring reminiscent of something he'd seen in pictures from India. Bailey Ann had at first thought it was too much, but Finn was glad he'd convinced her to go for it. It suited her. He could see it.

At last, they had the final piece of the bed together, and they unrolled a mattress that had come in the mail. Together, they watched it inflate itself, and put fresh bright blue sheets on the bed with a white eyelet comforter set that she had found.

"So I saw this in a catalog and I thought it might work in here. Can you help me angle the bed into the corner?"

Though he fully expected to be asked to pull it back out once she saw it, Finn found he was wrong. "This is really good. It looks simple but open."

Leaving the bed in place, Bailey Ann next had him hang rods for white sheer curtains that she draped around the sides, enclosing the bed in a way that was both exotic and a bit steamy. She laid out white plush rugs on the floor on either side, then turned a full three-sixty in the space that opened up since they changed where the bed sat.

While she was doing that, Finn installed a triangular shaped bookshelf behind the headboard with shelves climbing up to the ceiling and giving her some extra storage space. Or, he hoped, *them*. He so badly wanted her to invite him into this room. On a more permanent basis.

The faint odor of paint still clung to the air, but it made the whole place feel new. The attached bathroom had been upgraded. Though it was still small compared to more modern designs, he liked it. They'd changed out the pedestal sink for a more modern version with storage space underneath. Finn insisted on pulling out the old mirror/medicine cabinet and Bailey Ann had sighed in relief as the reminder had been ripped out and replaced.

Piece by piece, they'd been overhauling both houses, and they'd been eating about half their meals together. Standing in the finished room felt like a big accomplishment to him. And maybe an endpoint. Her house wasn't done yet, but this room was checked off.

He watched as she stood in the middle of the space and took a deep breath in. She didn't seem to notice the lingering paint smell as her shoulders dropped and she relaxed into the room.

But for Finn, he wondered if this was the moment she would tell him thank you, and send him on his way.

He pushed on the mattress, testing out the springiness. "Tell me I get to try it out with you tonight."

"Of course." She smiled, and he began to relax.

It was then that Finn realized what it truly was she was doing. "You just painted this room orange—"

"Peach," she corrected him with a grin. "It's peach."

"My point is that I'm painting my house in creams and whites. You used 'peach.' You're not moving out, are you?"

❧ 38 ❧

It struck Bailey Ann hard that Finn was right. She didn't want to move out.

She had just completed the bedroom in bright colors to her own taste, and chances were good no one else was going to appreciate it as much as she did, except maybe Finn Malloy. She stood, staring at the bed in the corner and looking up at the corner bookshelves, thinking what a great space it was and that he was right. She had not decorated to sell.

She'd chosen *colors* for the other rooms, too. She'd picked a pale tea-green for the bedroom that had been hers and Harper Rose's at alternating times. She'd left the queen bed in there, adding the new one in here and throwing out her Mama and Daddy's old mattress since she had no idea how many years old that thing was. It had all seemed practical at the time, but Finn's statement had jarred her, and she stood staring at him for a moment.

"No. I don't guess I am."

Though she felt the universe shift under her feet once again, he only smiled. Bailey wasn't sure if that meant he already knew what she was only just now coming to realize or if it simply didn't matter to him. She still hadn't asked what his plans were, what was going to happen when his house was finished? They weren't done with it yet, but the end point was getting closer every day.

So, as they'd stood there—Finn with almost no expression on his face, other than admiring the shape of the new room they'd put together, and Bailey Ann, in her own stunned silence—her phone rang.

Pulling it from her pocket, she found the face on the phone was another surprise. She tapped at the screen and smiled as she said, "Lennon! Good to hear from you. How are you?"

They chatted for just a few moments, catching up. Lennon had finished up the work she'd had left over from the previous semester. Given where she was in her degree, her coursework was slim, if anything.

"So," she said, "I talked to my professors, and they told me I can finish my final exam from a distance. It's going to be online anyway, and we just held our last class session. There were only three of us anyway."

Bailey Ann only nodded along, interjecting an occasional *mm-hmm*. Having been in finance, she'd taken a set of rigorous courses with large numbers of people in each class. The rooms were often so full as to require stadium seating, and she had no idea what it was like to be a science student in a graduate program. Three people in a class sounded both decadent and horrifying to her.

To Lennon, it sounded like just another day. "What it means, though, is that I can be there at the end of next week. I don't want to intrude, and I'll stay with my Mama and Daddy for the week, if you want, because I know you weren't expecting me."

Bailey Ann interrupted. "Don't you worry about that. You come on over whenever you're ready. Just give me a heads up so I can make sure I have clean sheets on the bed. I'm going to put you in Harper Rose's old room."

They went on for a few more moments, finalizing details— which day Lennon expected to arrive, at what time, and so on.

When Bailey Ann hung up and turned back to Finn, he had a different expression on his face.

"Your cousin Lennon's moving in with you?"

"Yes," she said. "She's doing a research project for her thesis." Though she'd listened carefully to every little bit, Bailey still couldn't have told him what it was about.

"So, you really aren't selling the house?"

"Well, I thought I still might be, but she was going to stay for a semester, and I thought I might . . ." She broke it off. She didn't know. She'd thought she might move back to Nashville. Or find a new job somewhere along the way. But the fact of the matter was she'd only put this one task in front of her, and she hadn't thought very far ahead of it, and she sure wasn't ready to tell Finn anything.

"She's coming in a week," she said. "Originally it was supposed to be in two more weeks. She offered to pay rent because she knew we were thinking about selling, but I told her she couldn't." Bailey heard herself rambling a little bit, and she decided it was time to buck up.

"What are you going to do when you sell your house, Finn, when you finish?"

He looked her square in the eyes then and answered cleanly and clearly. "I don't know. I considered looking around the area and seeing if there were houses to be restored. I have the credentials, and I could make a living doing it. I don't know what the local cities hold, though. I kept telling myself I would research it, but I've been putting it off. Another option is to go back to Atlanta, talk to my firm."

"You didn't quit?"

"No. I took an extended leave of absence. I honestly don't know if they're expecting me or not. I was pretty burnt out when I left, and when I hit that one house and the problem with the NIMBY laws, I cracked. I just turned around and came here. At least I knew I had it waiting."

Bailey Ann wondered then if he'd known she was here when

he came back. She just hadn't known that he was back in town. Somehow, she'd managed to go through a lot of her life with her eyes closed, she discovered.

They stood there like that, his answer hanging in the air, as much of a non-answer as hers had been. When the silence grew thick, Bailey Ann opened her mouth. Somebody had to say it, but Finn beat her to it.

"Are you asking about us? What do we do?"

She nodded. "To be honest, Finn, I don't even really know what we are."

"How can you not know, Bailey Ann?"

"What do you mean? We never talked about it. Am I your girlfriend? What would you call me? I honestly don't know if you're seeing anyone else or if you have somebody back in Atlanta."

His reaction to that was swift and fierce. He started to open his mouth in protest, his brows pulling down in anger, but she held up her hand.

"I have always assumed that you don't have some other girl-friend. Probably not even someone who might think she's your girlfriend even if you don't. If I had thought you might do that, I wouldn't be here. But, the fact of the matter is that I didn't ask, and if you do have someone, it's kind of my own fault."

"I don't, Bailey Ann. You know me better than that."

"That's just it," she said. "I do know you better. That's exactly why I didn't ask. It never occurred to me you would do something like that."

"Well, that's good, at least."

It seemed, then, to occur to him. "Did you leave somebody behind in Nashville?"

She shook her head with a self-deprecating laugh. "I've been single for a while. I liked my job. It was fun, and I had my friends. But my friends were getting married or having babies, and they didn't have much time for their single friends anymore. It felt awkward. I wasn't *doing* anything, just showing up and clocking my time. So when Daddy got really sick, I looked around Nashville and realized I could just leave. I wasn't convinced I would miss it that much."

"Do you?"

She shook her head. "I was thinking I could just put my resume out, get a job anywhere and move away to wherever I land once the house is ready."

This time, his voice was softer. "Is that what you want?"

Bailey Ann just shrugged at him. "Finn, I don't know what I want."

39

Bailey told Nana Rue exactly that the next day. "Nana Rue, I don't know what I want. I don't know what I want to do. I really thought I had my whole life planned out and it simply didn't happen that way. Now, I have to stop and make some new decisions."

She paused for a moment, and Nana Rue just smiled at her in that way she did.

Bailey Ann looked up from the salad they were sharing and said, "Nana Rue, what do I do? What do I do next? Do I put my resume out there and find a job and move away? I can sell the house when Lennon leaves." But she thought about keeping it.

Nana Rue laughed. "Sounds like you just painted it too many different colors to sell it."

"I can paint it white." Bailey Ann said. Lord knew, she'd become a good enough house painter over the past handful of days—and under the expert tutelage of Finn. It was a skill she'd never expected to acquire, but there it was.

"No," Nana Rue said, "Don't you undo all that good work. You picked it all yourself, you love it. If you sell, you sell it to someone who loves it as much as you do. I, for one, would love to have you stay here, but I can't be the reason you do that."

That was exactly the problem, Bailey Ann thought. She needed a reason to stay or to go and it needed to not be someone else. It needed to come from within her. For the first time she wondered if there were any jobs available in town for her. She'd never even considered it before.

She'd gotten that first job out of college, then she'd transferred to the second company and the third, and gotten herself raises, simply because the opportunity had presented itself. Not because she was intending to climb any career ladder. She had believed—as her mama had—that she would go to college and get her MRS degree. She was supposed to have a minivan, a white picket fence, and two car seats long before now, and it simply hadn't happened. She said as much to Nana Rue.

Nana Rue laughed at her. "Honey, you are the most ridiculous thing I have ever seen."

Bailey Ann wasn't certain she liked this new Nana Rue—interacting with her as though she was an adult.

"Do go on," she told her grandmother trying to sound wry rather than wounded.

"You had it. You had all that and more. Twice that I know of and maybe a few more times I don't know about. You had an offer on the table for exactly everything you wanted. You could've married that Todd Hooker right at graduation. Everybody knew you two were dating, and I heard from his grandmother that he bought you a very nice ring. Now, maybe you thought it was ugly, or maybe you thought something else, but whatever that was, if that made you turn down that proposal . . ."

Bailey Ann laughed. "His last name was Hooker, Nana Rue, and he was not willing to change it. He seemed to think I should become Bailey Ann Hooker."

Nana Rue laughed, too. "Well, whether it was that or the shape or the color of that silly rock, or the way he snored, you sure found something wrong, didn't you?"

That made Bailey Ann stop again. She did not like this. When she lived in Nashville she'd gone about her days, happily unaware of all these things in her life. She couldn't know what she now understood—not about Aunt Gigi and Lennon, not about her mama—and still go back to being that clueless woman. She had to go forward. She just had no idea where forward was.

Nana Rue kept poking at her, "You also had that nice Ray Haley boy. He was a sweetheart. He'd have built you a picket fence for no reason other than to say he'd given you one. He would have gotten you a minivan and the car seats. He'd have gotten you five or six car seats, if that's what you wanted. That man thought you walked on water."

Bailey Ann thought about that one too for a moment. All that was true, but that had been part of the problem. He had been so head over heels for her that she had no idea who he was really in love with. It couldn't have been any real woman. Then she'd made it all the way to the proposal again before she high-tailed it out of that relationship. She was looking like a runaway fiancé.

She'd thought she'd find the right guy and leave her job when she had kids. She thought she'd stay home, run them to ballet and soccer, have at least one boy and one girl. Mama and Daddy had had three girls and she thought that would be okay, too. Harper Rose had managed to pull it off.

She hadn't realized she'd said that last one out loud until Nana Rue commented, "And look what Harper Rose got for all that. Not to be too blunt, but Harper Rose has three tiny children and the only thing she's got in her favor is a big steaming basket of shit."

Bailey Ann had to laugh. Nana Rue had always been the proper Southern lady the whole time she had been growing up, but apparently adulthood had its privileges and detriments, and one of them was Nana Rue's straight talk.

"Sadly, that's true," Bailey Ann said, "I'm trying to help out and find some money as much as I can. Selling the house would help."

"No, it won't," Nana Rue said. "I don't know what you know

about your sister's situation, but I know this: you can sell that house and give her *all* the money from it, and it still will not cover the big old behemoth of a monster they've been living in."

Bailey Ann hadn't thought of it that way. She'd thought about giving Harper Rose some money, getting her out from under the crippling debt she'd been left with, at least starting to fill the hole. But Nana was right. If it wasn't decided that the San Francisco house outright belonged to Harper Rose—and even her sister had said that wasn't likely to happen—then there was no way she could afford to stay where she was with the kids.

Nana Rue jumped into her thoughts, "Your sister hasn't held a job in ten years. If she's lucky, she can get a secretarial position. Still, that's not going to cover daycare for her girls. Chances are, at the end of this she has no assets. It's possible they will sell off that house and give her something out of the goodness of their hearts, but she's going to have to play that widow card hard and keep everything else close to the chest in order to make that happen."

Bailey Ann got more serious. There really wasn't a place for Harper Rose. Her middle sister was holding out and holding on, making sure what was left of her family got to stay in that house until the case closed, but the case was going to close. Since the house had been owned by a company associated with her husband's banking, not anything in their own names, Bailey Ann knew how it would ultimately go. She'd worked finance long enough to understand when the law came down on that, they weren't going to give her sister any money they didn't have to, and they didn't have to give her a penny.

"Maybe it's better to give Harper Rose the house," she said out loud. It was the first time she'd thought it.

Harper Rose didn't want to move the girls. She liked the school they were in, but if she couldn't find something that covered daycare for the two littlest ones and put food on the table and paid their rent . . . and right there, Bailey Ann was tapping out. She loved her sister. Her sister had gone to college and gotten her MRS degree. But her real degree? She hadn't worked with it a day in her life. There was no telling what she might be able to get now, not when there were so many other women on the market who'd done the same thing. But while Bailey Ann was grateful not to be in that position—she earned good money and she could take care of herself—she still found herself wishing for the minivan, the car seats, and the picket fence.

"Do I give up on it, Nana Rue?"

"Why are you so clueless sometimes, child?"

Bailey Ann felt her eyes go wide.

"You've got that Malloy boy, and I know you've turned him down, and that's your own fault. You think long and hard about why Todd Hooker and Ray Haley weren't good enough for you. Maybe you've always known what you wanted, and you just didn't know how to go about making it okay. But I'm telling you right now, it's beyond okay to get what you really want, child."

Bailey Ann felt the anger flare in her chest. "You make it sound like I'm some kind of racist bigot, and that's not what it is. Finn and I don't work! We're in different places in our lives. Torrid love affairs don't last; I've read the psychology on it, Nana Rue. Maybe *you* don't know."

She sat still for a moment. Bailey could not believe she'd just spoken to her grandmother like that. She was waiting for the rebuke. For her Mama to come back from heaven just to slap her silly. But it didn't happen. Nana Rue took as good as she gave, and she came back with more.

"You be quiet. Don't tell me that I don't know what it's like to sneak out your window to meet the boy you love. I married him, and we lasted a good long time. Whether or not you last has nothing to do with how bright and hot you burn, it has to do with how well you love each other. And to be honest, Bailey Ann, I see him doing a good job towards you, and I don't see you doing that good of a job toward him."

She'd gone home from that lunch, barely managing to hold

herself together. She'd done it all the way back from the restaurant to dropping Nana Rue off at cluster F. Today, the name of the unit didn't make her laugh. She'd started shedding tears as soon as she faked a smile and watched her grandmother go through her front door safely. Bailey had driven straight home, crawled into bed, and cried herself to sleep. Apparently, it was "tell Bailey Ann how she was fucking up her own life" day. Nope, the whole week. The *month*.

She didn't want to make a mistake. She'd told Ray Haley *no* because she knew it would be good between them for a while, but she wouldn't change her name to Bailey Ann Haley. She also knew that they'd be bored to tears with each other very quickly. Then they'd be stuck with kids. She wouldn't be able to move to take a new job, and he wouldn't either because they'd have to stay near the kids. Todd Hooker had had the same problem. Her issues with her and Finn didn't have anything to do with Finn. They had everything to do with her and just how scared she was of picking the wrong guy.

❧ 40 ❧

S he didn't see Finn for two days after that. Every time he texted or called, she returned the message or she talked to him, but if he invited her anywhere, she'd shrug him off.

She should've been helping him lay his flooring. They'd put it off to lay hers and hers was fully installed now. It looked amazing. Her walls in the kitchen were painted all the way straight through into the dining room with blue wainscoting and a creamy pale color on top.

She only had to paint the trim herself and she immersed herself in the details, taking a tiny brush and a piece of cardboard to block the edges out. She put her face in close, breathed the paint fumes, watched what she was doing, and tried not to think that she was painting *her own house*. She tried hard not to think about how she was putting Finn off for several days when Lennon's entry into her life was so close. They were about to lose their chances to hang out together or at least to do it the way they had been.

As she did the meticulous work, Bailey thought long and hard about what Nana Rue had said. She quickly got over the idea that everyone was trying to "beat up on Bailey," because she couldn't imagine that Aunt Gigi or Nana Rue would actually be *mean* to her. In the end, that just made things harder because it meant they must be right.

Her big problem was Finn. If she threw herself in, and things blew up, she would hate herself. She couldn't do that to Finn. Ultimately, he wasn't really offering anything anyway. He might have come up to her on the street asking her when she was going to marry him, but it was probably just a joke. He'd asked her that same thing so many different ways, so many different times over the years. Even after they'd broken up, he'd greeted her with those same words more than once. Each time she'd easily brushed it off and now she had no idea whether he was really asking her or just kidding around. She didn't want to ask him either. If he said it was a joke, it would hurt. It would pinch way too tight in her heart. She wasn't sure she'd survive. She knew this because she'd always leaned on the idea that somewhere out there, Finn Malloy still loved her.

If he was serious, then she'd have to tell him that she was scared, that she thought they would burn out and things would fall apart. The last thing that she ever wanted in this world was to hate Finn Malloy. After all her long and hard thinking and painting around the dining room, she hit the end of the chair rail and realized she had to do the base boards. So she got down on her hands and knees and her thinking, along with the muscle tension in her back, became even more pronounced and painful.

She probably had been her mother's favorite, but it wasn't because of anything that she did herself. It was because she had tried so hard to be just like her Mama, and who wouldn't love someone looking up to you like that? Bailey Ann had been the *easy* child. Her mama had said so on multiple occasions and Bailey had always basked in the idea. But if it was her own children, she couldn't imagine loving one child more than another, easy or not. So her Mama surely hadn't loved her more. Maybe *liked* her a little better but even so, it turned out that wasn't something she should be so proud of.

Nana Rue had called her on it, told her to stop trying so hard to become her Mama, maybe figure out who *she* was. But Bailey Ann knew who she was would marry the wrong man and get divorced. Mama never would have. If her marriage had been bad, Mama would have stayed anyway, and Bailey Ann held on tight to that as the first solid difference between her and her mother.

She was so scared of getting married. If she screwed it up, she'd wind up divorced. What she didn't know was why she was so afraid of that. Maybe it was because her best friend in elementary school had been dragged through her parents' ugly divorce when the girls had been in fourth grade. The Mundys split had been terrifying. There had been custody battles, court cases and Allison's stark fear that if she didn't play her part right, she would lose one or both parents. Allison hadn't been able to tell her mom or her dad how she felt because each demanded that she feel one thing or another about the other parent. Eventually, Allison's mother had loaded up the old station wagon and taken Allison out of state, crying the whole way.

Bailey Ann hadn't ever seen her again. She's been ten years old. Old enough to understand what was going on and old enough to understand that kids were too young to have any say in it. There was nothing Allison could do about her parents and nothing Bailey could do to save her friend. Since then, she'd seen other friends have parents that got divorced and she'd seen it turn ugly in a heartbeat. Maybe that's why she was afraid.

It wasn't anything she could chalk up to her own upbringing, that was certain. Her parents would never have separated and Bailey had always been secure in that comfort for herself. But as she stood up and worked the kinks out of her back for a moment, she took stock. As she looked at the house a little more closely and sifted through her memories, she realized her parents had set it up so that they simply *couldn't* split. Neither of them could survive without the other. Divorce wasn't an option, not because of any social norm but because they simply had divvied everything up so tightly that either of them surviving alone would have been impossible.

On top of that, what would they have even fought about? They never shared decisions. Bailey hadn't really imagined it for herself because she'd imagined a life like her mother's. She would be the one taking care of the children. She would decide what sports or classes they did and how the family spent the money. That might have even been why she'd gone into finance in college. She wanted to be sure she did a good job as a wife and mother.

Maybe she'd wanted her mother's life, but as she finally imagined herself really in it, she found it petrifying. So all her visions of marriage had been so horrifyingly cloying that she'd had to turn them down. It was beyond scary to think that Finn's proposal had been real. How would a marriage between them even work? If you learned how to be married from your parents, then she had a good idea of what she had learned. She wasn't completely up to speed on what Finn might have learned from his parents though. She'd seen nothing of value in the time she'd spent at his house as a teenager. Sure, she hadn't been looking, but even stopping and trying to find some memory, Bailey came up short.

His mother was always cleaning the house. She did the chores. She worked a lower paying job than her husband and she ran the kids around when she could. A lot of times Finn and Sioban had been on their own though. But she had no memories of either him, his sister, or his parents saying anything about the quality of their marriage, but why would they? It wasn't the kind of thing you talked about in front of the girl your son had been dating for the past two years.

In the end, Bailey Ann had no idea what Finn might expect from a marriage. Other than the fact that his parents had never really shown each other any affection in public—nothing she'd seen, nothing she'd ever heard about, nothing she could detect. She wasn't even sure if his parents liked each other. If those two disparate ideas where what she and Finn had to build on, it was a disaster in the making.

So she crawled back onto the floor and got her nose back to the grindstone, kept her painting clean, and hoped Finn would be proud of her when he saw it. That was the moment she admitted that he would see it. Soon.

She had to figure her crap out right away. Lennon was coming in three more days and that alone was going to change things. So when Bailey finished the base boards and her knees were aching, her back pinching, and her forehead sweating, she called Finn.

She should have showered first because his voice came across the line like warm honey and he said, "It's so good to hear from you. What are you up to?"

He'd invited her right over and she'd had to say no. There was no way she was going over there like this, even though he told her he didn't mind. First, she climbed in the shower, soaped up, scrubbed her hair and let the heat from the water sink into her tired skin for a little bit. Then she headed over to Finn Malloy's house with hopes that she could let everything play out and see where this was headed.

❧ 41 ☙

Finn was working in the hallway, measuring for a chair rail when he heard Bailey Ann on the back deck. Though he was tempted to get up and get the door, it was nice to have her just let herself in. He hoped she understood she belonged here— or at least that he wanted her to.

He smiled as he listened to her reach into the fridge and grab one of the bottled waters he'd put there for her. He'd bought the brand he'd seen her drinking, hoping she'd show up, and then he'd have what she liked. When at last he heard her feet behind him on the carpet he looked up. Then blinked. "Something is different. What is it?"

Nodding a little, Bailey Ann bit at her lower lip but then shook her head no. She wasn't going to tell him. *Hmmmm.* He set down the long-handled scraper he was using on the subflooring and turned fully around to face her.

"Tell me, Bailey Ann," he coaxed, but still, she shook her head.

"It's something good," she told him with a nod. "Something I decided that I hope will play out well."

Now terribly curious, he pushed, "Does it involve me?"

All she could say was, "I'm not telling you this, because if I say anything else, I'll spill everything and it's too new. I'll just say that I'm hopeful." With that, she nodded and deftly changed the subject, sweetly asking him what he was doing.

Despite his now raging need to know, he leaned over and picked up the spackle and skimmed a spot. He needed it smoothed out before he hung the new chair rail. That dent had been there the entire time the Malloy family had owned the house. It seemed strange to be removing things that gave the place its character, but nobody seemed to want to buy anyone else's leftover "character," so he smoothed it right out.

Aiming for casual, he asked again, "So, are you staying? Are you going to live in the house that you painted for yourself and the master bedroom that you designed?"

"I haven't decided yet. I'm definitely going to stay until the house is put together. Lennon will be here in a few days. I'll have a roommate for a while and that will be interesting for me. I haven't had a roommate in a decade at least."

He nodded at each point she made but was calculating how long he had to win her over. How many days before her decisions became final?

"I painted all the trim in the kitchen and dining room area," she told him proudly and he looked up at her.

"You're better at that than the walls?" He shouldn't have said that, but was relieved when she grinned and narrowed her eyes.

"Hey! I'm better at the walls now and I'm better at the trim than I was when I started the walls. You should come over and look and you can tell me what I did wrong," she offered.

"I'll definitely have to inspect it," he replied over his shoulder, though he, too, was laughing. She was still wanting to meet up with him, work with him, spend time with him at least. So, he put the scraper down and left the spot to cure. "That has to stay for a while to set. No touching."

"Okay, what's next?" she asked, sipping from the water bottle again.

"A shower for me. Dinner for us," he said, pausing just a

moment as if waiting for her to refuse but she didn't. When she nodded in full agreement, he smiled.

"Movie?" He pressed his luck.

"Absolutely. Your choice. I don't even know what I want to watch. You decide," she said. She stayed at his house that night and they spent the whole next day together, laying the flooring in his place.

As she handed him board after board, he thought about the discrepancies between their houses again. His was dull. Her flooring was a beautiful, dark hardwood. She loved it, and he was hoping more and more she'd bought it to *live* with it. His was decided by budget. For once he wanted something that was his to show her. None of this did. He didn't say any of this as she sat back on her knees while he hunched over tapping the wood into place and laying the glue. But he did ask, "Can I ask a favor of you?"

"Of course."

"I haven't looked at the housing market lately. I was curious if you could work up a projection for me. How much I've put into the house, how much we think we can get now versus any other upgrades that need to be done. I need to know what's left, what's my best return?"

It wasn't a hard task. Bailey seemed to be thinking it through as she sat there and handed the pre-cut wood planks to him. She'd have to look it up, certainly, but she said, "You've already painted the bathrooms. If you're going to do much more upgrading there, we should have done it first."

"I know," he said. "I didn't think about the order—or I did, but it didn't include more."

"Where else could you do upgrades, if they would help?"

He was getting carpet installed upstairs. He was putting in the wood flooring down here. The walls were painted. "The kitchen is the big point," he said. "I haven't really done much with it . . ."

She probably already understood that kitchens were selling

points. Kitchens and baths, but he was done upgrading those. So he listened as she took stock. "You replaced the countertop but not the stove," she said. "Or the fridge or microwave. The problem is, if you're going to do it, you need to install everything and it all needs to match. That's not something that pays off if you just do part of it."

"I know. I thought about just hauling the fridge out to the dump and telling whoever moves in to bring their own. That's an option." He set the handheld trowel he was applying the glue with off to the side of the floor after wiping the blade and throwing the paper towel into the trash. "Can you work it up for me? Let me know if it's worth it?"

"I can do that."

When she handed him the next board, she also handed him an apology. "Finn, I'm sorry I wasn't around the past couple days. You helped me lay my own flooring and I'm hardly being much help to you now. I should have been here. I owe you for the work."

That was the only thing that interrupted his rhythm. "No, Bailey Ann, you don't owe me anything. I'm surprised you don't know that yet."

"We agreed, Finn, that we are going to help each other work on each other's houses."

"And we have. We never said we were going dollar for dollar or hour for hour. I don't keep track. I figured, if you weren't here, you had something important to do."

She paused at that and he wondered now just what she'd been up to. Her words were low-toned. "I just meant that I feel like I owe you more work than I've given you."

He'd stopped working then and sat back to look at her. "But you don't. You can walk out right now, and you won't owe me anything. In fact, if you never show up again, I'll still show up to help you because we still need to do something with those ugly baseboards and that quarter-round trim in the living room."

She laughed at him. The last time he had been over and

inspecting their progress, he had insisted on replacing it. Bailey said she could just paint it, but he'd pointed out that somehow, in all the furniture movement over the years—because her mom liked to keep rearranging that ugly, booger-green furniture in the living room—the family had managed to ding up the baseboards pretty badly. Flat out replacing them would be the easiest.

She'd simply nodded at him and that seemed to be the end of the conversation. He wished it wasn't. He wished he could tell her he was doing what he did because of how he felt, not because he was getting paid back. But her silence told him it wasn't the time for that. So they'd worked together in a rhythm too in sync for him to ignore and he wished she was truly his.

She stayed over at his house that night. The next night, when she tried to stay over again, Finn took a stand and flat out told her, "No."

"What do you mean no?"

Clearly, he'd surprised her.

Finn waited until he caught her gaze and tilted his head at her troubled look. "I'm going to pack a bag. I would like to stay over in that beautiful, bright, new master bedroom you created—"

"*We* created," she corrected him, but it made his smile shoot straight through him.

"Because we aren't going to be able to stay there once Lennon is moved in. You'll have to stay over here with me and my place is dull. New, but dull."

Despite her correction of "we," she protested then. "Finn, we can't stay over at all once Lennon gets here."

He felt his eyebrows jump sky high. "Because your college-aged cousin will know that you're having a relationship with a consenting adult male?"

"It's not proper. We're only getting away with this because nobody is looking."

"Trust me, honey, Mrs. Miller asked me the other day if I was headed to your house again."

He watched the flush climb her cheeks and her hands held onto her face as though she could contain it.

Finn laughed. "Mrs. Miller is ninety-five if she's a day. She has five kids. She seriously knows what's going on, Bailey Ann. She's probably done more than we'll ever see."

He watched as Bailey Ann laughed through her embarrassment and finally said, "Yes."

❦ 42 ❦

Bailey Ann woke up in Finn's arms in her brightly colored bedroom where the paint smell had finally faded. It felt more like her own real home every day.

Though they hadn't replaced the baseboards in the living room yet, they picked out the ones she wanted. She had them set up on sawhorses under the carport so she could paint them before Finn started cutting and sanding.

They discussed how to make the house functional and comfortable, both for herself and Lennon and then later for a family. She spoke in terms of Harper Rose and the three little girls, but she also kept saying "a family," wanting the idea to be more generic in case Harper Rose and her little girls never materialized here. In case it was her own children who lived here someday.

Finn talked animatedly about the possibilities with her and if he'd caught on to her vagueness, he didn't let her know. She rolled over in bed and kissed him awake. He answered in kind, until the two of them were doing more than just kissing and she screamed his name in that bed one last time.

"We won't be able to do this again," he pointed out when they finally caught their breath.

"Well, we can still do *this*, right?" she laughed at him. She'd been the one pulling the throttle before.

"Not in this bed!" He smiled. "Not if you scream like that."

Lennon wouldn't have a boyfriend here. She was coming in from out of state and was going to stay and do her research. She would likely be in the bed across the hallway every night. So, he was right.

"Well," Bailey offered, reconsidering her earlier hard-line stance, "if we sleep in long enough so Lennon leaves . . ."

"That would mean that we're staying here while Lennon's here, and sooner or later we're going to think that it's okay, and that we can be quiet." Finn laughed, "You can't be quiet to save your life."

"I would never think such a thing." She smacked him on the arm and got up.

Once again, she didn't take her normal morning shower. But it hadn't been normal since she'd started working on the house. Finn had bought her a slightly less unsexy pair of safety goggles and she carried them with her over to his house, grateful not to be stuck in the seventh grade chem-lab version that he had for her originally.

They laid the last of the flooring into the kitchen, carefully cutting around the wall that jutted out between the kitchen and the dining area, around the cabinets. They made sandwiches for lunch out of food she'd stocked in his refrigerator—the old refrigerator that she'd calculated the value for and decided he couldn't afford to keep. He'd been incredibly grateful when she found him a matching set of kitchen appliances on sale, because it meant his return on the house would be even better for having done the upgrades, but they would have to do the installation once the pieces arrived.

She was now constantly thinking of it in terms of *they, them, we* and *us*. And she liked it. When she got the text that Lennon was an hour away, she kissed him goodbye and headed home. At last, she popped in the shower and as soon as she was out and dressed, she started making brownies. They wouldn't be ready by the time Lennon arrived, but the whole place would smell of chocolate and they'd probably be good to go by the time her cousin got in and settled.

Sure enough, Lennon pulled up right after Bailey Ann pulled the toothpick out of the middle of the brownies. They were nowhere near done, so she hit the timer for longer, licked the toothpick and chucked it in the trash before heading out to the driveway to greet her cousin.

The Nissan Lennon pulled up in did not look like it was about to fall apart, but it had seen days when it was shinier and newer.

"Bailey Ann!" Lennon popped out of the door, coming forward to hug her cousin with no other fanfare. She grabbed nothing else out of the car and offered only herself and her happy greetings. Bailey Ann hugged her little cousin tight. She always thought of Lennon like Emma Kate, and she thought of Lennon how she wished Emma Kate would turn out.

Though Lennon was a year older than her own little sister, the two had been thick as thieves in high school. Lennon had gotten an academic scholarship and gone straight on to school— on her way to a likely PhD—while Emma Kate, already a year behind her cousin, had taken a gap year and roamed around doing pretty much nothing.

When the two finally quit hugging and squealing and saying how excited they were to see each other, Bailey Ann headed over to the car. It was packed with more suitcases than she would have imagined. Then again, if she was going somewhere for three months, she'd probably pack that much, too.

"All right kiddo, let's get these things into the house."

Lennon had laughed at her. "I'm hardly a *kiddo*. Pretty soon —another six months—and you're going to have to call me Master Mayfair. It's not fair. Everyone calls PhDs 'doctor,' but no one will call you 'master' for getting your MS."

Bailey Ann had laughed. She flashed to an image of Finn

standing by her side and welcoming Lennon into the house, insisting on carrying the heavier pieces of luggage but, in a moment, it was gone and it was just her hauling the big suitcase up the stairs where the wheels it was designed to easily roll on were of absolutely no use.

As she set the bag on the newly laid carpeting, Lennon looked over her shoulder into the room. "Oh my God, Bailey Ann. This is beautiful!"

"Thank you very much." She tried not to comment how'd she managed to do it on a budget or that Finn had helped paint and talked her through what the different kinds and styles of carpet meant. The oven dinged as they got the last suitcase up and Lennon had even said, "Please, tell me those are brownies I smell."

So Bailey went down the stairs to pull them out and left them on the counter to cool, then went back up to help Lennon as much as she could. The job wasn't complete, but they'd done enough, they thought, that Lennon could sleep in the room and be relatively comfortable for the first few nights. She had about four or five days before she had to appear before the city council and let them know she was getting started. Everything else for her thesis research was already in place.

Bailey Ann insisted on dressing up a little bit and heading up the hill to Zeal to go out for a very nice dinner to celebrate.

"Oh, Bailey," Lennon said, "I'm stuck on a school budget. I cannot even afford my half of that meal."

"No, you can't," Bailey Ann smiled, "because I'm covering all of it. I'm not rich. This isn't going to happen all the time, so say *yes* right now while I'm offering."

Laughing, Lennon had readily agreed, and they'd driven up the hill, chattering and catching up for the whole drive. They'd gotten stuck waiting a short while for their table, glad they had brownies for appetizers before they'd left.

When Lennon headed off to use the ladies room, Bailey sat on the waiting couch, looking at her phone and wondering if she should call Finn and check in, when a voice she knew said, "Hello."

"Gabe Zemp!" She'd jumped up and hugged him. She hadn't run into him since returning to town, and she wasn't sure how that had happened.

He'd hugged her back before the two of them took a polite step backward. "I'm sorry I missed your father's funeral, I was out of state."

She nodded at him, not certain if she should say she was sorry she had missed his father's funeral too, but he'd smiled, asked her how things were going. "I heard you're remodeling the house?"

She nodded—because didn't word just travel everywhere in Mayfair faster than the speed of light?

They were chatting about what she'd done and she was carefully editing out Finn, whom he hadn't brought up, when Lennon walked up behind him and froze. Bailey Ann made the wrong move apparently and openly frowned at Lennon. The stark expression on her cousin's face almost scared her. Gabe must've seen it and turned to look.

Though Bailey Ann couldn't see all that passed between the two of them, she watched her cousin turn stiff as a board and heard the coolness in Gabe's normally buttery voice. "Lennon."

Just that one word was clearly too much for him. He turned back to Bailey Ann, his earlier pleasure turned sour and hidden behind a mask of civility, and said, "Ladies, I will leave you on with your evening," and he walked away.

Deflating like a popped balloon, Lennon stalked over and plopped down next to her.

"Holy hell, Lennon, what was that?" Bailey asked.

"Nothing," Lennon said, her voice tight and her lips clenched in a flat line. Normally, Bailey would've thought to press the issue, but there was something about that look that told her there was more to this story than tonight could hold.

They were seated fairly shortly thereafter, and Bailey was

glad they hadn't run into Gabe Zemp again, because apparently there was some old blood there between him and Lennon. Though she admitted to being curious, she didn't push.

The women, now left to themselves, made happy conversation during all of dinner and Bailey Ann managed to put off her question, but later when they were sharing their second dessert of the evening, Bailey Ann lifted her fork and stopped before she got the cake to her mouth. "Lennon? I know I told you that you would have the house to yourself in a few weeks, but what would you think about really having a roommate?"

❧ 43 ❧

Though they paid their check and left, the two continued talking about the fact that Bailey Ann would most likely be staying at the house.

Lennon was excited. "I'm glad. Honestly, I thought I'd be a little bored living by myself. I miss having a roommate." Then she backpedaled a bit, "But I don't want to cramp your style. I can still go and stay with my Mama and Daddy if you need."

"Don't do that, Lennon. You're fine where you are, and I don't have any style to cramp," Bailey Ann added. Then she gave that a second thought. "Well, maybe I do."

She decided it was better to get out in front of things and tell Lennon what was going on between her and Finn, though it probably wouldn't take her cousin more than about five minutes to figure it out for herself.

"You've been seeing Finn again?" The incredulity in Lennon's voice was almost more than Bailey Ann could take.

Why did no one believe that? Or maybe they did. Maybe they believed it a little too easily. And Bailey Ann decided to get out in front of things again. So she asked her cousin, "What do you know about it?"

"Well, I was a kid, but you and Finn were on fire. Then if I recall the rumors, you broke up with him, right?" The way Lennon paused as she said the words made Bailey Ann push a little harder. She asked Lennon to clarify.

"Dumped," Lennon agreed. "The word was that you had dumped him."

Bailey Ann cringed. That was harsh. She hadn't thought of it that way at the time—or honestly, at any time since. She had thought of writing that letter to Finn as a way of making sure they didn't screw things up. She had been polite. She had been as kind as she could, but apparently, word on the street was that she *dumped* him.

She hadn't thrown him over for someone else. Nothing like that. She'd left relatively soon for college, so no one knew that it had taken her at least eight months before she dated again. Now that she thought about it, just thinking through how it had all gone down and wondering which parts of it she should defend to Lennon, she realized something else. It had taken her *eight months* to even date anyone new after she'd been the one to instigate the breakup. That was pretty telling.

"So, are y'all like officially dating?" Lennon asked. The awestruck tone in her voice once again making Bailey Ann wonder what the rumors were about the two of them.

"Well," she said, "We've . . . gone on some dates."

"Oh, it's one of those! Man, you really don't need a roommate."

"It's okay," Bailey replied. "He lives two and a half houses over. It's not like we no longer have a place to go. But, if I'm not home at night—" she cringed. "Don't worry about me."

It was the first time she'd ever said anything like that. When she'd been in college and had roommates, it was mutually understood that both of them would occasionally be staying out sometimes. But here, Lennon was her younger cousin. She'd felt the need to act the adult. It hurt to have to say she'd be breaking the protocols her Mama had set firmly in place, even though she knew it wasn't going to change anything.

She wasn't sure if she even could stay away from Finn Malloy now.

They stayed up into the late hours talking with each other, sitting on the couch—the booger-green couch that now horribly clashed with the colors she'd chosen for the living room. Bailey found she liked this new Lennon. Her cousin had grown up. Like Emma Kate, she'd always thought of her as a kid. She'd been a kid for a long time, even after Bailey Ann had become an adult.

So she found herself thinking through just how much to tell her cousin again. This time, she went for it and threw everything at Lennon's feet.

"Lennon, I am so messed up. I had two different men propose to me, down on one knee with the ring and everything! Because somehow, I managed to get that far into the relationship without realizing that I didn't really love either of them. I should have gotten out long before. I've spent most of my adult life either in a relationship that was over my head, or completely single."

When she was single—like she'd been these past handful of months before she'd come back to Breathless, and even when she was with her Daddy taking care of him—she did virtually nothing. She didn't date. She rarely went online to sign up for dating services. Not until her singledom had gotten so horribly lonely that she decided she needed to reach out. Most of the time, she was comfortable at home. She watched movies. She devoured books. She went to work like a good girl and passed her time.

It was no kind of life to live, she realized. She wasn't getting anywhere. When she wondered how she made it to thirty-four with no husband and no children, she could now easily see that was part of it. She probably spent six of those years not doing anything that moved her life into any direction she wanted.

So she laid out the nebulous ideas she had about where to aim her future and let her cousin help out. Lennon suggested there was a nonprofit nearby that might use her help. In fact, many of the nonprofits had paying positions, something Bailey Ann knew, but hadn't really considered before. Maybe part-time work would be good for a while. Maybe she could put together two part-time jobs and do something that really made a difference.

"I've been in corporate finance for so long. I'm good at it, but I just *do* it. I don't even pay attention to what's happening on the other end of my work." She'd always seen the job as a place-holder until her real life began. What a mistake.

Lennon asked after Harper Rose and the girls. When she didn't ask after Emma Kate, Bailey turned the tables and asked her. "Please tell me she's got a thesis. Tell me you know something I don't."

Lennon then laughed. "She has the start of it, I think. She's working on it. Emma Kate just works at her own speed, and you know that."

Unfortunately, Bailey did. "But she's okay? She's not unhappy?"

"I don't know if she'd tell me if she wasn't." Lennon laughed. "She's fine. She's doing all right, chugging along again, doing it at Emma Kate pace."

Bailey crossed her fingers and hoped it was all true. It seemed Lennon had a better impression of her younger sister's work ethic than she herself did. She prayed that Lennon was the one who was right.

They talked about Lennon's project, and Bailey Ann got more details on exactly what it was Lennon was going to be digging up for her master's thesis.

"I'm petrified about going before the town council," Lennon admitted.

"Why?" Bailey Ann asked completely surprised by the admission of her usually confident cousin. "I thought you already had your ducks in a row on that."

"I do. But I'm afraid they're going to tell me they've pulled my permit. Or they're going to restrict me, so I can't dig certain places. It's just . . . it has literally been a month since I got that paper. And all I can think is they will have sat there, and they will have written out these parameters, and made decisions about what I can and can't do, and it will ruin my thesis."

"Can you get another thesis?" Bailey asked. She wasn't trying to get rid of her cousin, but she wanted her to have a backup plan in case she was right.

"I could, but then I would probably leave Breathless and have to go somewhere else if the thesis changed." Lennon sighed and scrunched up her face. "I could find another topic, another loca-tion, but this is what I *really* want to study. It's right here under our own feet. It's been there all the time. I have funding for ground penetrating radar to find where the bodies are, and someone to operate it."

Bailey Ann had to ask what all that meant, and Lennon explained. She went on, though, about the town council and her concerns. "Some of them are just crotchety old men."

"That's true," Bailey laughed. "I don't know if it helps put your mind at ease, but I can't imagine the council would change your parameters. None of the things you suggested are things they even know about, let alone would analyze and change. *I* didn't even know they were a thing."

Lennon took a deep sigh and thought about it, and then nodded. "That's a good point. They can't stop me if they don't understand what I'm doing, or if they just don't know."

Bailey laughed. Eventually they'd gone to bed, to their sepa-rate rooms and curled up. Bailey climbed under the white eyelet lace comforter by herself and thought about how it felt to be in there all alone. It didn't feel right, that was for sure.

❧ 44 ❧

Your home, even if it is just a small apartment, reflects you. You had better be reasonably neat and have lemonade on hand.

LENNON TOLD BAILEY ANN THAT SHE MADE IT THROUGH HER town council meeting with flying colors. She said she stood up tall and proud and told the council exactly what she would be doing in no uncertain terms. Well, not all of it, but she got her paperwork signed and decided she was going to begin her work the next day.

Though she'd been in and out of the house frequently to have lunch with her Mama or Daddy or to meet up with Nana Rue and see old friends, she'd been around most of the time. Starting the next day, Lennon had gotten up early and put on work boots that Bailey Ann had never seen before. With her hiking clothes on and a hat in hand she headed out the door just after the break of dawn.

In the intervening days, Bailey had made the decision not to reupholster the couches her mother had always loved. She'd wanted to hang on to them for sentimental value, but they weren't the most comfortable pieces of furniture, and while she believed her Mama had possibly done that on purpose so that guests would sit upright and no one would go lounging in her living room with their feet up, Bailey had different ideas of what the room should be and how it should be used.

She remembered she and her sisters had found it to be unwelcoming. Bailey wanted a room that was as comfortable for reading as it was nice enough for greeting guests. So, she bit the bullet and spent some money and bought a new comfy, squishy couch and the armchairs that went with it. She splurged for the ottoman and a matching end table set.

Finn had gone along to help her pick them out, laughing at her choice of the most expensive set in the store. "That's a bit of a budget buster, don't you think?"

"It is." She couldn't help being smug.

He'd smiled back at her. "You really are staying."

"I think I might be." True to her decision not to stay over at her house with Finn, with Lennon in the room next door, she spent the night at his place about every other night. They ordered his kitchen appliances, and when they arrived a handful of days later, she did her best to help with some manual labor.

While she handled the microwave excellently, the stove and the dishwasher proved too heavy for her skills. But each time they fixed something, Finn stood back and admired the work and her stomach twisted a little tighter. It took four days to figure out why.

The following night when she'd stayed over with Finn, she'd curled up naked next to him after he'd made love to her until she screamed his name. Again, pointing out why they couldn't stay at her place, but she'd gotten quiet and he'd noticed. "Bailey Ann, tell me what's going on in that brain of yours."

She didn't know how to say it and it took a while to work out the words, even though in the end, they were pretty simple. "You're getting close to finishing the house, aren't you?"

"I am." That was all he said.

She'd wanted him to offer something more. Undying love?

She didn't know if she could handle that. But he'd only said he was getting close to finishing and it made her stomach twist even more.

So she pushed forward, "You really only have the outside left to do. There's some landscaping, and you said you were going to paint it."

He'd had the new windows installed first and the outside still looked pretty rugged, without painters having come to repair and cover all the pieces that had been rearranged. He'd had a landscape artist looking at the front and back yards. Bailey Ann had been there for all of it; she'd helped him find the guy and was considering him for her own place.

She wanted to keep going the way she was but she wasn't sure she could, and that was the problem. She wanted to find herself and she wanted to move forward, but Finn was the piece holding both of those things together. So she made herself ask the big question looming over her.

"What are you going to do when you finish the house?" Her voice came out quieter than she intended. She wished she could have sounded bigger, bolder, braver, but she was none of those things.

"I don't know."

She felt her stomach twist more. Then Finn rolled closer to her. He put his hand against the side of her face and gently nudged her to look at him. "What do you want me to do Bailey Ann?"

"I shouldn't get to decide your life," she chided him. Even though she shouldn't, she was trying to let him decide hers. She didn't know how to do it otherwise, even though she told herself that wasn't the way it should be.

"Bailey Ann, you're not going to decide my life . . . I don't think. But I do want to know what you want. It may make a difference." He paused for a minute. "No, it *will* make a difference. If you want me to stay here, that may change things, and if you want me to go, I will leave because I can't be here if you don't want me here."

"I want you here, Finn." She tried to say it, but ultimately, she only barely whispered the words into the space between them, so she tried it again, bolder this time. "I want you here, Finn."

"Do we need to be *here*?" he asked, "In Breathless."

She shrugged. "I don't know. What are you thinking about?"

This time, he rolled onto his back, further away from her. He was looking at the ceiling, one arm thrown over his head, the sheets slung down around his waist, making him into an art piece that she wanted to take the time to admire but couldn't. She was far too nervous about where this conversation might lead and whether or not, in the end, it might break her.

"There's a plantation between here and Atlanta, and the owners are looking to redo it, but probably not until sometime in the next year. I'm considering putting a bid in on it."

Just the tone of his voice made her push up on one elbow. "Finn, you should! That's what you like doing, but why are you hesitating?"

"It would be a bit of a commute, I don't know where I'd live if I don't have this house. It might make more sense to live in Atlanta where there's more work."

She nodded slowly as she took that in.

Finn then rolled up on his elbow to face her again, "Please remember though, what makes sense and what happens can be very different."

"What does that mean?" she asked, again, her voice lower and less clear than she'd intended it to come out.

"It means that if you wanted me here, there are things I can do here if I stay."

"Like what?" Her heart was beating faster though she tried not to show it.

"Well, I discovered I really liked redoing this house. It felt weird because it was my own, and I'm glad I had you on it. Some of the decisions were easier with you along, because it doesn't have the emotional meaning to you that it does to me."

She reached out and put her hand on his arm. "I am not immune to this house, Finn. This place means a lot to me and I have so many memories here. I'll be sad to see it sell. I'll be sad not to walk down the wall behind the two houses."

He smiled at her, seeming grateful that she'd said that.

"Do you have to sell it?" she asked. Maybe he would decide to stay put, too.

But he quickly dashed that idea. "I do. I've been draining my savings to fix it up. I have to pay myself back. I need to pay out Siobhan. She's sitting in a hole of epic proportions as far as her student debt goes."

"Is this going to fix it?" Bailey Ann asked.

"Oh God, no. She's been very clear she'll only take her half, but it will make a reasonable sized difference, enough to change what her payback is. It means she'll actually be earning some money as a surgeon when she gets started."

Bailey Ann nodded. That would make a world of difference, she understood. While she was thinking about his sister who didn't like her too much, he tossed out more bait.

"There are houses in town that I can flip and sell."

"That sounds like a neat idea," Bailey Ann said. "And you're good at it."

"I'm good at *pieces* of it," he said. "That's the problem."

She'd laughed. "How is that a problem? You did a great job here. This place is going to sell for far more than it would have. You'll get all your investment back."

But he shook his head at her, "No, Bailey Ann, I didn't do a great job here by myself. *We* did a great job here."

This time, she was the one who flipped over and laid on her back, putting her arm over her head while she stared at the ceiling and thought long and hard about it. How much effort had she really put in here? When she thought back, it was a decent amount. He didn't need her to help lay flooring, and she said so.

"Actually, I do. You may think you're just being an assistant but having somebody hand you the boards and having it all lined up makes a difference. It's less than half the work when it's a two man job."

She nodded, but his next words struck her, and she wasn't sure if she should laugh, or cry, or scream. "What would you think about getting into this business with me, Bailey Ann?"

❧ 45 ❧

Some people have trouble parallel parking on an empty street. If this person is a real belle, she'll apologize and leave her car crooked.

BAILEY WANTED TO SAY, "YES."

She wanted to yell it to the heavens. She also wanted to ask him where in God's name they were going to get the money to purchase the first house. Was the sale of this house going to be enough? She didn't quite think so. She had some savings to contribute, but she wasn't sure it would be enough. She'd always heard one should flip houses with other people's money—things like credit cards or loans.

She wanted to ask him all the questions suddenly swirling in her head, but she also wanted to say, "Yes." So for the first time in probably her entire adult life, Bailey Ann Mayfair threw caution to the wind and looked at Finn Malloy and said, "Yes, let's do it."

If felt like she was on drugs—if she knew what being on drugs felt like. She was excited, elated, soaring, and a bit petrified. And Finn was laughing at her.

"What are you laughing at?" she asked him.

"You're about to start shaking. The idea of doing this scares you so much, you're about to rattle apart."

"Well, thank you for laughing at that. And no, I'm not scared," she said, even though it was a bald-faced lie, and even though he completely saw through her. So she admitted it. "Okay, I am scared. But I'm also really excited. It sounds like so much fun. It sounds like a good job and a wild adventure."

"It will be. And don't worry, it's okay if we suck at it."

"Is it?" she asked, thinking about winding up owning four houses that no one wanted, or tens of thousands of dollars in lost revenue, or trying to get another job and having to explain in an interview that she'd gone into business for herself and sucked at it.

"Of course, it is. We're smart people. We each have an education. We have homes. We'll be okay."

"You don't have a home," she pointed out. "At least not as soon as this one sells."

"I'll live in it until it does. And actually, I do still have my apartment in Atlanta."

That made her pause and she replied rather quickly, "Atlanta sucks."

She'd lived there, and she didn't mean the city itself sucked. She meant Finn being in Atlanta would suck.

"I'm not intending to move back. I'm just saying, I'm not homeless."

"I thought you would have given up the apartment."

He shook his head as though the reasons almost didn't make sense to him either. "The lease isn't up, and I didn't know how long it would take to get my parents' house ready or if I needed to go back for anything. My leave of absence is indefinite, so I really don't know what that means. But I've got another two months until that lease goes up, so I've been paying it."

That was interesting. She hadn't known he still had a place in Atlanta. It was always surprising to her when she learned something about Finn Malloy that she didn't already know. Because she thought she knew everything.

They spent the next several days rebuilding his back deck and talking to the landscaper. This time, though, when Finn asked her opinion, she stepped in a little bit more forcefully. His house still wasn't her project, but Finn was encouraging her to act as though it were.

They plotted out the best landscaping bang for their buck. A little bit of work would make it look a lot nicer, they decided, and so they went for the lower-end version that the landscape gardener had offered.

Replacing the deck was hot, sweaty work and, as each afternoon wore on, Finn would look over at her and say, "You should go in and shower. I'll finish up here."

The first day, Bailey Ann laughed at him and replied, "Are you just dismissing me? I'm not as useful out here as you are and so I'm getting sent in?"

"Well, kind of. Your skills are not in laying planks on decks. But we need a future projections budget. We need to figure out how much we can spend on the next house, and we need to know what houses are selling for in this district so that we can figure out what to buy. Do we want to buy inside the city limits or outside? What schools is each possible house zoned for and how does that affect the resale value? Yada, yada, yada."

She'd been thinking about that, too, so it was nice to know she wasn't alone. That he hadn't just pitched her a business idea without having thought about it. He did seem to know what he was doing, and truth be told, most days she got her fill of cutting boards on the compound miter saw.

While this was a business she had never expected to get into, she found out it was one she was truly excited about. When she ate dinner with Lennon that night she blurted out, "I'm going into business with Finn."

Lennon had almost dropped her fork. "You are shitting me, Bailey Ann Mayfair."

She'd not expected the swear word from her young cousin and Bailey had laughed outright. All this was very unlike her. Construction work was unlike her. She normally worked at a desk, in a business suit, from nine to five, and then she went home. She collected a very regular salary and lived in a townhouse condo with one bedroom. That was the Bailey Ann Mayfair that everyone knew.

While she hadn't disliked it, looking back now, she couldn't say for certain she had liked it either. This idea certainly had its ups and downs, too. Sawing boards for the deck was clearly not her strong suit nor the thing she liked best, but she really enjoyed the work. She enjoyed that her tasks changed each day. She enjoyed, so far, finding the bargains and making the place look amazing.

It took her most of the meal to convince Lennon that she hadn't been joking and she thought that was the funniest thing ever. When had Bailey Ann Mayfair ever pulled a prank like that on anyone? Emma Kate would have done it, but Bailey? No.

Though she hadn't been in any hurry to get Finn's house done and ready for sale before—and she still wasn't now—she found at least it didn't make her heart pinch each time another project in his place finished. In fact, in her own home, she was ready to put everything back together.

The baseboards had been painted. Finn had crawled on his hands and knees, installing them all the way around the borders of the rooms. It looked gorgeous now and Bailey couldn't have been happier with the results. The house felt both new and familiar, and it was something she found she was sitting in pretty well.

At last, she reclaimed her dining room table. Though she'd managed to clear a few spots at the end, she'd still left the drawers with her grandmother's china and silver all stacked over it. She and Finn had come across a mirror while they'd been out bargain-hunting for his house and Bailey had snatched it up for herself. The wood tone exactly matched the sideboard that had been handed down through her family for generations. She'd been really considering getting rid of the old behemoth, but now she thought if they put the mirror on top . . .

The old, silver-backed mirror had needed work. In the end, it looked perfect and allowed her to keep her great, great, great-something grandmother's family heirloom intact and still look like something Bailey might have in her house. The idea of "Bailey Ann's House" was still something new to her. She was shocked how much she *wasn't* becoming her mother. Even so, parts remained.

"No, Finn," she protested when he questioned her choices. "I think we need twelve place settings of the good china."

"You can't get rid of any of it?" he asked.

"But what if . . . what if you have a dozen guests and need shrimp forks?"

"Bailey Ann, what would you even use shrimp forks for?"

"Shrimp!" she retorted in a tone that said it should be clear to everyone.

He laughed and shook his head. "You're like a prepper, but in reverse. You're prepared for every formal situation that might come up."

She'd smiled and shrugged. It was true, she thought. Couldn't fault the truth.

Again, he laughed at her. "You're so busy being perfect, that you have twelve ice tea spoons and twelve shrimp forks and twelve dessert spoons."

And she looked at him as though *what could possibly be wrong with that?* She even shrugged and said, "And they're mono-grammed."

They were sliding the drawers back into place when it occurred to her that Mayfair and Malloy meant she wouldn't have to change her monogram. For a sliver of a moment, Finn looked at her while she stopped dead from sliding the drawer back in. She was doing it again, thinking about what it would be like to be *Mrs. Bailey Ann Mayfair Malloy.*

✲ 46 ✲

Finn enjoyed standing in the doorway of the house admiring the newly finished back deck, though it was a shame he wouldn't be the one enjoying it. "I wish we could throw a party here and just enjoy it once."

"Is it worth it if it causes any damage?"

"Oh, Lord, no." He polished off the tea he'd made and that she'd insisted sit on the deck while they put the final stain on it.

After painting themselves in through the door, Bailey showed him three properties that looked like promising flips and brought the paperwork to Finn to look over. They wound up discussing how they could get the money together to get the next property paid for. They decided to start with a smaller home out of town. Though it would strap them—taking the remainder of Bailey's savings and Finn's portion from the sale of his house—it would serve them better to buy it outright, according to her projections.

The next day, she told him she'd found four more options beyond the city limits and she'd begun speaking to a real estate agent about getting in to look at them. Finn would be the major voice on what work was needed. Bailey Ann would calculate whether or not the houses would generate a profit. Though they'd discussed working without a real estate agent, Finn was glad that someone Bailey Ann knew from high school was willing to help. When the three of them got a chance to speak on the phone, he was proud that Bailey dove into talks of their business and wanted to know if the real estate agent could cut a deal.

When they hung up, she'd turned to him and surprised him. He was expecting a business analysis, but she said, "You do realize that the news that you and I are looking to buy a home together will be all over town in minutes."

He had not thought about that, but he watched as Bailey Ann tried her best to brush the thoughts aside. So he grinned at her as though he thought it was a great idea.

The first house was twenty minutes out of town and they had taken a break from putting the final touches on his house. They showered off—together—and headed out.

"My God. This place needs more work than anything I've seen," she whispered to him as she walked through the place, her hand tucked in his, until she needed it for notes.

Sherry, the real estate agent, had shown them the house exactly the way that Bailey and Finn wanted. They weren't prospective homeowners, they were business people looking to buy for profit and not comfort. Finn was glad that when Bailey Ann showed up with a spreadsheet and a calculator, Sherry hadn't even batted an eye. Finn tapped at the walls and checked the foundation. He talked opening the space up and modern-izing it, about how far out of town they were. Bailey discussed school districts and together they pondered who they might sell this house to. Large family, small family, couple with no kids? That would help them make decisions about how they would change it and if it would be worth it.

They'd driven home, talking over each other the entire way. Finn even managed to throw in, "I put a bid on the plantation just outside Atlanta."

"Oh wow," she said, "But does that mean you wouldn't flip the houses?"

"It might mean that we would do a small house and then the plantation would be our second house to do. Would you be up for that?"

"I don't know anything about historical buildings. I'm looking at return on investment for people coming in as the buyers. My guess is, you don't need me for that if you're putting it back the way the owners want. They'll decide the budget, not me."

He'd nodded, reached across the console to hold her hand. "I do want you to know that if it doesn't work out for both of us, I won't take it."

Bailey had shaken her head, "Look, if that's what you love, then that's what you need to do. If we flip a house and make a profit, and that's the only one we ever do, I'll be okay with that."

Though she'd said it with some solid conviction behind her words, Finn was still weighing them. Did she mean that? He reminded himself that though she'd thrown her lot in with him businesswise, was she all in for the rest of it? He still didn't know.

As they pulled up to the house and Finn let her off—heading back to his own place to take a shower and maybe meet up—she walked up the front walk, put the key in the lock and waved at him as he pulled out. But Finn didn't quite know if he was solid yet.

Though he'd showered and changed as usual, he'd felt uneasy all afternoon. Was she telling him to go do his own thing because she wanted him to be happy? Or because she wasn't as attached to him as he was to her? He wished he had the answer to that, but he wasn't even sure that she did. So he didn't ask.

Finn headed over and cooked for the three of them that night, glad that the plans had already been made. Lennon came in and showered as he fed rice into the pot and pulled down the big pan for the chicken and shrimp he'd diced.

As Lennon came back down the stairs a few moments later, Bailey said, "You look a sight better."

Lennon had only laughed in response.

Bailey replied again, "I think you've been coming home dirtier each day," to which Lennon had told her, "Well remember, I was grading out the area at first, so I wasn't actually digging in the dirt, just putting stakes in. Now, I've actually got the trowel out and I'm starting to bring the soil up and sift it."

Finn paused, spatula in mid-air, "You're sifting dirt?"

Lennon went over and sniffed at his cooking, nodding her head, "I have to find finger bones and foot bones and they may be really small. I suspect they're a lot further down in the dirt than where I am now, because I haven't found any yet."

Bailey cringed, "Can we please not talk about dead bodies at the dinner table?"

Lennon, once again, had laughed, "I will be very quiet, I'm not sure I have much else to talk about."

Later that night, they'd headed back across the wall, hand in hand. He wondered for the first time how many more trips across this wall there were, and how they would end up. Instead of jumping into each others' arms—which he would have chosen —Bailey Ann stayed awake and worked at his desk, calculating numbers on the first house listing they'd visited and trying to come up with a rating system.

Eventually, he'd decided that he wasn't going to win her over by letting her crunch numbers, and he'd turned off the TV, grabbed her, and pulled her up the stairs to bed. "It's time to stop. You can always do more tomorrow."

She explained the numerical system she was trying to develop, and he'd merely laughed at her. "You know, all that silverware, all those drawers, all your preparations for everything that might come up, I would think you were neurotic, except you're too perfect to be neurotic."

They'd gone to bed and made love and he'd tried to show her what he was feeling, but she didn't shout out that she loved him. Instead, she stared at the ceiling as though she wasn't tired.

Unable to withstand not knowing any longer, he whispered

into the dark, "Bailey Ann Mayfair, when are you going to marry me?"

This time, she grinned and said, "I think maybe we can work on something."

He'd shot bolt upright in bed, his breath catching on the edge of excitement. That was not the answer he'd been expecting. She smiled up at him, serenely having finally said anything close to *yes*. "Wow, a *maybe*. I was thinking I'd get a flat out no again."

"I've upgraded to maybe," she told him, glad her voice held her conviction, even if it was just a maybe.

When he finally let himself down on his elbows, he hovered a little bit over her but looked down at her and asked, "Why *maybe*? Why not *yes*? I need to know what my goals are."

She'd smiled through terrified eyes and that's how he knew it was the truth. "I'm petrified. I'm petrified of failing."

"How would you fail?"

"What if we wind up divorced, Finn?"

"You can live through a divorce," he told her.

"What if you don't really love me?"

He'd almost bust a gut he was laughing so hard, but she pushed on. "What if you just love the idea of me?"

"Bailey," he replied, glad he could answer this one. "I'm *confident* that's not the case. I'm not just in love with the idea of you. I was already married to the idea of you."

47

Bailey didn't know what to say. But she also couldn't figure out what *not* to say. So she said everything and asked every question, pretty much all at once.

"You were *married?* For how long? *Were* married, right? You're divorced now? *Jesus, Finn!* When did this happen?"

Eventually he got tired of listening to her questions without the opportunity to answer and held up his hand. "Did you really not know?"

"No, Finn. I didn't. Apparently, nobody around here is telling me anything. Did you hide her?" Yet another question, and still she hadn't had a single answer.

"I didn't hide her. I mean, I didn't flaunt her. But we came back to visit my parents. We saw people in town. Everybody knew I was married. Seems to me, everybody knew I was divorced, too. By the time I came back solo no one was surprised when they saw me alone. My mother must have told people."

"Did you live in Atlanta?" Bailey asked.

"Yes."

Getting answers to some of the basic questions led her back around to the big one. "What do you mean you married *the idea of me?*"

Finn, in the stance she was coming to know well, flopped back down on the bed, one arm over his head while he stared at the ceiling. It seemed to be his answering-Bailey's-questions position. Or maybe his thinking about things he maybe didn't want to talk about position. "Should I start at the beginning?"

"Sure," Bailey said. But as soon as the word was out of her mouth, she regretted it. Maybe she didn't want to know. Somehow, she'd managed to stay single until thirty-four, and Finn had gone and gotten himself hitched. Worse, Finn Malloy had fallen in love with someone else.

She took a deep breath, except it wasn't deep, it was shallow. And so was the second deep breath she tried. And the third. Pressure pushed to the back of her eyes, and she realized she wanted to cry. She didn't know why. It wasn't as if he was still married, she told herself. But he'd *been married*. Finn Malloy had married someone, and she hadn't known.

So she lifted her eyes to the ceiling too. Thinking that maybe if she wasn't looking at him it would be easier to take. Then she waited for him to speak.

"Her name is Amanda," he said, finally.

Is Amanda, Bailey thought, not *was*. She wondered if he still loved this Amanda.

"And she was everything that you were. Except she wanted to be married to me."

"What are you talking about?" Bailey asked. She'd wanted to be married to Finn for a long time. But after the words were out, she wished she hadn't asked. Surely, Finn was going to tell her.

"I waited for you, you know," he said, still looking at the ceiling.

No, she hadn't known. She always assumed that Finn had gone on with his life. She assumed he loved her the way she'd always loved him. She didn't know that she was always *in love* with him. She didn't think they belonged together. She told herself she'd fallen in love with Todd and then with Ray, but she'd always carried that space in her heart for Finn.

She would have done anything for him, even if she'd married someone else. That's how she loved him, and she thought he loved her the same way. Maybe he did, but he hadn't been *in love* with her. No. He'd taken that and given it to somebody else. To this *Amanda.*

"We met at my first job at the architecture firm. She was in finance. She did not have a finance degree like you, but she had a minor in economics, started as a secretary, worked her way up." He paused, and his voice came close to cracking. "Bailey. I did something so stupid."

Now she was intrigued. She still felt like she was going to cry, but Bailey wondered what Finn could have done that was "so stupid."

"Bailey, she even looked like you. It was awful."

How is that awful? Bailey thought, but out loud she offered a sarcastic, "Thanks."

"She was homecoming queen at her small town high school. After I got to know her a little bit, it seemed she was just like you. She was the inevitable homecoming queen, the princess of her town. Her family had been there for years. Get this: she was captain of her cheerleading squad. Just like you." He didn't say "head cheerleader" the way some of the people in town had, because when they'd been dating, Bailey had always been sure to correct him.

"She went to college on a cheerleading scholarship."

Bailey had not done that. She hadn't been good enough. She'd told herself she hadn't wanted to continue as a cheerleader, that she had a sorority to join. Either way, Finn had gone on and married the idea of her and the idea of her was better than the reality.

"We fit," he said. "Everything about us *fit.* We wanted the same things: a family, a house, a life together, someone to grow old with. And I told myself I loved her. But she left me."

Great. So he did still carry a torch for Amanda, because Amanda had apparently dumped him, too. Although Bailey Ann hated the thought of that word, she still never thought of their breakup as her dumping him, merely as ending something that wasn't going to work. But now, now she thought she was stupid. She'd had something that would work. She was watching it as it worked now. Except *now* he was telling her he'd been in love with *Amanda*.

"She asked me something one day. I don't even remember what it was. Something about her. Did I know it? She asked me about her birthday or her favorite color, something like that. Apparently, she'd been quizzing me for a while, she said. She would pop these little questions once in a blue moon and see what I would say. This last day, she said she realized why I kept getting the answers wrong. It was because I wasn't answering *her* favorite color, and apparently not even *her* birthday. She pointed out I'd answered all her questions with your answers."

"What?" Bailey whispered into the air above her head, up toward the ceiling, as though the ceiling might understand what was so confusing here. She certainly didn't.

"What it is," he said, "is that I never really got over you. Amanda was the one who figured it out. Poor Amanda, stuck married to me, and me not really being there for her, because I was just using her as a replacement. It was terrible of me . . . I don't know what you thought of me or if you ever wished things had gone differently. I know you got a couple of proposals in the interim. I heard you turned them both down."

"What?" Bailey asked again, sounding like a broken record. "You know that?"

"Please, this town grapevine is unreal. I may have been an outsider, but I still heard the gossip."

"How?" she asked. "*I* didn't. Seriously. Something's going on with Lennon and Gabe Zemp. And I have no idea what it is, and Lennon won't tell me. So where's the town grapevine on that one?" For a brief moment, she appreciated the change in topic, the opportunity to think about a problem other than the one looming with Finn.

"Oh, you don't know," he said.

"*Know what?*" Bailey practically shouted.

"Lennon dated Brodie Zemp for a while, and it did not end well."

"Lennon dated Brodie Zemp?"

"Yes."

"Why does no one tell me these things? How can I be here and not know this? I was the homecoming queen! I feel like I should be at the center of this town gossip mill. No," she quickly self-corrected. "That sounds really snotty of me."

He laughed. "It's not snotty. It's true. You are the reigning Princess of Breathless."

"I'm the princess of Breathless?" Her incredulity had to be clear in her tone.

"You are. You were the obvious choice for homecoming queen and you got the crown. You were the obvious choice for prom queen and you got the crown. And even though I was your date, I was not prom king because I was not the obvious choice."

Bailey remembered she'd not expected him to get the crown. She'd been well aware there would be a prom queen and prom king dance and that she would do it with someone else. She had, then she'd returned to her date for the night. Finn had been pleased to be there with the prom queen, but she had always wished it had been him up there with her.

Finn kept talking. "Your last name is Mayfair. The town is in Mayfair County. Your ancestors established it. There has been a Mayfair family here since what? The fourteen hundreds?"

She laughed. That was far too early! The area had not been settled by then. Her great, great, great, whatever, grandfather—and even as she thought about what year it might have been, as she tried to align what she knew of her family history, she realized he was right. She was Breathless royalty.

"I think," he said, "no one tells you these things, because no one wants to tell the Princess of Breathless anything bad."

"Well," she huffed, "they're not telling me *anything*."

"If it's any consolation," he offered, "I don't think they tell Harper Rose either."

"I'm sure they tell Emma Kate," Bailey said wryly.

"I bet they do," he agreed. And though he was laughing, she stayed where she was, still looking at the ceiling, still shaken to her core.

❧ 48 ❧

B ailey lasted two days after Finn's little revelation.
Only it wasn't little. It was massive, and it stood in
her way.

Finn had been married. Finn had gotten divorced.

She asked him, "Do you think it's okay that you got
divorced?"

"I don't dwell on it," he said. "I made a mistake, Amanda did
too. She didn't realize what I was before she married me, and I
apologized."

"Are you still friends?" Bailey had asked.

"Yes."

That was it, all he said. Nothing about if he'd been speaking
to his ex-wife or even still seeing her, and Bailey didn't press the
issue further. She'd thought about it, but then decided she really
didn't want to know.

She pressed a different issue, trying to get at the heart of
what was bugging her. "Do you think it's okay to get married and
just get divorced?"

"Yes and no," he'd shrugged as he stained the last of the
deck. She was supposed to be helping but she ended up standing
there, questioning him and staring at his back as he worked and

offered answers she didn't like. "I mean, it happened. Staying married would not have been the right thing. I wasn't even treating her like herself. That was terrible of me. I thought I was in this relationship and that everything was moving along, but I wasn't even fully participating. And I wasn't letting her either. Was I supposed to stay in that?"

"Well, no," Bailey conceded, "but this idea that it's just okay to get married and get divorced, I don't know what to do with it."

"It's not okay, but it is okay. I mean, I didn't get married thinking I would just sign my way out of it when the end came. That wasn't my goal. I really thought I was getting into it the right way—"

"And that's the problem," she interrupted him. "Everybody thinks they're getting into it the right way. Then you wind up divorced."

"Sure you do, Bailey Ann, but it's not that terrible. I'm okay. I'm still standing. So is Amanda. And so are you. The deal is you've never even tried."

She stiffened and stood stock still as she stared at the back of his head. Is that what he thought of her? That she was so afraid she'd never even tried? Was he right? She didn't know.

Now she was reconsidering if she wanted to stay with a man who thought it was so easy to walk away. What if they didn't work out? Would he just divorce her as well? When she asked him this, he told her *no*. He didn't waver, only said that Amanda had not been the right person, partly because he'd been in love with Bailey since he was sixteen.

She thought about it. She'd been in love with him too, but she hadn't made the mistake of marrying someone else. She hadn't gotten herself divorced. She'd kept her nose clean. She didn't have a picket fence, a minivan, or car seats, but neither did he. And she didn't have a divorce under her belt.

When she'd asked him this point blank, he'd shouted at her.

"Are you serious, Bailey Ann? You're upset with me because

I've been in love with you since the day I met you? I screwed up. I married the wrong person. Should I still be with her instead of here with you?"

There was no answer for that. It was a mess. In fact, it made her think maybe she'd been right when she was eighteen years old. They weren't a good fit. He didn't believe in the things she believed in. She was shaking and nearly in tears, but she didn't know what to say in response, so she told him she was going home, and she left.

She stayed in her house that entire afternoon waiting for Lennon to come home for dinner. However, when Lennon arrived, she immediately asked Bailey what was wrong. Pressing her lips together, Bailey could only shake her head *no*.

Lennon, of course, understood that did not mean nothing was wrong because clearly something was. So Lennon began playing "twenty questions." It had only taken two to figure out that Bailey and Finn had had a fight.

"It's not a fight," Bailey finally said. Still close to shaking, she had come home and cooked up a storm just for something to do. She was both not fit for human company and in desperate need of a friendly ear. Though she didn't like the way she was getting questioned, there was nothing she could do about it. It wasn't as if she could shut Lennon up.

"What do you mean it wasn't a fight?" Lennon asked as they ate their way through everything Bailey had prepared.

"It was a fundamental disagreement," Bailey told her.

"*Fundamental disagreement?* Like, you want kids and he doesn't?"

Bailey shook her head. That hadn't been it.

"You want to get married and he doesn't?"

She shook her head again. She didn't like making Lennon guess, but it was difficult putting everything into words. By the fifth question, when Bailey had shaken her head yet again, she blurted it out. "He thinks it's okay to get divorced. He thinks if he gets married and he doesn't like it, he can just walk away."

"That's not good," Lennon replied, and Bailey was ready to yell, "*Yes!*" and pounce on it, grateful for the validation, but Lennon wasn't giving any.

"How do you know that's what he thinks? Because I don't know many people who actually think that way."

"He told me."

"He *told* you this? He flat out said you can get married on a whim and just get a quickie divorce if you don't like it?"

"Not in those words . . . He got *married*, Lennon."

"Yes, he married that woman down in Atlanta."

"*Good God, Lennon!* Does everybody know these things except me?"

"Apparently," Lennon shrugged. "I didn't realize you didn't know my Mama's stories from Mississippi."

"Nobody tells me anything! Finn seems to think that Harper Rose doesn't hear any gossip either, that we're somehow these Princesses of Breathless and no one wants to tell us anything negative. Well I'm thirty-fucking-four years old and I can handle the real world." Even as she said it though, she wondered if anybody else heard her, if they might laugh. Maybe she couldn't handle it. She'd been so sheltered for so long that all the real world had come at her as a big shock.

Mama and Daddy had stood sentry, despite the fact that she moved away, even out of state, and only now that they were gone was anyone telling her anything. Maybe she just gave off that vibe of "princess in need of protection," and everyone had hopped on the bandwagon.

She noticed Lennon didn't correct her and she finished her dinner in relative silence.

Over the next two days, Bailey tried to get things back to normal with Finn. She went over and worked with him, but for the first time, the conversation was halting and stilted.

He finally gave up and threw down a board he'd been hauling out of the house and demanded, "What do you want me to say? Do you want me to lie and say I'd never gotten married? Then I could lie again to say I'd never gotten divorced. But I never lied to you, Bailey Ann."

She shook her head and thought, *I want you to be who I thought you were.* And that was a terrible thing to think. She knew it, but it didn't make her not think it.

"Because here's the thing," he told her, standing in his kitchen, the last pieces of the house finally in place. He looked at her hard and said, "If I hadn't married Amanda, I wouldn't have realized that what I wanted was you. So you should tell her *thank you.* She's the one who figured it out. Not me. If anything got me back here and got us together, it was her."

Bailey clenched her fists and stood so rigid, she almost shook. *Really?* She should thank his ex-wife?

"Maybe you shouldn't have come back," she said. That had been the final blow.

The house was clean. The work was done. And she was finished. She'd walked away, angry. Angry that no one had told her these things. Angry that she spent all this time trying to be a woman who didn't exist. Even her mother had never been the woman that Bailey saw. Aunt Gigi and Nana Rue had taken care of any illusion she might have clung to on that count. And her goal of trying to be like Mama? Well, look how it had worked out. It left her standing here, madly in love with the Finn Malloy that she wanted to exist and not the man who really did.

Here she was thirty-four years old and really in love for the first time. Only she'd just discovered she was in love with someone that could never be.

She'd walked out of the house, climbed onto the wall separating the back yards between the houses, and for the first time, it was not fun. It was hard to walk along the top, even though she now knew where each crumbling rock was and each place her ankle might slip or the rock under her foot might twist or give a little. But it was hard to see for the tears forming in her eyes.

By the time she got to her own back yard, she wanted to run.

So she bolted across the grass, up to the back door, and threw it open.

Two days later, she hadn't spoken to him and he hadn't reached out to her either. That's when the sign appeared in Finn's front yard.

For Sale.

❧ 49 ❧

It was another two nights of just Bailey and Lennon eating dinner at the formal dining table before Lennon noticed that the For Sale sign was up at Finn's.

"Bailey, did y'all finish with his house?"

"Yes." The word hit like a dull thud in her chest. She thought about that being sufficient as her only reply, but this was Lennon. They'd become closer since Lennon had moved in. And Bailey needed a friend right now, so she told what had happened. At least a little of it. "We finished it two days before the sign went up. And the sign's been up for two days already."

"Wow. I missed it. I only came back that way tonight because I was dropping off some additional paperwork with the town council." She said it somewhat cheerfully, the words rambling. But her voice trailed off as she caught sight of Bailey's face. "I know you two haven't been talking. What happened, Bailey?"

"I don't know. We were talking, and he dropped this huge bombshell. I tried my best to ignore it, but I couldn't. Then we had a disagreement and we haven't talked since."

"You had another disagreement and haven't spoken at all?" Lennon looked incredulous.

Bailey shrugged. "He was mad. I was mad."

"But it's been . . . four days!" Lennon wasn't eating, and Bailey had gone to a lot of trouble to cook it.

She kept eating the food herself and, while mentally she knew it tasted great, she wasn't able to enjoy it. Her cousin's next question wasn't helping.

"You have lost your mind, Bailey Ann! Or," she frowned now, "you're seriously afraid of something. What is it?"

"I don't know. What was I afraid of?" Bailey asked as though Lennon might be able to answer it. But she could answer it, and that was the problem. It was the thing she'd always been afraid of, hanging in the air, waiting for answers. Only, there were no answers.

There was nothing she could fix. Finn hadn't called her. The next day, she'd finally given in and gone over and climbed the back steps. She told herself she was just checking the house to see if he was home, to see how much he was asking for it. To see anything. Just some contact with him—even for something mundane—would have been welcome.

She traipsed the back yard and climbed the brand new deck stairs and found only a doorknob that refused to give. Since she'd come across the wall, she was left heading back down the deck steps and walking around the side to the front. She headed toward the front door, despite the fact that she looked like a burglar. Raising her hand to knock, she wondered if Finn had locked this too. But even before she managed to rap her knuckles on the door, she saw the realtor's lockbox hanging on the front.

It was for showing the house, and Bailey knew right then that Finn didn't live there anymore. So at dinner that night, when Lennon asked, Bailey held it together for all of two sentences before she burst into tears. "Lennon, he's gone."

"Do you know where he went?" Bailey shook her head.

She didn't know. He hadn't told her. Then, she nodded as it dawned on her. "He has an apartment in Atlanta still."

"Then drive down and find him, or at least text him. What is wrong with you?"

Bailey pulled back as if slapped. "What do you mean *what's wrong with me?* I told you what he said."

"Yeah, and you're crazy if you let what you two had just vanish into the air."

"I'm not crazy. I want something real. I want something that lasts. And I want it with someone who will fight for it."

Lennon only stared at her. "Girl, if you think he's not the right man for that, then don't follow him. Don't give him anything else to pin his hopes on. I remember when the two of you were dating. I mean—Em and I—we were just kids, but we thought you guys were the coolest couple in all of school."

"That doesn't mean anything, Lennon," Bailey protested. "We were in high school. We were a couple of kids and we were crazy about each other. That's all."

"That doesn't make it less real," Lennon said. "I may have been nine then, but I'm not nine anymore. I saw you two together these last few weeks, and I know what I saw."

"It doesn't change what he said," Bailey protested.

"It doesn't. You're absolutely right. But," Lennon told her, "if that's how you feel, if you're willing to let a guy like that go over something like that, then do it! Let it go. Let him finally, maybe get over you."

Bailey didn't think that was necessarily the issue, and it bothered the crap out of her that her younger cousin seemed to be so much saner than she was. Then again, Bailey was the one who'd been sleeping with Finn. Bailey was the one who'd thrown caution to the wind and decided that she could go into business with a man she was sleeping with. That she could let Finn Malloy change her life this time, when they hadn't been able to figure out how to do it last time. This round, they'd been together for six weeks. Last time it had been almost four years and it still hadn't worked out.

So she had gone to bed that night by herself in the wonderful, bright blue and peachy-orange room that she so loved. She wondered if she still loved it, or had she only ever loved it because Finn had helped her create it. She didn't know the answer to that question either. Though, when she woke up the next morning, the bright colors made her feel better, but everything else made her feel worse.

Everything in her whole life now hung in the air without anything to anchor it. Without Finn, there was no business, no job. Her house was finished. Everything finally put in its proper place, ready to leave with Lennon if Bailey decided to move away. Ready for Harper and the girls to move in if her sister needed a home. Ready for anything the house was needed for. For anything Bailey decided—to stay or go, to get a job or try something else, everything was wide open. Too wide. She'd rolled the dice, and been excited at her high score, then crapped out on the very next move. It took two more days with no word from Finn before Bailey got her shit together and got out of the house.

Then again, maybe she hadn't gotten herself together. Maybe she just ran out of food in the fridge, and she didn't expect Lennon to replace it. Lennon, it seemed, was living off ramen noodles and boxed mac and cheese when Bailey wasn't feeding her. Bailey wanted slightly better fare. It had been awhile since her own ramen days.

Once the grocery shopping was done, she needed something else to occupy her mind. So she turned toward the couches her mother had loved. They remained in the den under tarps, where she and Finn had stashed them to make room for the new pieces. Bailey thought now about what to do with them. She could take them to a charity, though she wasn't sure which ones accepted furniture. Or, she thought, she could go to the church and see if there was someone specific who wanted them.

Somehow that seemed the better idea to her. Unable to haul the furniture herself, and thinking that Finn would have merely picked it up and found a way to get it in the back of her car,

Bailey resorted to taking pictures. Then, she headed into her old stomping grounds. The staff at the Methodist Church greeted her on sight. She was, after all—as Finn had called her—the Princess of Breathless.

"Bailey Ann Mayfair! Why, it's been years. I heard you were back in town."

"Bailey Ann Mayfair, how are you doing? I heard you fixed that house up real pretty."

"Bailey, it's good to see you back. Are you coming to services?" Of course, that's what Reverend Roberts had asked her.

So she said yes. It wasn't a lie. She hadn't been intending to rejoin as the faithful member she'd been as a kid. In fact, she'd been avoiding it most of the time she'd been home, despite the chiding looks that Nana Rue, Aunt Gigi, and Uncle Dawson had given her. Uncle Dex had merely accepted it at least. But now, point blank, she answered on a whim and decided she would follow through.

Once she said *yes, she was coming back into the fold*, she talked to Reverend Roberts about the couches.

"Is there anyone you know who could use them? I want them to go to someone who will love them. But they don't fit what I have now."

"I'm sure we can find someone worthy, Bailey Ann," he had told her, as he'd motioned her to sit in the seat across from him.

She found it odd, given that she'd come to talk about couches, that he bade her sit down. "Can you tell me what's troubling you?" he asked.

Her immediate thought was to deny it. To say, "Nothing's troubling me." But that would have been a lie. She didn't pour her heart out, but she did offer him pieces of the truth. The parts where she was at a crossroad, or maybe no roads at all, and she couldn't tell the difference.

She told him that she'd been mulling over Lennon's idea of applying to work for a nonprofit, only now part-time probably wouldn't cut it. There would be no income from flipping houses. Not unless she wanted to do it on her own, and she was confident she did not have the knowhow to go it alone.

Thirty minutes later, she found she'd told him about her Aunt Gigi, about the things her family had withheld from her, and the things she'd never seen. Then he asked her, "Do you want to help?"

❧ 50 ❧

When Reverend Roberts asked if she wanted to help, Bailey Ann once again found herself saying yes, though that hadn't been her intention when she walked in. She suddenly agreed, and the decision felt right. The problem was, she didn't know how to help.

"What can I do?"

"It's my understanding you have talents in finance."

She nodded. Everyone wanted her to work the numbers, but what could she say? She was good at it. She always had been. She'd gone and gotten herself educated with the idea that she'd be useful. Her intention was to be useful to her husband and her family but, since they didn't exist, she should at least be helpful to someone who needed it.

"Recently, things have been harder. The church isn't in great shape financially. We need expert advice."

She'd never even thought about the monetary stature of her church. Her parents had always given money, the other families gave money. The church helped the people who needed it. It was a cycle she didn't think twice about. As she mulled it over now though, she saw the carpet in Reverend Roberts' office was the same as it had been when she'd been there in high school.

The outside of the church, though still white, was now a bit dingy. Without more to go on, she could only ask what he meant. Two hours later, Bailey Ann found herself neck deep in the church's financial records.

They had some financial status of course, as a church, but they drained many of their accounts helping families who'd been long-standing members but had fallen on hard times. The church had paid off medical bills for one member, tried to pay off more for others, and helped one family with a loan so they wouldn't lose their house. But the bank had foreclosed the house anyway and the loan from the church had not been repaid. Bailey looked through all the pieces. She came back to him with her recommendation and he called in Mrs. Patel who worked at the front desk. The two sat together to listen to Bailey Ann's pronouncements.

"You can write some of this off and, if we want, we can turn around and look at the medical records of these families. You've offered to help them, but maybe the way we help is by calling the collections companies and getting the bills put on hold for a while. It looks like your record keeper just paid the bills but didn't try to barter them down. That's a must in this situation. I know you want to help, but if the church keeps paying out the way it has, you will lose what small buffer you have."

She paused and took a measure of their expressions. It looked like the information was new, but they weren't surprised that she sounded a bit dire. So she went on, "The problem with having no buffer is that, well . . . that's up to you. But you would be depending on God to make up for it. You may want to be a little more fiscally conservative."

Reverend Roberts nodded. "It's hard to press the members of the church when I know many of them are giving the most they can, and others are giving the most they will."

That struck a nerve with her. She wondered what her parents had given. Had they been in the "can" category or the "will" category? She'd been in neither. She herself had given no money to the church. Though she'd never taken money from the church, she'd definitely benefited from it. She was low on her own money, but in a moment of faith, she handed over a check for a thousand dollars into the church coffers.

Reverend Roberts smiled and held his hand up, palm out to her. "You don't have to do this Bailey. My intent was not to guilt you into giving the church money. I just thought you might know places where we could find more or hold off some of our bills."

"I know," she said, and pushed the check on him. Then she took a more serious note. "Have you not had an accountant or someone professional to look at this in the past?"

Mrs. Patel shook her head. "We couldn't really afford it. Reverend Roberts and I have been doing the books together for years and we'd been holding on, so we counted it as okay."

The grim look on Reverend Roberts' face told Bailey what he thought of them "holding on."

"I think you can do better," she said. Bailey started to lay out a few short-term investment ideas that would help the church turn around, if they could hold off some of the bills that wouldn't hurt some of the church members in the meantime.

She asked, "Did the money used to look better than this?"

Reverend Roberts nodded. "The economy took a hit. Some people didn't hold on well enough."

She understood. She'd been lucky. Some people were. She realized now that she had every advantage and paid no attention to it. It was time she started giving something back. She'd gone home that day feeling better about herself as a person than she had in a long time.

So the next morning she got up and went back. She left the church that day at noon, claiming she had appointments of her own to make. Though the appointments were with no one other than herself, they were real. She had to get herself on track. She knew that now.

She had not been a person that she felt very proud of, not

before just recently. A few good deeds for the church weren't going to make her into what she wanted to be. She needed a job. She'd written that check to the church on faith that she could find something that would give her some income before the rest of her money ran out.

She was not selling the house. She was lucky, though. She had a cushion of some of the money from her parent's things. She could liquidate stuff if she had to or *who knew?* The way her parents ran, she would find more, but she didn't want to spend her part before she knew what it was. She had to admit though, those were problems she was grateful to have.

Spending the afternoon online, she scoured the job market for non-profits in need of someone in her division. She applied for three positions before the afternoon was over and it was time to get her butt to the grocery store again and get some fresh vegetables for her and Lennon. This time she shopped with an eye on the budget. No more salmon. She wasn't headed down Lennon's path of ramen noodles and pasta yet, but she wasn't on Bailey Ann's-cooking-up-a-storm track anymore either.

The good news—or was it bad news?—was that Finn was no longer eating with them. He'd eaten as much as the two women put together and her grocery bill was almost cut in half once she ignored the fact that he'd been feeding her some of the time too.

She'd gone back to the church each morning, though the past three mornings she'd had Lennon help her wrestle one piece of furniture into the trunk of her car. The day it had been the couch, they'd wrangled it upside down and backwards, the feet of it sticking out while her trunk hung open, held only with an ugly orange bungee cord. It was a look she was not overly fond of, but nothing she could do anything about.

Father Robert split up her offerings, surprising her. Ultimately, she decided her Mama would probably be pleased that two families were enjoying the furniture she had so loved. At least Bailey Ann felt good that it was in excellent shape. There was nothing she could do about the color.

She'd gone home that afternoon and this time she applied to two non-profits that were in different parts of the country. If she got one job, she'd wind up moving to Colorado. It would be the end of her work with the church, but it'd be full time. This one was offering a good salary, though not as good as she'd been making before at the bank. She hoped it would pay off in other ways and if it didn't work out, she could find a different job. She hadn't stayed in anything for more than about three years in the past anyway. Why did she think that would change now?

The other job—if she got it—would take her back to Nashville. She knew the area and even had local references. She thought her shot at that job was better than most, though she wasn't keen on the pay scale. Then again, non-profits and beggars and choosers and all that.

She'd gone out to the box store for paper towels and other little things she noticed she was running low on. It was just another thing to keep her busy, but she kept at it. If she found enough things to *do*, maybe she wouldn't *think*.

So when she found a man selling winter squash on the side of the road, she decided to take him up on a couple of his best offerings. She'd gone an alternate route, thinking it was time that she headed by Finn's place. If she couldn't even drive by, what good was she?

That was when she saw the sign had been changed. It now bore a new sign, stuck on top that clearly proclaimed the place *Sold!*

❧ 51 ❧

Finn dragged himself in to his apartment and fell back on the couch. He was usually happier after a night out with his friends. He'd come back into town and done only the necessary things for the first few days.

He'd turned on the thermostat and headed to the grocery store. He changed the sheets on his bed and watched whatever TV the recorder had grabbed here that he'd missed while he was in Breathless. He'd not called the office to let them know he was back in town though.

When he'd run out of things to do, he called around, letting his friends know he was back. Five of them had headed out to their favorite sports bar to watch the game, eat the best chicken wings in town, and drink beer. They'd all been glad to see him, moving plans to hang out since he said he didn't know how long he'd be back.

He should have been happier.

He loved a night out with no responsibilities but cheering for one team or another. But he almost asked if the restaurant had changed their menu, because the wings didn't taste as good. The game was a dud, teams he didn't care about—though he used to.

Lying back on the couch, his head rolled back, his eyes staring at the ceiling, he had to admit nothing had changed but him. He wasn't going back to his job. He would explode if he had to face someone throwing NIMBY laws at him when he felt like this. He felt hollow, gutted, and he remembered the feeling from last time.

He loved Bailey Ann Mayfair. He hadn't said it, but maybe it was better that he hadn't flat out handed her his heart to toss back in his face. He'd asked her to marry him—more than once —but she was too afraid. And when she finally wasn't too afraid, she revealed that she didn't trust him.

She was perfect.

She needed everything around her to be perfect, too.

And he—clearly—wasn't. He hadn't fought for her the first time. And she'd made it clear this time that they didn't fit. Period.

He understood that now. Maybe she felt like this around him: that all the old stuff that was good was just . . . nothing.

He sighed into the night air and when his phone rang, he picked it up, answering with hope rather than looking at the screen. "Hello?"

"Finn!" He knew that voice.

"Amanda, good to hear from you."

"Is it? You sound like crap." She paused. "Was it hard, selling your parents house?"

"Yes." That was the truth, though probably not for the reasons she was thinking. Then again, Amanda was smarter than him. She'd figured him out early enough to question him. She'd figured out all of Bailey Ann's answers, so she knew what he was choosing when he didn't choose *her* favorite color or favorite date night.

When he thought of it that way he realized he'd been left by the idea of Bailey Ann, as well as by the real Bailey Ann—twice. He needed a beer.

"I need a favor . . ." Amanda's voice cut through his thoughts as he reached for the fridge.

He paused. He'd screwed her over by not ever really letting go of Bailey Ann. He owed her. "Anything. Name it."

❧ 52 ❧

L ennon set down her fork with an unceremonious thunk a
   few nights later at dinner. "Bailey, you said no one in this
town ever tells you anything and that you didn't like it."

Bailey nodded, wondering where this lovely line of thought
was headed.

"And you said you can handle things. That you needed to
know the truth. Right?"

Bailey nodded again, though this was sounding more and
more ominous.

"Fine then. Bailey Ann Mayfair, you look like shit warmed
over."

"Thank you," she said wryly. She thought about fighting
back, but she was exhausted.

Lennon didn't let up though. "You haven't spoken to Finn in
almost two weeks now."

Bailey nodded one more time. That was a statement of fact,
and it wasn't like Lennon was telling her anything she didn't
already know.

"Well, it's time you said something. Have you called him?
Texted him?"

Bailey shook her head. *What was the point?*

"Well, get off your ass and do something," Lennon told her, her tone getting sharper with each command.

"You know, he hasn't called me or texted me, either," Bailey pointed out, and tried to calmly go back to eating her pork chops. Her cooking skills had improved, at least.

Lennon still hadn't picked her fork back up and continued to stare. "Of course, he hasn't."

Bailey raised her eyebrows. *Well, dinner wasn't going well.* Lennon had been relatively subdued the last couple of nights. Mostly, they'd eaten in silence, sharing occasional information about their day. So Bailey guessed that all that was left was for Lennon to yell at her about her life choices.

"You know, Lennon, I'm a decade older than you, and I don't need this. I don't see you making your life into sunshine and rainbows."

"Actually, Bailey, you do. I'm here getting my Master's degree because it's going to get me where I want to go in life. And I'm not trying to be snobby or anything, but you're turning yourself backwards."

Bailey thought about that for a moment. "No," she replied. "I'm not turning myself backwards. I went and made the same mistake I made last time, and it blew up in my face. Instead of me getting out, this time, I got dumped."

Lennon was eyeing her oddly. "Is that the story you tell yourself?"

Bailey felt her mouth drop open. She felt horribly affronted, and she was about to say so, but she didn't get to say anything before Lennon was speaking again.

"You *told* me. You told me when it happened, that you two had a fight and *you* walked away, so are you changing your story now, or are you lying?"

"What is with you, Lennon? I don't need this. I feel like shit as it is." There, she'd gone and said, *Shit.* She'd said it at her own dining room table over the good china that she kept pulling out because it wasn't getting used for any other reason. Great-

Grandma Mayfair may have emblazoned her initials on every piece of silverware, hoping to one day hand it down to her great-granddaughter, but she would have a conniption fit and roll over in her grave right now if she saw what Bailey was saying over her pork chops.

"So what was it, Bailey? Did he say the words that he no longer wanted to see you, that he didn't think you were a good fit, that he thought you were a terrible person, that he was leaving?"

Bailey finally held her hand up. It shouldn't have hurt hearing Lennon say the words, but it did. Finn had not said those things to her, but she'd felt each cut as though he had, as though he'd been throwing knives.

"Did he?" Lennon pushed.

"No! He didn't say those things. We had a fight, and it was too big."

"That's just it, Bailey. Whether or not that fight is too big is up to you."

"Well, it was."

"No, it wasn't! You're the one who says you want to get married and you want to settle down and you want to have kids. You had several opportunities if half the rumors are true, and you fucked up every single one of them, Bailey."

"Jesus, Lennon."

"No. You said you wanted people to tell you the truth."

"Is this what people are saying around town about me?"

"No," Lennon conceded and looked away for the first time. "No one is saying that Bailey Ann Mayfair is a coward. They are saying, however, that you did it to Finn again."

"I did not."

"Well, Bailey, if you're so concerned about what people think, fix it. You want me to go out in town and tell people that Finn is the one who blew it up this time? I can't do that."

"What would you have me do?" Bailey asked.

"You need to reach out to him."

"Just send him a text?"

"Good God, Bailey. Don't do that. If he texts you, you can text back that you want to speak to him, and . . . I can't believe I'm having to tell you all this. Call him. Leave him a voicemail. At least let him hear a tone in your voice rather than trying to make one up from a text."

It all sounded perfectly reasonable, but, "I'm looking at jobs all over the country, Lennon. What if I move away?"

"Do you want my honest opinion?" Lennon paused and let the question hang there in the air as though Bailey would answer her honestly.

Of course, you were supposed to say you wanted someone's honest opinion, and, right now, she didn't, but the etiquette that had been drilled into her came to the surface at that moment. Funny, she'd just been swearing over her grandma's china, but this, she couldn't seem to break out of. "Of course."

"My honest opinion," Lennon began, "is that the two of you belong together. I don't know what bullshit you've decided to believe about Finn getting divorced, but from what you told me and from what I heard around town, that wife of his left him. He decided to be okay with that, and he understood what had been going on. He is not the one who walked away from that marriage, and, Bailey, you should be grateful that marriage broke up. It's the only reason you've had another chance with him. The two of you were always the best thing since sliced bread and, now . . ."

What? Bailey Ann thought. They'd gone stale? Moldy? None of that was true. The way that analogy was headed, the loaf of bread should probably have blown up in her face.

"What would you have me do, Lennon?" She sighed, wearily, knowing she wasn't going to do it anyway, but hoping if she let her cousin talk it out, it might turn out okay.

Lennon must think she was as dense as a brick. "I get it. From your side, it looks like he left you. But you've left him *twice*

now. This one's your turn. Call him, Bailey. Pick up the phone
right now and call him."

"What if he doesn't answer?"

"Then you leave him a voicemail telling him you want talk
with him. Do you not understand how technology works?"

Bailey sighed again. That was not the point.

"Right now," Lennon said, pointing into the other room.
Bailey didn't keep her phone at the table, but Lennon demanded
that she go to her purse and get it, and unless she was going to
flat out refuse her cousin, there wasn't much she could do.

So she dialed, and when Finn didn't answer for her—*shocking!*
—she wound up leaving him a voicemail.

But Lennon was right. Even telling her sisters that their
Daddy had passed was not as hard as leaving that message for
Finn.

❧ 53 ❧

Ultimately, that voicemail was the worst possible outcome. It left her with no gauge of how he felt or thought.

Was he going to call her back? Had he even gotten the message? Some people didn't check their phone messages, though she thought Finn definitely would.

By midnight when he hadn't called her back, she hauled herself up the stairs and crawled under the covers. Though she loved the room, it felt colder and colder each night. She missed Finn and she loved him. She knew that much. She wasn't sure she could live with him, but she wasn't sure she could live without him either.

Despite Lennon's angry tone, her cousin was right. Bailey was being a bear. Even Mrs. Patel at the church was recently being very cautious around her. So Bailey apologized the next morning when she went in, even though she hadn't slept very well the night before and felt like being even more cranky than she had been.

Lennon had convinced her that if Finn wouldn't speak to her, or if he did and it all went south, Bailey should take the job offer in Colorado and flee the state. That was tempting, and it was maybe the only thing that made her brave enough to do what she did. Still, it didn't matter. By noon, her phone hadn't rung.

When her phone did finally ring at one, it was Lennon's face on the screen. "I've hit a roadblock and I'm tapping out for the day. I'll just be home to shower before heading out again."

Bailey, on her own way home, had pointed out, "I'm not even your landlord, really. You don't have to report all your movement to me."

"Oh," Lennon replied flatly. "That's a bummer. I was hoping Finn was there and you two are making out like wild rabbits."

"Yeah, right." Bailey said.

"That didn't happen?"

"Well, he hasn't even called me back."

"Call him again, Bailey," her cousin pushed.

"No, Lennon. I have some pride left."

"No, you don't. You can't afford any."

There was Lennon, telling her she had no pride left, and Bailey thought about that a little bit more. What Lennon had said at dinner the night before made sense. She and Finn had broken up once. This time, they hadn't really gotten together or broken up at all. Now they were at kind of a stalemate.

At two, when they were both home and Lennon had climbed in the shower and then quickly turned around and left for the library, Bailey knew she couldn't hold it off any longer. She picked up the phone and called him again, fully intending to leave a voice message, only his voice had answered this time.

"Bailey?"

That was it.

No *Ann*, she noticed. He called her *Bailey Ann*, one of the few to always use her full name. Somehow his tone was both flat and wonderful at the same time. No matter what he was saying that sound of honey and whiskey hit her in the gut and she knew she loved it.

Shit. She was in way over her head.

"Bailey?" He asked it again as a legitimate question, but by now, he was probably thinking she'd butt dialed him.

"Finn?" she spoke just to let him know that she was there.

Shit. Damn. Crap. She'd not been ready to speak to the man. She expected to have a chance to leave another voicemail, telling him once again to call her back, trying to sound calm. But it was harder right now, when he was on the line and her heart was pounding.

"Finn," she said, when he offered nothing into the silence. "I think we should talk."

"Didn't we do that? Didn't you already make your decisions about me?"

"I did," she admitted. Then she said what she hadn't expected to say. She'd thought she would ask him to talk. She'd thought they would get together and make a decision about how terrible they were, but at least she would know she had followed through. Instead, the words that came out of her mouth were, "I'm sorry."

Again, another long pause hung between them, until at last, he asked her, "I don't understand. What are you sorry about?"

She didn't even know, or consciously she didn't, but she must have felt it somewhere inside, because the words rolled off her tongue. "I'm sorry about the way I handled things. I'm sorry about the way I judged you. You don't deserve that. I'm sorry that I walked away, and I'm sorry that I let you walk away without us figuring this out."

Again, another long silence went on between them.

"I just . . . I was hoping we could talk." She put it out there and waited.

"I was there for several days. Just a short walk away," he pointed out the obvious facts. Things she already knew she'd fucked up. But then he added, "I came over and knocked on your door and you didn't answer me."

"I didn't hear it! I would have answered," she protested that one. He'd come over? He'd actually tried to talk to her? But he hadn't taken up the conversation. Maybe he didn't believe she hadn't been ignoring him. Her heart twisted in her chest.

"I'm in Atlanta," he said flatly.

"I know. Will you be back?"

"Why?" The one word was soft, and it hung there between them, cutting a hole in her as surely as if he'd been standing right in front of her and taken a knife.

Why should he come back? What had she offered him that would make him come? While she pondered that, his voice filled the space again. "If you really want to talk to me, Bailey, you can do it."

He rattled off the address for his apartment and hung up the phone while she scrambled to get paper and write it down from memory. She was pretty sure she'd gotten it, but she stared at the post-it note in her hand for a solid five minutes.

❧ 54 ❧

Bailey arrived in Atlanta just a few hours later.

She'd stood in her living room, staring at his address. With Lennon's words ringing through her head, she'd immediately gone out the back door and climbed into her car.

She was still wearing what she'd worn to the church that morning, but she didn't care. She had nothing on her, except her purse. No change of clothing, no extra cash, nothing for a trip. She'd simply gotten in the car and driven.

Lennon was right. Bailey needed to know what Finn thought about them before she made any big decisions, like taking the job in Colorado, or even the one in Nashville. Though she fully expected the two of them to have another knock-down drag-out fight about his beliefs and hers, she could handle it. If they did, she would know for certain where she stood, and she would turn around and go back to Breathless. She would pack her things, email Colorado and tell them she was coming and take the job that looked the best on paper.

She told herself she'd make new friends and build a new life there and she would get over Finn Malloy. But first, she had to come down here and see him. It wasn't until she was driving around his neighborhood—having finally located a parallel parking spot almost two full blocks away—that she admitted to herself that the outcome she envisioned was not the one she wanted. She wanted to find something between them again. She wanted to bridge the gap that had opened up. *She wanted Finn back.*

Her heart was pounding as she walked in the front lobby of the nice glassed-in, modern building. This was not where she had expected Finn Malloy would live.

For some reason, she'd expected an older building, shorter, dingier, less in the heart of the city. Something that more resembled what she imagined of his family, rather than what she knew of the man he had become. As she looked around at the gleaming lobby she saw herself reflected in the mirrored panels. Her outward image looked pretty today, but her thoughts about what she believed of others wasn't reflecting well on her.

No one was at the front desk of the building. However, from the looks of it, someone was coming right back. A coffee cup with a white lid bearing a fresh lipstick stain sat next to the computer. So Bailey sat down on the waiting bench and thought hard about what she'd been doing.

Had she been seeing Finn through old lenses? Or maybe even lenses that nobody had but her? When they were teenagers, she'd loved him. She'd known it. She told him that. But when she was looking back honestly, she had judged him. She had tried to train him out of his accent when hers was as thick as his, only hers was different, more local. She hadn't accepted him exactly as he was. He had allowed it, asked for it, and she wondered now why he had. Had he loved her that much that it was worth it? Or had he simply not known his own place in the world and it was good to be with the Princess of Breathless?

She was petrified that he'd loved *what* she was more than *who* she was. She was well aware that was a possibility. Apparently, he had married someone just like her and it hadn't worked out. She wasn't sure what made him think the two of them would be okay, since he had already done the whole thing so similarly before.

From her own perspective, she'd always wanted what her mother and father had, but it was past time to admit that she'd missed that train. Her mother and father had gone together in high school, though they hadn't married until they graduated college—because to do so before that simply wasn't done. But her mother had been captain of her cheerleading squad, and her father had been the quarterback on the state champion football team. They'd been big fish in a small pond even then, even before they'd gotten married, even before they'd had their three daughters and continued the Mayfair legacy in town. She could have continued on a track close to theirs, if she'd stayed with Finn through college. But it was her mother who'd convinced her they didn't fit. She could see that now, even though Bailey still hesitated to call it manipulation. Her mother wanted her to marry someone with a bigger name. And Bailey, though she hadn't seen that as an end goal, had followed right along.

Now, though, she realized she'd done Finn a disservice. And she couldn't recall a single thing he'd ever said to her either when they were together in high school or this time around that had ever made her think he didn't understand exactly who she was. When the clerk came back, she'd made up her mind, given the apartment number, and was let into the elevator.

Though she hadn't thought it possible, her heart was beating even more rapidly than before. Little fluttering strokes let her know just how frightened she was. Still, when the door dinged, she got off at his hallway and began looking at the numbers on the doors. Down the hall, one of the doors opened and a woman walked out.

She started toward Bailey Ann, clearly heading to the elevator when she stopped dead and stared.

"Well," the woman said, the sweet Southern drawl dripping from her lips. Dissimilar to her own, Bailey couldn't quite place its origin. Then the woman stunned her, "You must be Bailey Ann Mayfair."

How in hell would anyone know that? Bailey stopped and stared back.

"I can tell by your stunned expression that I got it right." She held out a hand with perfectly manicured nails—nails much prettier than Bailey's own after weeks of working on houses—and said, "I'm—"

But Bailey figured it out. "Amanda," she whispered as she shook the woman's hand, not because she wanted to, but because it would be impolite not to.

"Exactly." Amanda paused for a moment, looking Bailey up and down as Bailey did the same. Finn was right. Though it was easy to see that Amanda was simply gorgeous, there were similarities between the two of them. She had dark hair, a nice chestnut brown—the same shade Bailey dyed hers to match when she got up the nerve to get her hair stylist to do it. Where Bailey's own eyes were brown though, Amanda's were a golden amber that shined in the dim light of the hallway. Amanda was two inches taller and still proportioned like the high school and college cheerleader she'd been. It only took a few seconds for the two women to size each other up. And Amanda came out the winner once again.

"I see you don't even know my last name," she said.

Bailey scrambled, searching through her brain, and found nothing. So she took a stab, "Malloy?"

"No," Amanda said. "I went back to my maiden name."

Bailey nodded, though she realized Amanda was right and Finn had never said it.

"I know all four of your names," she said, "and that I think tells you everything you need to know about how he feels about you and me. I will tell you this though, he's in a mood like a bear that's been stung by a thousand hornets. So good luck in there."

She offered the last bit on an upbeat note as she brushed past Bailey and headed down the hall. Though Bailey didn't turn, she heard the doors ding as the waiting elevator opened to take Amanda away.

Why had Amanda been here? It was a question to which she didn't like any of the answers she thought up. Still, she pushed forward.

Knocking on the door, she called out, "Finn. Finn!"

She knew he was in there. Amanda had said as much. Unless the woman was lying—and she hadn't seemed outright mean—then he should hear her. Reluctantly, he opened the door and let her in. He didn't say it was good to see her, though she had expected as much.

She wanted to start with something different, but what came out of her mouth was, "What was Amanda doing here?"

He looked at her, the stare letting her know it was none of her business what he and his ex-wife did or discussed. Still, when she stood there frozen, he said, "I told her the lease is up in several months. So if she wanted to come and check and see if any of her things were still here."

He let it trail off as Bailey Ann put two and two together. This wasn't *Finn's* apartment so much as it had been *theirs*. She hated the thought of that even more. They stared at each other for a while, and she wondered if he would offer her a glass of lemonade or a beer, but he did neither.

Despite being a gentleman, maybe he was still just some Irish rogue at heart. So she repeated her earlier words from the phone. "I'm sorry. I'm sorry I judged you like that."

He nodded, accepting it. "Is that all you came for?"

"No Finn, I wanted to talk. I wanted to work this out. I . . ." At least that changed his expression a little bit.

For a moment, she was hopeful, but then his face took on the expression of a thunder cloud again, "I don't know, Bailey. I don't know what to do. If you think I could walk out on you like that, then I'm not sure there's anything more for us to say."

❧ 55 ❧

Lennon came home at noon the next day, not in the dark clothes that she'd been wearing, but in something a little less rugged.

"Where were you?" Bailey asked. As soon as the words were out of her mouth, she realized she had no right to demand to know where her roommate was. "I'm sorry, I shouldn't have asked you that. I'm not your keeper—"

"I was at the library." Lennon interrupted. "Where were you?"

"Atlanta," Bailey replied, trying to think if there was anything she could add to that. There wasn't.

"Then what the hell are you doing here at home?"

"Well, we talked."

"And you came home?"

Bailey nodded.

"Then you didn't do it right." Lennon told her.

"Lennon, I can't put back together what's broken. He doesn't want me."

"That's not true." When Bailey raised her eyebrows as if to ask how Lennon was somehow more knowledgeable about her own relationships than she herself was, her cousin jumped back in. "There's not a single person in this town that would agree with that statement."

Bailey stared hard at her cousin. "Look, I don't know when you think you became the lord of all things *love*, but . . ."

Lennon was *laughing* at her, and Bailey was in far too sour of a mood to take it. "Thank you, so very much."

"Bailey, go pack your bags and turn around and go back to Atlanta."

"You cannot be serious, Lennon. I talked to him. I told him I was sorry."

"And what did he say?"

"He said, 'If I can't trust that he wouldn't walk out on me, then he can't be in a relationship with me.'"

Lennon stared at her hard. Bailey just stared back.

"What?" Lennon uttered the word then didn't say anything.

"What do you mean *what*?"

"Bailey, get your dumb ass out of here. Get down to Atlanta and tell him you do trust him. That boy is right."

She almost laughed at the idea of Lennon calling Finn—a full decade older than her—a *boy*.

But Bailey did stop, and she thought about it. Maybe she was being an idiot. Finn had said if she didn't trust him, then they didn't have anything. And she hadn't trusted him.

Lennon was looking at her askance again. "I get it. I get it. It's easier not to trust. I've trusted people and been completely dicked over by them. But I don't think he's like that."

"What are you talking about Lennon?"

"It's a story for another day. *If ever*. But having been completely dicked over by a man, I can tell you that Finn is not one of those guys." Lennon paused a moment. "Maybe you don't know, maybe you've never been on the receiving end of that. So you're imagining monsters under the bed. But in this case, Bailey, they're not there. You got one of the good ones. And if you don't grab him, he's going to get over you one of these days. Then you'll regret it for the rest of your life."

Lennon then grabbed her by the shoulders, turned her, and aimed her up the steps.

"Go, pack an overnight bag this time. Get your ass back to Atlanta, tell him that you're wildly in love with him, you trust him beyond measure, and get your shit in gear, Bailey."

Bailey almost laughed. "Why are you doing this?"

"Because I don't see my own future working out well, and I love a good love story. You're about three inches away from one and you're struggling to take those final few steps. So, I'm going to push you."

This time Bailey did laugh. She headed upstairs and packed, a new lightness in her heart as she put pieces into the small overnight bag. She put gas in her car and waved at people as she drove out of town. She was going to get Finn Malloy back.

Lennon was right. And this time, Bailey's heart was right. It was her brain that had always gotten in the way.

Another half hour down the road, and she realized her brain had not gotten in the way all the time. She'd been right not to marry Todd, and she'd been right not to marry Ray. She'd never really gotten over Finn, and she was lucky he'd never really gotten over her, either.

This time she won a parking space nearer to his building. Grabbing her overnight bag, she swung it up onto her shoulder and climbed out. Her heels clicking on the sidewalk, she headed confidently into the front of his building.

It was two in the afternoon now. Surely, he would be home. Unless he'd gone back to work, or . . . She didn't know, but she didn't let her optimism flag.

This time, she walked right up to the front desk and was once again waved to the elevator. Only now she knew exactly where she was going. Nothing hit her until the elevator doors opened, and she was suddenly afraid she would see Amanda again.

Seeing the woman once was something she could stomach, and she could handle Finn's response that Amanda had just been there to see if she'd left anything behind. But if she saw his ex-wife again . . . Now, Bailey was worried that he'd come back to Atlanta and picked up the pieces of his old life. That maybe he'd remembered something about Amanda, or realized she was better than Bailey.

Heading down the hall and feeling her confidence flag a little, she was grateful when, this time, no woman came out his door. Bailey knocked lightly on it. When nothing happened, she knocked again and then again.

He didn't answer. Fifteen minutes later, she was still standing in front of his door, now fully convinced that he was not at home.

What was she going to do? Where could he be?

The problem was, he could be anywhere. She had no idea. What if he'd driven to Breathless to find her? She'd be here, and he'd be there . . . But she didn't think he'd do that. He'd been adamant, the decision was hers.

So she made it.

Setting her heavy bag on the floor, she turned around and put her back to his door then slid down. There she was sitting in his doorway, cross legged, in his hallway at his apartment, waiting. Twenty minutes later, when she still hadn't decided quite what to do other than wait, and Finn still hadn't shown up, she texted Lennon.

"He's not here. It's been over thirty minutes and I can't find him."

"Do you think he's on his way here to find you?" Lennon asked and Bailey smiled about great minds thinking alike. But Bailey replied that she didn't think so. He'd told her if she didn't trust him, there was nothing he could do. Why would he come back for that? The ball has been placed firmly in her court, and it had taken a while, but she was returning it.

So, she sat there and tried to figure out what to do. Should she have messaged him? Another thirty minutes later—after she'd played on her phone for a while then scoured her social media for anything interesting—she decided to do just that. She'd shot a text to Finn, and half an hour later, he still hadn't responded, and she was getting concerned. This was not the happy reunion she'd hoped for.

When her stomach growled, she got up and went downstairs, headed down the street and found herself a sandwich place. Instead of eating there, she'd gotten half a sandwich and a drink to go and gone back up the elevator to sit in front of his door again. She wasn't going to miss him, she told herself. She trusted him. And she had to trust that he would eventually come home.

She messaged him again, and it was three hours later that she stopped just asking if he would text her back and finally typed out the words, "Finn, I'm sitting in front of your apartment door waiting on you. If you're in the area, and you want to come home, I'll be here." *There,* she thought. That should get him.

Still, she'd sat and waited. Her commitment not wavering, even when a neighbor walked by with groceries and asked if she needed help. He'd offered to get the super for her, but Bailey thought letting herself into Finn's apartment wasn't a good idea at this stage of things. Though it was Atlanta, in the big city, it was still the South. And she'd assured the nice man that she was simply waiting for Finn to come home.

"Well," he said, "I'm in seven. If you need anything, just come knock."

"Thank you," she replied with a smile.

She didn't know how long she'd been there, but she felt a hand on her shoulder shaking her awake sometime later.

"Bailey Ann, what are you doing here?"

❦ 56 ❦

The Four-Season rule states that you should know a man for all four seasons before you agree to marry him. What if he knits with his Aunt Edna every winter evening?

GROGGILY, BAILEY TURNED HER HAND SO SHE COULD SEE THE face of her phone. It was well past eight p.m. She didn't answer Finn's question. Instead, she tried to slowly stand up, but her legs hurt, and her back hurt, and her butt was asleep.

"Where have you been?" she asked.

He shook his head at her. "I went to work. I went out after for drinks."

"Work?" she asked, latching onto the one thing she hadn't expected. "Did you go back?"

He shook his head, "No, remember I won the bid on the plantation? I'm not going back to the firm. I'm letting the lease run out on the apartment."

She nodded slowly, still trying to get fully upright and finally making it with the help of the hand he held out to her. She was standing there in the hallway looking at him, and she thought she didn't want to do this out here, not where the neighbors could open their doors and walk by, not where anyone coming out of the elevator could interrupt. She didn't know how sound-proof these apartments were or if the neighbors were listening to everything, but the deal was she didn't get to choose. She'd fucked it up, and she had to make it right whether his neighbors heard or not.

"What are you doing here?" he asked again now that she was more alert.

She looked up at him then. "You said if I couldn't trust you, we didn't have anything left, and I went home. That was a mistake, a big one. Because the fact of the matter is I *do* trust you. I have no idea how this will turn out, and I'm petrified. I'm so scared that one day you'll decide you don't love me anymore."

When he only stared at her in response to her pouring out her heart, she asked him, "What? What are you thinking?"

He was scowling, and it wasn't what she'd expected. Instead of answering, he fit his key into the lock, picked up her bag, and walked into the apartment in front of her, fully expecting her to come along behind him. When he turned and closed the door behind him, he flipped the bolt. She had no idea if that was a good thing or a bad thing. He dropped her bag unceremoniously on the ground in the front hallway and stared at her, his hands on his hips now.

"Bailey Ann, what are you doing?"

"I'm ah—ah—*apologizing*," she stammered. "I'm sorry. I screwed it up. I should have told you a long time ago."

"Damn it, Bailey Ann. Do you have any idea how hard I've been working on getting over you?"

She stood stock still and stared at him, her heart clogging her throat and making it impossible to breathe. "Is it working?" she whispered.

He threw his head back and laughed a deep, hearty laugh that would have made her smile under any other circumstances.

"No," he said bitterly. "It never does."

"Good," she whispered. "I don't want you to get over me. I never want you to get over me."

He stared again for a moment and said, "That's just lovely."

Again, she was shocked at the sourness of his attitude. Here she was telling him she'd been so wrong, that she did love him. Why wasn't he picking her up and swinging her around? Why wasn't she happy? She'd decided not to go home until she was fully defeated. Deciding she wasn't there yet, she asked him, "What do you want from me?"

"I want you to have the same trouble getting over me that I have getting over you. I want to know that you're not going to walk out on me again."

Her heart soared. She could do that. "I do. I can."

Shit, she thought. She wasn't making any sense. So Bailey Ann started over. "I will not walk out again. I promise you that right here and right now. If you let me, if you come back, I promise I will stand and I will fight for us every step of the way. I have never said yes before, Finn, not to anyone, even to the guys I knew would never leave me. *I didn't say yes*. I'm saying *yes* now. I want to be with you, and if nothing else, you can trust that I'm too petrified of losing you to ever walk away on my own."

This time, it was Finn who whispered, "Do you love me?"

"Finn Malloy," she said, standing and staring at him, wishing there weren't four feet of space between them, wishing his hands weren't still on his hips, but clearly it needed to be said. "I didn't know it, but I never stopped loving you. You were always the only one."

In a heartbeat, the distance between them was closed, and she'd thought it was him, but she was no longer standing in the same place, and she was in his arms. Their mouths sought each other out as he held her tight as though he would never let go. Or maybe that was her clinging so tightly.

Their mouths fused together. They tore at each other's clothing, a difficult task while they were trying to get so close. They tumbled onto the couch and never made it to the bed, and this time, when she screamed his name, she didn't wonder if the neighbors could hear, because she didn't care.

Let Atlanta talk. Let them gossip. Let them know she was crazy in love with Finn Malloy. She was done hiding from it.

Even when their breathing had returned to normal, and they were curled up on the couch together, they didn't put on the TV, and they didn't talk. He just held her close, and she felt for the first time that she was where she truly belonged. She hadn't felt this way since before she'd written that awful letter in high school. So, this time, it was finally the right time.

Wondering if he was asleep, she put her hand on his chest and watched as his eyelids fluttered open to look at her. For a moment, there was a question, but eventually that wonderful shade of blue that was the window to Finn's soul settled on her and seared into her, and he smiled. He started to open his mouth, but she beat him to it.

"Finn Malloy," she said, "When are you going to marry me?"

He smiled and said, "That's a change I didn't expect."

"When?"

Finn reminded her then. "What if we look up the date of the first day of school in the year we met? I saw you and I knew something big was happening. I didn't know what, but I knew you were important to me."

"I knew I'd just seen the hottest boy in the whole high school and I had to make him mine. It took me way too long to realize exactly what a wonderful thing I'd found."

His arm tugged her tighter against him, almost as though it was involuntary. "It's been a long way. But let's go home."

She smiled and laughed. "It's been twenty years exactly, hasn't it?"

He nodded. "Sometime this September."

She flashed back to being a freshman in the halls at the high school and seeing that stunningly good looking boy, tall and lanky, trying to work the combination on his new locker. She'd volunteered to help and hadn't known that she was changing the course of her life forever.

"Yes, Finn, it's the perfect date. That's when I'm going to marry you."

✽ 57 ✽

Lennon wound her way through the produce section of the local grocery. She needed apples and raisins for dessert. She needed fish fillets for dinner and . . . she mentally ticked off each item on her list.

Usually, she bought what was on sale, and what was cheap. She was eating a bunch of noodles, cereal, and the occasional apple or salad to attempt to stay healthy on her student's budget. She'd likely go back to that method next time she shopped, but she had a celebration dinner to cook tonight. Bailey Ann had stayed in Atlanta for three days.

The first night she'd texted back late—*I'm staying. Thank you.* —So Lennon had breathed easier knowing all was finally well between her cousin and the man she loved.

The second night Bailey Ann had sent a picture of her left hand and possibly the most gorgeous engagement ring Lennon had ever seen. Then another text had immediately followed— *Please don't tell! We'll announce it when we get back.*

So Lennon was expecting the household to go from one—her alone—to three tonight. And she was going to plan a nice dinner for the happy couple. After all, she was the one who almost yelled at Bailey to go to Atlanta and fix things. She wanted to believe she was in some way responsible for getting them together.

At the fish counter, she pointed to fillets and had them weighed out and wrapped. She picked up the bacon wrapped asparagus they had on display, too. As she turned away, she saw him, and her heart stopped.

Gabe Zemp, at the other end of the store, checking out eggs.

For a moment her whole body froze. Should she keep heading that way, act like it was nothing? Or turn and try to avoid him?

The way her heart had started pounding just from seeing him made the decision and she turned away, moving quickly until she was out of sight. Anyone who saw her would think she was having an anxiety attack. Who knew? She might be actually having one.

It shouldn't still bother her after all this time.

But it did.

Checking her cart, Lennon told herself she had everything she needed. As she headed to the front of the store, she both prayed that Gabe wouldn't see her and that she would be fine if he did. She promised herself she could pull it off. After all, they'd been friends once.

Still, she scanned her groceries with as much care as she could while speeding through the task. She bagged them, practically raced out the door, and climbed into her old dinged Nissan like she was being chased and she tried not to peel out of the lot. Only when she got about three blocks away did she start to breathe easy again. But then the tears started to threaten.

She'd told herself she could come back to Breathless and it would be okay. She wanted it to be okay. But clearly, it wasn't.

Brodie Zemp was dead and gone. So was Brodie and Gabe's father, Robert. Gabe was the only one left. While Gabe hadn't done the things to her that his father and brother had, he had heard things she was ashamed to admit. He also seemed to believe she'd done things she hadn't done. She didn't need that. The reality was bad enough.

On the drive home, Lennon talked herself through the last lingering strands of her fear. She wasn't giving up her thesis over this man, over an old embarrassment. No, she was fine. She'd stand firm. She could do this. Besides, she'd been in town for several weeks and she'd only run into him twice.

Both places she'd seen him were places she could avoid. She just wouldn't go to Zeal—the restaurant his family owned. That had been her mistake to let Bailey Ann take her there. And she would switch grocery stores. Done.

Lennon breathed easier.

She could both stay in Breathless and stay away from Gabe Zemp.

By the time she pulled her car under the carport, she'd convinced herself she was golden. This would be fine! Now all she had to do was convince Gabe to stay out of her way, too. That was probably easier said than done.

AFTERWORD

Dear Reader,

Thank you for coming along to Breathless, Georgia with me. I have to admit I love the South, but—like in my books—it's real love, not just lust. I see her faults and I know we have a lot of work to do here, but it's gonna be amazing when we get there. I grew up in East Tennessee and my first husband was a golden boy in a classic Southern Family. My family is *not* Southern Royalty...nope, but watching his family taught me a lot. That was over twenty years ago, but the history I love of Southern Women and their strength has finally made it to paper (or ereader, if you will.) Bailey Ann is the perfect Belle. I saw these modern women, I know them, and sometimes the rules just have to be broken. Finn is her perfect foil, lover, and other half! I loved writing them and I hope their (second) first kiss took your breath away as much as it did mine!

If you loved falling in love with these two, it would mean the world to me if you left a review. Thank you so much, and thank you for reading.

PREVIEW OF RUINED
(BREATHLESS, GA - BOOK 2)

Ticks—there's a little bit of Satan in each of them.

Lennon sat back on her heels and surveyed the damage she'd done to the ground in front of her. She felt a lone bead of sweat run down her spine, and she pressed at her shirt to make it stop. She hated the feeling of sweat rolling along her skin. But the work she liked.

She'd dug small holes at various points on her patch of ground. None of the holes was wide but each was several feet deep. Before she abandoned one, she would look down in to see if she could spot changes in the soil pattern, maybe see layers where dirt had been moved in recent centuries, or even find human bones or pieces of ancient clay. She'd already spent weeks getting a ground penetrating radar specialist out here to mark her spots and then gridding the area with stakes and string. It felt good to finally be digging.

Some people didn't realize how much of getting your degree was about navigating the bureaucracy. Her last year had involved getting her thesis approved by her committee at school and then getting the town council of Breathless to approve her digging on some of the public lands.

Three years earlier, Lennon had found a good-size piece of pottery while out for a walk on this patch of ground. That's how long it had taken to get far enough in her degree to propose a thesis, to get that idea approved by the research board, contact the local native tribes, and get them to agree to what she had suspected all along—that the piece of clay pot and the design on it were definitely not theirs. Then, she'd had to get the Breathless town council to write up extensive paperwork, saying it was okay for her to come out and dig up some random test spots.

She'd kept that piece of clay pot to herself. She could have told one of her professors what she'd found. It was an interesting discovery. But being who she was, she'd wanted to do the research herself. She was pursuing a joint anthropology/archeology degree. And handing over the discovery would have meant the dig would fall into the hands of a professor and she'd be lucky if she was even allowed on the student team.

Keeping it to herself had been a gamble. She'd had to both downplay the find enough that no one stole the research from her, but make it clear enough what it was to justify doing the dig.

But here she was—*finally!*—with her fingers in the soil.

Her back hurt and her gloves were sticking to her hands. She didn't take them off; the alternative was blisters. Still, if she got lucky, this would possibly become an important dig showing roots of North American human history right in her hometown.

The other possibility was that the piece she had found had traveled some distance from its origination point, and—for whatever reason—gotten lodged in the soil here in Breathless, Georgia. Lennon did not like to entertain that possibility.

The good news for her was that there existed evidence of ancient cultures having migrated through here. They could have come north, through Central America, and passed through this section of Georgia even before the known natives. It was a hotly-contested issue since the vast majority of names of the Native American tribes literally translated to "First People." But there was a growing body of evidence that others had come through and died out maybe even long before that.

If she already had her doctorate, if she was running her own dig, she would have a bevy of graduate students doing this work for her. Instead, she was on her knees and troweling the dirt herself. To be fair, her thesis was only about the preliminary research to determine whether or not more digging was required. It was still a lot of work.

So far, she'd found nothing. Exactly jack squat. Day three of truly digging and she was out here again, sweating into her uniform of work boots, tank top, and old cargo pants. The pants themselves were lightweight but she'd filled all the pockets until she looked lumpy. The outfit was practical and not much else.

She'd come home every evening, peeled all of her clothing, and stuck it directly in the washer. Then she'd stuck herself directly in the shower. She'd do the same tonight, though *home* wasn't even *her home*.

While her Mama and Daddy lived in town, Lennon couldn't quite face moving back in and settling into her old room and the old rules. She loved her parents, but they were a bit on the strict side.

Instead, she'd moved in with her cousin. She'd been excited to have a roommate. She and Bailey Ann were nearly a decade apart in age. But as they'd become adults, she'd realized what an amazing person Bailey Ann was. They had lived together for almost two months while Lennon finished up all the paperwork and started her planning phases.

However, over the course of the past several weeks, Bailey Ann had moved out. She'd moved in with her boyfriend, now fiancé, Finn Malloy. Those two had begun dating in high school and broken up in college. But whatever they'd worked out this time was jealousy-inducingly solid. So Lennon now had the house to herself.

She'd once again offered to pay rent, but her cousin refused. She told herself to enjoy having her own home, and at least she tried. It was strange being an adult back in Breathless. Luckily, all her cousins were turning into good friends, even if the youngest Mayfair sister, her best friend Emma Kate, was still at UCLA finishing up her own degree. Lennon and Bailey Ann were establishing a new relationship as adults now. And she was trying to establish one with her older brother Jackson, who also lived in town.

Though none of it had turned out the way she expected, Lennon was still doing her best to enjoy it. Though she was rattling around in a house by herself, it was good not to be in her parents' home. She would always be her mother's daughter, but it was harder to be herself at home.

Leaning back over the hole she'd been working on, she stuck the trowel in and widened it. Her lack of finding anything for three days was not discouraging. In any other job, it probably would be, but in this one, she knew she could dig for months and not find what she needed. What she was looking for was likely broken, tiny, and muddy enough to not be seen until she was directly on top of it. So with plenty of enthusiasm still in place, Lennon went back with her little hand shovel, carefully scraping the edges of the hole.

She couldn't even really dig. If she did, she might break something and damage the very artifacts she was looking for. But twenty minutes later, she heard the first telltale clink.

Her heart soared. She knew that was odd. Who got excited about pot sherds? She and her archeology friends did—the same people who liked to explain that they were, in fact, "sherds" and not "shards." That's who.

Setting the trowel aside, Lennon shone her flashlight into the hole as she leaned over. She couldn't quite make out what she'd hit. So she reminded herself it could be a lost dog tag, a bottle cap, a scrap of an old wooden sign . . . anything really.

After a few more minutes of work, she identified it. It was a broken bit of a baked clay pot!

As she smiled and stared at the small piece in her hand like a long-lost lover, she heard a noise off to her right. Turning her head, she spotted a pair of expensive and too-clean-to-be-used hiking boots. When her gaze lifted, following long, lean legs, a cut torso and striking brown eyes, her heart plummeted.

Of course.

Who else would possibly be standing there but Gabriel Zemp?

Thank you for reading! I love romances with real love and believable characters, and I hope you found all that in these pages. I want to fall in love right along with the characters, and I do, while I'm writing it.

About Savannah

I started writing when I was eight—I hand wrote an 80-page novella that I believed to be (adult) romantic suspense. I'm proud to say, I've gotten a lot better since then. I've grown up to be a nerd at heart! I love neuroscience and people watching, and if you look, you'll find some of that in each Savannah Kade book. Most days you'll find me in my office, looking out my window at a handful of the neighbor's cows, or watching my dogs or my cat roam the backyard.

Follow me, find me, ask me questions! I would love to hear from you.
www.SavannahKade.com
Savannah@SavannahKade.com